Liz,

egg dancing

egg dancing

Liz Jensen

THE OVERLOOK PRESS
WOODSTOCK • NEW YORK

First published in the United States in 1996 by
The Overlook Press
Lewis Hollow Road
Woodstock, New York 12498

Library of Congress Cataloging-in-Publication Data

Jensen, Liz
Egg dancing / Liz Jensen.
p. cm.
1. Mothers and daughters—United States—Fiction.
2. Television in religion—Fiction. 3. Genetic engineering—
Fiction. I. Title.
Originally published by Bloomsbury Publishing Plc
PS3560.E592E48 1996
813'.54—dc20
95-34134
CIP
ISBN: 0-87951-645-3
First American Edition

ACKNOWLEDGEMENTS

With warmest thanks to Polly Coles for her sharp critical eye and her friendship, and to Michel Coleman for his love and support.

For my beloved father, Niels Rosenvinge Jensen.
Whose fault everything is.

PROLOGUE

'Expect a new world,' said the evangelist, 'and the Lord shall provide it.'

But he was lying, as usual. The Lord provided nothing. Why should He? I've worked in the holiday industry, and my theory is this: the planet God designed for us to inhabit is strictly self-catering.

So dates shift, and one century becomes another amid much ballyhoo: fireworks, champagne, suicide. But the world doesn't change. It's people that change. Take me.

Have I changed?

Are courgettes green?

Was the *Seismosaurus archipelagi* the largest dinosaur that ever stomped the earth?

This is my story. Mine, and Ma's, and that of my excruciating sister Linda. It charts the chain of homely atrocities that began that winter and led to the downfall of the Perfect Baby Project. The snowballing saga created other casualties, too: the greenhouse, my husband's reputation, the regime in one of the nation's leading mental institutions. It nearly destroyed the evangelist, too, but the Born Again have a habit of resurrecting themselves. So despite the public humiliation, the Reverend Carmichael is doing well enough to get back on prime-time TV and say, 'Expect a new world.'

I was out to lunch, in one way or another, for most of that year, so I had to piece it all together afterwards – from what emerged at the trial, from the confession of my husband's mistress, from Ma's epistles to Dad, from the recollections of my aforementioned sister (including details of the Reverend's hairy penis), and from the rigorous Stasi-style inquiry at the Manxheath Institute of Challenged Stability.

Everyone exaggerated their own heroism, of course, and played down their cowardice, greed, duplicity, stupidity, et cetera. They all, interestingly, made a point of insisting that their sanity had been intact throughout. Not least Ishmael, the great pretender. Thus is history enacted and recorded: in jigsaw fragments.

Just as well, then, is it not, that jigsaws are one of the few things I'm good at?

The media knew me as Dr Gregory Stevenson's wife, of course, but not being great cottoners-on, the journalists only ever got a fifth of the story. They never discovered, for example, that I was personally involved in the whole scandal on a grand scale. Nor did I, until it was too late. When the story finally broke, the papers called me a 'suburban mother-of-one'. One article said I had a 'chilly smile'. This was one way of describing the weird rictus that gripped my jaw, which not even alcohol would loosen.

This was the new me.

ONE

M y so-called delusions started around the time I
went to visit Ma in the loony bin. To me they
were just ideas that began to gel in my head, but my
husband Gregory, being a doctor, insisted they were
something more clinical. He's not one to use a medical
term like 'delusion' lightly.

'Delusions' such as: I had become invisible. I meant
invisibility in the metaphorical sense, but Gregory is
a literally minded man. 'Delusions' like, for instance:
Gregory was in love with a woman whose long dark hair
and sloping shoulders gave her an uncanny resemblance
to the Virgin Mary. That was no metaphor. That
was fact.

Another fact – that my mother was winding down
in a loony bin – didn't help. Like mother, like daughter,
I could hear my husband thinking. It had been eighteen
months since I had visited the Manxheath Institute of
Challenged Stability. How peaceful the grounds were,
with fat oaks, and clusters of silver birch which has
that white, shivering way about it in a cold sun that
can make your blood hum. I can see Ma there now, her
thick outline filling the doorway: she blocks entry. She
clutches her handbag level with her sternum like a heavy
platter. She rhinos forward to greet me, but when she
comes close to kiss the air next to my cheek (she prefers

3

not to touch, especially bare skin), she panics about what to do with her bag. She has had this bag for years; it is a too-big one in artificial leather, and the inside smells of ink, onion, and dandruff. It is empty now, I imagine. She checked in her belongings long ago, at the front desk. I can see she wants to make a gesture of contact, but the bag is in the way, and her big mitts are locked so they can't loosen their hold of it. We fumble about a bit, in a hopping dance, and in the end she compromises by keeping a grasp on both straps but letting the bag swing low by her knees, a giant scrotum.

We are standing in the porch, where noticeboards flutter with hospital messages and photocopied posters: 'Relax with yoga'. 'Family Help Network – a listening ear'. 'Support your hospital radio'. 'Institute of Challenged Stability dancing lessons: JIVE IT UP!' 'Patchwork for Pleasure'. 'Lost: child's shoe, red, size 28'. 'Ever thought of bowls?'.

'How are you, Ma?' I ask. Old habits.

'Dry all the time. I have to keep licking my lips.'

She has a Scottish snob's voice. She comes from near Inverness. She came to England, to Gridiron, when she met my dad, but her accent hung on at home. When you grow up with a voice, it goes unnoticed, like the smell of your house. But now her accent seems like a stranger's. In fact, it has broadened since she's been at Manxheath: the words come out as 'lucking ma lups'. And to prove it she licks them slowly, like a camel.

'Nice trees, don't you think?' she says, as I follow her down a windowless corridor.

I have come to have a look, of course. To inspect her, in fact. I feel quite cold-blooded. I had been expecting a caged animal, gnawing at the bars, or asleep in a corner, a drugged ball of sawdust and fur – but it was a mistake to think of cages. A mistake, because you can tell at a

4

glance that she is at her most free. My mother has turned a frightening colour: a pale, waxy yellow. Her obesity still gives her the look of freight, but she has shrunk a little. Her outsize skirt hangs loosely round her middle, showing a strip of grey nylon petticoat.

The first thing she wants to know is where I've parked the car. It seems important to her.

'It's in the Pay and Display,' I reassure her. 'Five hundred spaces.'

'Oh good,' she says, a weight lifted from her mind. She licks her lips again, very slowly. And then she looks away from me and says abruptly to the air, like a blind person, 'You can go when you want: don't feel you have to stay long in this – environment.'

It hasn't struck me that I might not be welcome. Am I not doing her a favour? I feel wounded. Bugger her. Bugger challenged stability. When I was little she was a story-book mother with a pinny, who sang songs and rolled shortcrust dough, up to her elbows in flour, with the sun streaming in the kitchen window and outside, the bright garden. A garden of apple trees, pumpkins, marigolds. Parsley. I'm sure of it. Then one day, there were real mud pies for lunch, a foul-smelling knickerbocker-glory of a mess seeping under the bath-room door, and a laugh we hadn't heard before, wild and free and dangerous.

'I'll show you round my greenhouse when it's in better shape,' she is saying airily. I have seen no sign of this greenhouse. And nice peaceful trees, my mother is repeating proudly, as if she were showing off a new home with the help of a brochure. Good food, too. Not your traditional bland hospital food at all. They do some quite imaginative modern things, interesting salads and curries with turmeric and whatnot, mixing things you wouldn't normally put together at all, except next to each other on a shelf.

'I've liked everything so far. Oh, except something Caribbean, grapes in spicy mayonnaise. I spat *that* out in a hurry!' And she makes a child's 'yuk' face, her cheeks creasing behind her glasses like slabs of putty.

'I'm re-reading Iris Murdoch and Virginia Woolf,' she tells me.

We come out and walk down a path along the outside of the building, making dragging progress because the drugs have side-effected to her feet. She stops now and then to gaze around, as though the activities of walking and seeing are incompatible. The Victorians built Manxheath in the blood-red brick of conviction, rooting it in a broad park, where crows now stand hacking obsessively at the frozen earth like tiny motorised pickaxes. I watch the white vapours of my mother's breath curdle into the frozen air as she speaks. We discuss the family in quite a normal way, except that she gets me and my sister muddled up.

'Honestly, Linda,' she says at one point. Linda is my sister. I am Hazel. Hazel and Linda: the two daughters of Moira Janet Sugden. There was a boy, but he died aged three months, and her brain began to make the wrong connections, like a knitting machine that creates a complicated garment no one can wear. It annoys me that she calls me Linda.

'I'm Hazel,' I say – but she has not heard, or does not want to.

'Honestly, Linda, I wish you'd do something about your sister with her strange baby, who by the way keeps sending me messages, and that gynaecological man of hers. I don't trust him. He looks voluptuous.'

Hang on a minute; she's talking about me. My baby.

6

(What messages?) My 'voluptuous' husband. *Voluptuous?* Even though I know she's mad, I want to take her by the throat and shake her and hit her. It is something I used to have dreams about – nightmares, in fact. Hitting her but the blows bouncing off, *boing, boing!* as if she was rubber.

But I say nothing. She comes to a halt in front of a door.

'You should see the other patients, good gracious, Linda.'

'I'm Hazel,' I say patiently, but she ignores me again. (I should put up a notice on the board. Lost: Hazel's identity. Small reward.)

'They're *really* mad. There's an Indian woman who walks round and round in circles, and a man, must be thirty-five–forty, thinks he's a divorce lawyer, which is complete phoney-baloney, because he's also a pathological liar, but he's actually been divorced so he must have gone through some legal books because he knows all the Acts and details of it and jargon and everything. And an Italian Signora who's been pregnant for months now, years even, but the doctors don't believe her. She's my best friend, actually.'

She pauses slightly and I notice her eyes flicker at me sideways, checking that what she's said about having a friend – a best friend who thinks she's pregnant – impressed me. I let my mouth twitch in acknowledgement, and she carries on.

'Then there was this one man, funny glasses with sticking plaster everywhere but otherwise quite unnoticeable, suddenly flipped and attacked this poor little Jamaican and then had a sort of fit, shouting some very nasty racist things. The staff were there in a flash; you think they're not watching but they are. Then there's this man called Max, hates women. It's neural. And another one

7

who's convinced he's got a contagious disease, several contagious diseases, in fact, and I think he has because he comes out in boils but they just ignore him, say it's psycho-something. Well that's what he's here for, isn't it, to be cured of his psycho-something, but *they* don't care. We had a Mrs Cramper, too, but she's gone now; she had a wee, wee microchip computer implanted in her head, controlled by the Driving Vehicle Licence Centre in Swansea. Anyway, I look completely sane next to some of the others.'

It's as though she's describing a tankful of exotic fish, with herself as one of the plainer ones. I've never seen her so animated, or so happy.

She glances at me sideways to see how I've reacted. She is obviously pleased with the result. I am dry-mouthed, speechless. After all these years, I still don't know what to say to my mother. The State of Absolute Delusion, Linda and I used to call it. It was a territory which was home to her and us, and yet far away from Gridiron City and all the things we knew in the normal world outside – pop stars, the Dress-for-Less shop, make-up, department stores, Wimpy menus.

'Abandon hope all ye who enter here,' we would laugh, coming home from school and entering Ma's domain. But it wasn't in fact that funny.

'I've found a new word in the dictionary,' Ma is saying.

I'd forgotten: she's a beachcomber for words, picking over the shoreline of language for lexicographical detritus. She used to be a librarian.

'It's under K. It means 'the government of a state by the worst of its citizens'. It's what we live in. As do the Portuguese, the New Zealanders, the Colombians, the Austrians, and many others. You've only to look at the globe. The word – ' Here she paused for effect, and I find myself stopping, too. 'The word,' said Ma, 'is "kakistocracy".'

And she moved off again.

Now we enter an annexe of Manxheath's main building and Ma leads me down a draughty corridor that smells of paint. Now and then she still calls me Linda, but I find myself making excuses for her: Linda (being unmarried and self-righteous) comes to see her more often, after all. Always has; ever since way back. I'm shocked by the way Ma shuffles along, dragging her feet behind her as if they're paralysed — especially when otherwise she seems quite alive. An alarming thought crosses my mind: I'd quite like to poke the back of her calves with a stick to see if they mottle or discolour. I stifle a giggle.

We reach the Day Room, a desolate, shambolic place in which lumpen chairs and sofas are moored on a disinfected linoleum lake that stretches to the horizon of the far wall. The wallpaper strikes me as inappropriate; it's a Regency floral pattern, in stripes. I have always thought that vertically striped wallpaper is a mistake. Another oddity: a large chandelier, to which the dust is welded by means of grease. Ma sees me looking at it and says, 'Quite a bugger to clean,' as though she's in charge of it.

Despite its size, the room smells closet-like from stale cigarettes. Around a formica-topped table there are three men watching a Kung Fu video and an elderly woman playing Scrabble with a fat youth. He has a shaved head and a dangerous, pudgy expression which horrifies me. I see the words 'COLDER', 'IT', 'JINX' and 'FINANCE' on the board, and wonder if they might mean something to the psychiatrists.

'That's Dr Stern,' whispers my mother, nodding to indicate the man who has just entered. She is glowing with pride, as though he is the president of a very exclusive club she's joined. I notice that she's swinging her handbag in what I take to be a flirtatious way. 'I'll introduce you. He's a very brilliant man. He does *The Times* crossword every day and has published all sorts of case studies.'

She's wriggling, and her man's slippers are making squeaking noises on the floor.

I look at my watch. I've been there fifteen minutes, but it feels like hours. Dr Stern, now talking to a nurse, catches my mother's eye and smiles. He gives her a little friendly wave and she blushes with pride.

She calls, 'Dr Stern! Come and meet my other daughter, Linda!'

The nurse leaves and Dr Stern comes over, hand outstretched, a wide smile. He is small, with dark eyes and a dark moustache. Beneath his white coat there is a green silk tie and a green-and-white-striped shirt. He could be a cardboard cut-out of a man selling something. His smile shows even, cared-for teeth. He seems so normal next to Ma that the frank sanity of his handshake chokes me.

'Pleased to meet you, Linda,' he says.

'No, Linda's my sister. I'm Hazel.'

We are still holding hands. I want to explain that my mother gets us muddled up, but I can't in front of her. I find suddenly that I have used up the last ration of optimism I'd brought with me for the journey. I've been dosing myself frantically, not heeding the limited supply, and now it's gone. And I want to go too – not formally, but just to fade to blackness in the way some documentaries do. Perhaps it's the presence of the psychiatrist, and the odd constriction he has caused in my chest, as though Polyfilla has been shoved in there to fill a hole I didn't know I had, that also gives me an urge to disintegrate into hopeless blubbing. The psychiatrist and I let go of one another's hands, suddenly conscious that we have held on too long, and that my mother's bag is swinging violently close to us. I'd thought it was empty, but it's suddenly rattling with small dry things like a desert snake.

'Your sister!' sighs Ma theatrically, rolling her eyes. 'You wouldn't believe the worry I had with both of them, Dr Stern. And *God*, the relief of being away from them. Cats. Bitches. Words cannot describe. The whole family, in fact. They were wreckers, I'm afraid. Some people are born wreckers. And I gave birth to two. If that isn't statistically significant I don't know what is. Look at the way I am. I have a degree, you know. I was just telling – '

And there she breaks off, because there is a huge bellow and a thud as the table in the corner crashes to the floor, and Scrabble letters skid across the lino. The fat youth has fallen to the ground screaming, with his hands over his eyes. Two nurses grab the old woman and rush her away to wash the blood off her hands. She doesn't resist. She seems to have gone limp and floppy, but she is smiling. In ten seconds she and the nurses are gone, and Dr Stern is seeing to the boy. He won't stop screaming. It is a thin, high-pitched scream like a pressure-cooker makes. His face is badly scratched, but his eyes are safe. My mother is excited, and the waxy yellow of her skin has flushed to pink.

'Never a dull moment,' she says proudly, and begins picking up Scrabble letters from the floor, leaning over so that her grey petticoat lifts high. The backs of her knees look like pinched buttocks.

She picks up the Scrabble pieces one by one. 'F for Freddie,' she says. 'J for Jug.'

I remember 'J for Jug' from my alphabet book when I was little. In some books it's 'Jam'.

'C for Chlorpromazine . . . A for Afterwards . . . D for Dog . . .' Then she finds an X and gets stuck. Suddenly, her mood changes and she snaps, 'Well, help me with these letters, will you, I spend my whole life clearing up after you. This isn't a hotel, you know.'

Dutifully, I help Ma gather up the rest of the letters and we put them in the Scrabble box, while the fat boy continues his whistling scream without ever seeming to stop for breath.

'Monopoly's worse,' says my mother. I can feel her getting rapidly more tense.

I say, 'I have to go.'

It's as though I've flicked a decompression switch: her face instantly radiates profound relief.

'Well, I said you shouldn't feel you have to stay too long. And of course you've left your car in the Pay and Display. You don't want to run over the limit. They can hit you with a hefty fine. You can meet Dr Stern properly another time, if he's not too busy.'

We leave Dr Stern crouched over the boy, who has rolled himself into a ball on the floor. Dr Stern begins murmuring to him soothingly, like a father, and rubbing his back. There is a ghastly intimacy about it. I follow my mother's slow shuffle along the corridor.

'The drugs have all sorts of side-effects,' she is saying. 'I'm on seventy-five milligrams a day now. That's why I'm dry all the time. Parched. Absolutely *parched*.'

We said goodbye, fumbling again to avoid flesh meeting flesh, and I left her. Halfway down the drive I turned back to see if she'd gone in, but she was still standing in the porch, with her handbag lifted in a sort of salute.

As I walked away I felt something envelop me like a bubble or a shroud. It was a feeling of invisibility. And sure enough, although there were many people in the Pay and Display car-park, all loading their shopping and messing with children and keys, nobody glanced at me even once.

I grew up near the Works, on the Cheeseway Estate, known in Gridiron as 'the Cheeseways'. The Works manufactures moulded plastic kitchenware, mainly pedal-bins, and its burnt acrylic smell was part of childhood. We were never away from it. So naturally, in later life, I'd wanted to be rid of it. Linda and I grew up believing that, as daughters of a librarian, we were posh intellectuals. Our mother, who raised us in the Cheeseways in her State of Absolute Delusion, told us we were. Ma drew us a map of the class system once, in green felt pen, so we could place ourselves. Aristocrats/the upper class were at the top, and upper middles (e.g. Mr and Mrs Roberts) on the next level down, because they had a dishwasher and he was a dentist. Below that came the lower middle (e.g. us, Mr Staples, Mrs Carnie), followed by upper lowers/the working class (e.g. Dad, the fallen woman from over the road, my schoolfriend Nicky), and finally, at the bottom, lower lower. There was only one example in this category: Aunt Marjorie, Dad's sister, whom we didn't officially know.

Some things stick. Oakshott Road, where I live now, is leafy. Everyone has a quality paper delivered, and knows how to ski. It's at the smart end of Gridiron, as far from the Cheeseways as you can get, I reckon, short of going to live on the moon.

I chose the road and I chose the house.

My next-door neighbour Jane was at home, baby-sitting Billy. Looking back, I realise now that Jane and

I had a strange relationship built around mistaken pity. I pitied her her childlessness, and she pitied me my ball-and-chain of a son. When she baby-sat, each of us thought we were doing the other one a favour. We drank tea and I told her about the Scrabble. I cried slightly, without really knowing why. Jane was kind, in her suffering divorcée's way, but I think she was afraid she might be exposing herself to contamination from the hospital. I can understand that, because I felt it, too.

'Don't dwell on it, love,' she said as she put on her coat and turned to me. 'And just remember,' she added with glassy eyes, stabbing her forefinger between my breasts to emphasise her point, 'the only person who counts in this world, at the end of the day, is you.'

I think this was an idea she'd picked up on one of her Weekends.

Billy doesn't like to see me cry. He looked at me distantly, like his father would, then tottered off to the other side of the room to play with his toy ambulance. He doesn't say much, but he's good at noises: ambulances, cars, aeroplanes, pneumatic drills – city noises. He did the ambulance noise and I tried to smile.

'Very good, sweetheart,' I said in a cooing sort of voice, which sounded phoney.

'I've been to see Granny in hospital,' I told him. 'I saw a big ambulance.'

He looked up at me sharply, his blue eyes coins of quizzical light.

'Yes, sweetheart. An ambulance. Granny's living in a place with lots of ambulances.'

That set him off again. By the time Linda phoned, he had torn up a whole newspaper into small pieces. A day's information lay in shreds on the floor. He began stuffing it into an old carrier bag he'd found. Linda wanted to know how the visit had gone. My sister is difficult on the phone. She has never coped with the lack of eye contact, or understood the nature of telephone etiquette, and it makes her even more blunt and aggressive than in the flesh.

'I don't suppose you stayed long,' she said.

'She's looking well,' I said. 'She seems happy.'

I didn't mention the fat boy and the blood.

'Did you see Dr Stern?'

'Yes, why?'

'Oh, she's obsessed with him, that's all.'

'How d'you know?'

'I saw something she made from clay.'

She refused to tell me what it was. My sister is quite prudish.

'She's been there for two years and you've visited her once. At least when she was over in Coxcomb you had the excuse that it was a long way to go. I bet you didn't stay more than ten minutes. If you'd been seeing her regularly you'd know about things like her clay.'

When Linda was seven she was Ma's little girl.

Ma loves me more than she loves you. You're just horrible, and you'll fall in a 'normous gigantic cowpat and go to hell, so ber ber ber.'

'She's got us muddled up, you know,' I told Linda. 'She thought I was you.'

There was a silence from Linda as this sunk in.

'Well, when I go to visit, she knows exactly who I am,' said Linda.

'Good. but she thought I was you today. She kept calling me Linda.'

'Well, I must go. A pile of work to do.'

Linda is a civil servant. She hung up.

Later it snowed, heavy flakes that were dirty before they hit the ground. Gregory came back from his conference in Manchester. Billy was already in his cot asleep, and Gregory was annoyed that he'd missed an evening with him. He was leaving again the next day for a week-long symposium. That night we made love. Gregory is a gynaecologist. He'd made a special chart so that we knew when we could and couldn't. We didn't bother much about sex though. We were both too tired, usually, and to be frank the thrill had worn off a bit. It hurt.

The snail has the best sex life, I reckon: no limbs, and no capacity for guilt. Hermaphrodites do as they are done by. No wonder they blow bubbles. My husband's behaviour in bed was peculiar, but perhaps no more than most men's. I had had one boyfriend who liked me to pretend I was asleep, and another who always kept his socks on, and another who insisted that I suck his nipples while he twiddled with mine like they were radio dials. So Gregory's cleanliness thing didn't seem too way out of line. (And if I still find myself scrubbing my nails four times a day, long after the decree nisi, I have him to thank.) He always insisted that we wash with soap before and after sex, and once, memorably, during. His bare body was so scrubbed it reminded me of Spam. Gregory would always shut his eyes, so I had no idea what was going on in his head, but it must have been something musical because as matters progressed he would start to hum and then burst into a type of marching tune in rhythm with his thrusts. It was always the same tune, and it wasn't one I had ever heard elsewhere, so I think it was his own composition. It got faster and faster as he approached orgasm, and ended on a loud, triumphant note of finale. When he finally opened his eyes afterwards, he would often look quite surprised to see me.

'I think I have a yeast infection,' I said when Gregory's tune had collapsed in a dying tuba-honk.

Usually he took an interest in these things, but he just rolled off and grunted.

Perhaps it was at that point, just before the Politics of Reproduction Symposium in Madrid, that I should have started to wonder, but I didn't. I'd never thought much about him being a gynaecologist until I married him, and I began to worry about all the other vaginas in my husband's life. He assured me there was nothing in the least bit sexual about looking up women's orifices – 'birth canals', he called them – all day long. But I wondered sometimes. He had certain preoccupations. All the monitoring he insisted on. Urination, defecation, menstruation: he'd make me register all my bodily excreta in a notebook in the bathroom. I felt like one of the early astronauts from the days when human guinea-pigs were shot into space for the greater glory of mankind. Then there were the pills: pills for conceiving, folic acid pills for maximal maternal health in the peri-conceptual period, blue pills in the morning, red at night. I'd been taking two of each every day for the last three years, and I was rattling with them. I wondered sometimes if other doctors took such methodical care of their wives, or whether it was just those on the obs and gynae side. Habit didn't make it any easier. I'd pretend to read a magazine when he gave me my monthly check-up. My bare feet in the stirrups, he'd glide the Vaselined speculum in, open it with a screw-turn and peer in to take his swab. By the end, my brain was on the ceiling, flattened and clinging on.

He delivered babies and did abortions, too. They said he was very talented.

I couldn't sleep that night. I kept thinking about that

word 'voluptuous', which was the last one I'd use to describe Gregory's tight, disinfected looks.

I went shopping the next morning when I'd dropped Billy off at playgroup. Gridiron is at its most stark in winter, whittled down to the bare essentials of a generic Lego town: red-brick buildings, themed shopping malls, grimy pubs, churches, hospitals, Jaycote's Park with its ancient sycamore trees, their bark almost black from car exhaust, the Cheeseways Works in the distance. Ma always used to say she liked Gridiron because it 'wasn't too big and it wasn't too small'. For what, we never knew. But walking about that morning, it seemed to make some kind of sense. Gridiron is a place to lose yourself in, almost-but-not-quite. A medium-sized pond for medium-sized fish. And a few big ones, like Gregory. He'd always wanted to move to London, but I didn't. Gridiron is my city. I like to know where I am.

Walking along the High Street I caught sight of a woman in a mirror outside Boots. She had longish, wispy hair and a thin, quite attractive, raddled-looking face. I recognised her as one of the mums from Billy's playgroup, Mrs Something-or-other, but it wasn't until I'd got home and unloaded my shopping that I realised with a shock who it was, and that I'd become invisible even to myself.

The invisible woman. I'd first sensed it when I was leaving the hospital after seeing my mother. It was then I put a name to it, there in the Pay and Display. When it was nameless I could dismiss it. But now, having just walked straight past my own mirror image without recognising myself, I could no longer afford to ignore it. When I told this to Gregory he just laughed and gave me a look, the look he gave me when I reminded him too much of Ma.

All winter I was thinking about it, though. 'Fostering my delusions', as Gregory would have put it. I tried to keep quiet about them for the sake of peace. Meanwhile Gregory was very preoccupied with the desire to be famous. It was wearing him down, this obsession with renown. Every night he lectured me about his prospects. He'd stand there in the kitchen with his hands deep in his pockets, making himself taller every now and then by standing on the balls of his feet, while I was giving Billy his dinner or cooking. He'd pour himself a whisky, and a gin-and-Slimline for me, and hold forth. He always made me stop at two measures of gin because of my uterus, but more often than not I'd slip myself another, and sometimes I got quite drunk. Then one night in late January he came back excited and flushed. I've seen mountaineers on TV with the same look when they've planted a flag at the summit of something. I couldn't help wondering if it was to do with Dr Ruby Gonzalez, but it turned out to be something else.

It's not enough to be talented, Gregory was telling me, not for the first time, but with an extra gleam in his eyes like he was building up to something. He makes Airfix models, and it was that Airfix look, the one when you're putting the last piece in place – usually the pilot's seat or the tail-lights. You have to be brilliant to get anywhere worth going in gynaecology these days; brilliant or lucky. That was it. Gregory thought he was about to get lucky. Some very promising tests had just come through, he said; a sort of breakthrough he and 'a colleague' had made. I wouldn't understand the detail of it. He was talking about the drug he'd invented. He'd been tinkering with it for years, and he still didn't have any concrete results, but he'd always had faith in it, ever since he started working on it way back when we were first married. (The Airfix stuff, I reckon, was a way of coping with the long-term nature of his research. You get a quick result with a model glider.) 'Genetic Choice', it was called. The tabloids called it the 'Perfect Baby drug'. Reverend Carmichael of Channel Praise called it 'the Devil's work'. He'd been lobbying against it, intermittently, ever since news of Greg's work first emerged in the scientific press. Gregory got so irate at one of the Reverend Carmichael's smear campaigns that he had the TV in his clinic waiting-room fixed so that Channel Praise became a jumble of dancing lines, with fuzzy, indecipherable sound. If women want to listen to that maniac, Gregory said, they have no business coming to my clinic. Anyway, he was saying, Genetic Choice still didn't actually work. Yet. But he'd had a small, important breakthrough.

'Some tests have come up positive,' is all he would say about it.

I was glad for him about the breakthrough. But I felt uncomfortable as well; always had. To be frank, the whole enterprise gave me a slightly odd feeling – a bit like the excreta-monitoring thing. But I'd tried to be supportive, in the way I was about all the aerodynamics cluttering the loft. There was still a lot of lab and rat work to do, and then the clinical trials. They'd take years, and then there'd be all the battles with the licensing authority, not to mention the Reverend Vernon Bloody Carmichael's lot.

'Plus Christ knows what else,' he added, with that weary breadwinner look on his face.

So in the meantime he was planning his own trial. He wouldn't say precisely what, though. The Perfect Baby. What a thought. Not that Billy's not perfect. Though Gregory said to me once, let's face it, he's not showing any signs of great intelligence – he thinks he's an ambulance.

'We have a normal boy on our hands here, Hazel,' he said, in a rather wistful way. 'A perfectly normal, average, ordinary boy.'

20

Which goes to show he knows nothing, I thought afterwards.

A few days later, I could tell that Dr Gonzalez had been working at the clinic again. She and Gregory 'collaborated' sometimes, and it always showed on his face afterwards. There was that look about him. Distant. Voluptuous, even. He always said she had a very womanly way of carrying herself. I suppose it was true, though I could only ever see her faults. I'll admit, though, that she had a certain light in her eyes, which were dark, lovely eyes, the kind men call mysterious, slightly greasy on the lids, but not unpleasantly so. Bedroom eyes. I'd only met her three or four times, over the course of a couple of years. I suppose she was exotic: she was born in Caracas and had spent most of her life in Croydon. Funny, but she'd always looked six months pregnant to me, though logically I supposed it wasn't possible. Gregory always liked visibly pregnant women; he said they were a heavenly sight. As I expect they were, in his line of work. I'd always tried to avoid meeting Ruby. She gave me a bad feeling. Inadequacy, I think.

I reckoned that, with a name like Gonzalez, the chances were she had Catholic origins. Gregory was a lapsed Catholic. Well, you have to be pretty lapsed to perform abortions, don't you. He said he was thinking of making Dr Gonzalez a 'member of the team'.

'Don't you think she looks like the Virgin Mary?' I asked him, remembering the way she'd sat once, in her blue-and-white clinician's garb, with sloping shoulders and upraised palms.

'Yes,' he said, with a strange, soft smile. 'It's funny you should say that, because it's her nickname at work.'

So someone else had spotted it, too, that weird resemblance she had to the mother of Jesus.

TWO

D r Stern sent his letter to Linda. It was a short note to say that our mother, Mrs Moira Sugden, was entering a 'crisis period', and could the family refrain from making any unexpected visits over the next two weeks, as she was always 'agitated' after seeing blood relatives, and any kind of shock could 'precipitate a mental emergency'. Linda came round and read it to me aloud, in a censorious voice, her clever steel eyes cutting through the text. She was wearing one of her frumpy frocks and a huge brooch of Ma's, and her winter hat, which she bought in Leningrad, on a package tour of the Soviet Union, as was. Despite the cuddly headgear, she was all spikes. Even after all these years, and all we've been through with Ma, my love for Linda is no more than a bad habit. The proof of it is that I can't get to like her much: I'll make an effort to, and she'll spoil it.

'It's all your fault,' she accused. 'I've been visiting her twice a week for months on end, and then three days after you decide to show up at the hospital, this happens.' She slapped the letter in disgust. 'What does he *mean*,' she complained. 'How can anyone get *agitated* after seeing blood relatives?'

With Linda trembling with righteous fury in front of me, dragging on her cigarette like she was giving it artificial respiration, and scraping at my pine table with her car keys, I knew exactly what he meant. She never fails to agitate me. But I offered her a coffee.

'Instant please,' she said. 'It's quicker. I have a lunch meeting.'

And she blushed a frantic, beetroot red. This meant only one thing; a man in her life. At a guess, someone she'd met at one of her gawkish Mensa Club get-togethers, where members bring their own sandwiches.

'What are you staring at?' she asked. 'Is instant not posh enough for you?'

Linda, the girl no one loved much, except Ma, who sort of love-hated her, which is worse.

I was too young to be a person when our dad left to live in New Zealand with a floozie of loose morals whom he'd met (according to Ma) at a petrol station near the flyover. But when he walked out with his one suitcase and kissed Linda goodbye on the doorstep, it hurt her a lot, because she was old enough to think it was her fault, and my mother was strange enough, even then in the days when she wore pinnies and rolled pastry, to encourage her to think that too.

Dad worked in double glazing, but he had plans to move into the conservatory and greenhouse market. He'd worked on a project for a pagoda of glass in Jaycote's Park which was to be the pride of Gridiron, but it came to nothing. He had a fondness for stock-car racing and was a great attender of carpet auctions, where he once obtained in great bargain quantities some rolls of carpeting which had fallen off the back of a BBC lorry. From then on, our living-room floor in the Cheeseways was tattooed all over with a grandiose logo and the motto 'And Nation Shall Speak Peace Unto Nation'. Dad also went to the pub a lot.

'At least that's where he said he went,' said Linda bitterly, on one of the rare occasions I could get her to speak about him. 'He took me to the fair once. We played Roll the Penny all afternoon. I won two goldfish but they died of fin-rot.'

That's all I knew about Dad.

'Not much call for greenhouses and double glazing in New Zealand,' my mother said when he'd left, rubbing at her eyes with her yellow washing-up gloves still on. 'He'll be a nobody out there.'

And he must have been, because we heard no news of him after that, until one evening, years later, when I was ten, a woman we didn't officially know, in a red flowery dress and a face that kind of matched, came knocking at the door, nearly broke it down, in fact, and barged in past my mother into the living-room and threw herself on the sofa in tears. It was Marjorie, my father's sister.

She wouldn't say anything until Ma had poured her a large whisky.

'Brendan's dead,' she said, and took another large gulp.

Linda left the room very quietly. She couldn't face it. Later I kept telling her about how he'd died, but she didn't want to know. And even then I'm not sure she believed me.

One of the features of Christchurch, New Zealand, is that, normally, nothing much happens there – so Dad's unusual death really put it on the map for a while. It was quite big news at the time, not just in the national press but in all the international medical journals, too. He'd been poisoned by water. I know it sounds ridiculous, but it can happen. He'd drunk a lot of water – no one knew why, but there was a rumour that it was some kind of elaborate bet – so much water that his blood became too thin, and he was intoxicated. He fell down in the street stone dead, and carried on passing water for another two hours, according to the pathologist's report.

'I just can't believe it,' Marjorie kept droning into her whisky.

By the time Ma sent her off in a taxi she was reeling about blind drunk, but quietly, like a hefty zoo creature with a dart in its arse.

My mother wouldn't discuss it, but she had a wreath sent, with the message: 'In loving memory of Brendan, misguided husband of Moira and father of Linda and Hazel. Despite the agony of your betrayal, you stay for ever in our hearts.'

I think it was mainly to make that petrol-pump girl feel bad.

When he died it was much worse for Linda, because she could remember him and still loved him. It didn't bother me at all, because to me he was just an old over-coat that hung in the wardrobe smelling of mothballs, an overcoat that I somehow knew had been there as a symbol of hope, 'waiting for Daddy to come home'. My mother's big idea was that he'd been enchanted by a bad fairy who'd cast a wicked spell on him, and that, one day when the spell wore off, he'd come home and wear his smelly old overcoat again. It never got that far, but that was the unspoken happy ending she had in mind, before he died in a pool of his own urine, having drunk enough water to fill a bath. The overcoat went to Oxfam.

'Daddy's coat's going to fill the bellies of starving Africans,' Ma said as she bundled it into a plastic bin-liner.

I noticed that, like me, Ma developed a fear of drinking too much water, and never had more than one glass no matter how thirsty she was.

Linda never really recovered from Dad's death. She developed an 'attitude problem' towards men, and they responded in kind. She tended to attract the faithful-dog types who were in thrall to her powerful brain, but in fact all she wanted was for them to destroy her self-esteem, like Dad did. So when they didn't, she had to tell them to go. Having once read a questionnaire entitled 'Your Man's Personality: Angelic or Monstrous?', I knew all about this syndrome. Linda's faithful ones were angels, or the psychologists' Type One. While the ones with *I am a shitty, selfish bastard* printed on their foreheads, the Type Twos who treated her badly and let her down with a sickening and predictable thud, who left her soul collapsed on the floor like a discarded condom – they were the monsters she'd fall in love with. Later she would return to her books. Linda had academic pretensions. But behind the façade of the blue-stocking, Linda's bad love experiences would be pickled in the venom of hindsight. If Linda had filled in the questionnaire, and read the accompanying article, she might have had more understanding of passion's mechanics.

'Why don't you leave all that stuff to Ma?' I asked her once. 'You don't have to go through everything she did.'

'Every woman goes through what Ma went through, one way or another,' was Linda's cryptic reply. 'You'll see.'

She was reading feminist critiques of various things at the time, and studying sociology.

So I just laughed.

I decided to go and have a word with Dr Stern about Ma. I wrote asking for a meeting 'at his convenience'. 'Any time is convenient for me,' I said in the letter, 'as I'm relatively free during the day.' I have time on my hands. I don't work, not since shortly after I married. Well, when you're a doctor's wife you don't strictly need to, do you? That's what Gregory says anyway. Unlike my sister Linda, I'm not much of a feminist. And as it turned out it suited me, too, because of all my pregnancy and

26

miscarriage problems. Three little ghosts I carry with me wherever I go. And then Billy. Being a mother is full-time work, says Gregory.

'I look forward to hearing from you soon,' I wrote. 'Yours sincerely, Hazel Stevenson.'

I wondered about Ma's clay thing.

Gregory had invited Ruby Gonzalez to dinner the following Friday. I asked if her husband was coming too and he told me she wasn't married and she hadn't got plans to bring a boyfriend. And I could have sworn she was pregnant. I invited Linda, too. I left a message on her answerphone saying she could bring a friend. I spent hours polishing and cleaning the house, with Billy chattering away over his cars. Then I brushed my hair – the tangle-prone, wafting kind of hair that shampoo manufacturers call 'damaged', or 'flyaway', or simply 'problem'. Then I applied make-up: foundation, blusher, lipstick, the works. I don't know what came over me. Perhaps I was sick of being invisible. But I might as well not have bothered, because Gregory didn't notice the difference and afterwards it left a tenacious brown rim round the washbasin.

As the days passed, I felt increasingly fretful and restless, and had a feeling of foreboding about something too vague to name. On the morning of that Friday, the day the dinner party was scheduled, I went back to Manxheath. Dr Stern's secretary had rung with a ten-minute appointment at eleven. I got there early and wandered about the grounds, the thin snow creaking under my feet. Once again I was struck by the trees. This time they were lumped with snow. I found them restfully static. Gazing at them, I managed to shove the usual lurking memories of my mother – her monstrous size, her facial tics, her grotesque flirtation, her swinging bag – to the back of my mind.

At eleven I knocked on Dr Stern's door. He opened it, patted my upper arm, and waved me to a big leather chair.

'Just excuse me a moment,' he said, and shuffled some papers on his desk. 'I've just finished this article about autism for the *Lancet*, and it has to be faxed this morning.'

He smiled briskly across at me, and pulled the top off his pen. I remembered how we'd kept hold of one another's hands after the handshake last time, and wondered whether the feeling that had passed between us was being echoed when he touched my arm. But maybe it was nothing. Doctors are taught to touch their patients, and it extends to relatives, too. A nice warm feeling is so easily aroused. Gregory does it to everyone.

Through his window I could see a patch of snowdrops and crocuses. On his desk was one of those heavy glass paperweights that look like they have squashed sea anemones inside. When Dr Stern finished feeding his paper on autism into his fax machine, he got straight to the point.

'Your mother is suffering something of a relapse,' he said.

He had soft dark eyes like I imagine Jesus Christ, or Judas Iscariot, had; the kind of eyes you see in religious paintings in poorly lit museums. I stared into them sort of mesmerised, and he stared straight back, radiating infinite kindness, and gentleness, and understanding. Again he had that strange effect on me of making me want to cry.

'Paranoid schizophrenia is a tricky disease to *treat*,' he went on. His voice was very gentle, but very decisive, and he stressed particular words carefully, like a teacher. 'I hope you won't be *offended* if we restrict all visits for a while.'

They were trying to modify her medication to cope with her current state of mind, he said. The results were somewhat *distressing* – for her and for other people. She was in isolation *for her own protection.* I pictured her alone, playing patience, writing her mad letters, reading Iris Murdoch, and making little effigies in clay with her big fingers. Farmer's fingers. The thought of them for some reason churned up a great clod inside me. I said I wasn't offended, because I didn't visit her much anyway. In fact only twice, and the last time – but I couldn't help wondering. If that. If that had something to do with it. If it was my fault. My fault, Doctor. Dr Stern. If my visit had. You know, distressed her. If I had wrecked his work on her. If, if.

I was on the verge of tears – not for my mother, but for me, I suppose. Dr Stern was making me cry. I couldn't stay. Really couldn't, Doctor. Not like this. Not usually like this. Snuffling into the tissue he tactfully handed me, I wrote my phone number down on his pad and rushed out.

'Can we talk about my mother some other time?' I blurted at him through my tears as the door swung shut.

I didn't know if he heard. Linda would have taken a dim view.

I had to prepare dinner for six people that night. Stuffed mushrooms followed by peppered duck followed by lemon mousse and cheese. Ma once made me do a cookery course.

'I told you it would come in useful,' murmured a Scots voice, far back in my head, as I prepared the ingredients. 'And remember that more salt's better than less.'

29

I poured quite a lot in.

You think you'll always stay young, don't you? I do. I'm thirty-two, which isn't so young really. It's the age by which you should have achieved something, if you were ever going to, even a bit. Look at Christ. He was only a year older when he was tacked up on the cross. I spent so long at the poly doing this and that – interior design, business studies – and going on holiday and having boyfriends and all that eighties stuff, getting drunk on *sangría* in Ibiza, wearing white high-heels to discos in Club Med, working in travel agents' offices. I went on holiday a lot, being in the business and getting the discounts.

Slowly work the flour into the fat, and remove the garlic clove.

That's how I met Gregory. He was booking a holiday for him and 'a friend', and then the friend pulled out and I said to him as a joke, because he couldn't get a refund, 'Oh, I'll come with you, if you like.'

It was just a joke, but he took it seriously, because he's that way. We had nothing in common, but Spain is quite a good place for that. I sunbathed while he read books; he was studying for his obs and gynae exam. The sex was quite a challenge, as was the compulsory musical accompaniment; I found out he was a Catholic and not really used to seeing fornication in recreational terms. This turned me on; I felt I liberated him. I didn't realise that it would leave me chained instead. Now I wouldn't know how to seduce a man if I tried. For eight years, it's been a solid diet of Gregory and fertility charts. And then when Billy came along, I disappeared. Nobody seemed to miss me.

Baste the bird regularly, and add the sauce at the very last minute. Carve and replace under heat before serving as this is a dish that must always be piping hot!

Dr Stern phoned while I was cooking. I had spilt some lemon juice on the floor and Billy was sliding about in it and I was yelling at him when the phone rang, so I shouted, 'Yes?' down the phone, assuming it was family.

'Is this a bad time to call, Mrs Stevenson?' he asked.

'No, it's fine,' I said, adjusting my voice, reaching for the biscuits. I gave Billy three, so he would shut up while I was talking. That's one of the things I do that makes me feel like a bad mother.

'I'm sorry I got so emotional, Dr Stern,' I said. 'I just feel ripped into minuscule shreds about the whole thing, like it's my fault she's having a new crisis.'

'I know that's how you feel, but it's quite unjustified,' he said. 'You really mustn't worry about any effect you might have on your mother. It might well have happened anyway. The disease she suffers from is very, er ...' There was a very long pause while he searched for the word. It was worth waiting for: '*cavalier*'.

'Can something be done? I mean – permanently?'

'We pride ourselves in our *pharmacological* approach to illness in Manxheath,' replied Dr Stern. 'No point treating the underlying emotional problems until we've tidied up some of the more alarming and florid *symptoms*. The brain is the most intriguing organ in the body,' he went on. 'Did you know, Mrs Stevenson, that we have only managed to map a *tiny area* of it? It's like ocean on the globe. Uncharted, for the most part. *Ignored*. And your mother's is no exception.'

Guilt again. And surprise: this doctor seemed to find my mother interesting.

'See her brain as a *vast sea of chemicals*, Mrs Stevenson, whose balance has been disrupted by, say, an earthquake on the sea-bed which has set off a series of underwater explosions.'

'Or something that's come along and polluted it,' I said.

'Absolutely! I see you've got the picture. Anyway, we're trying to restore the chemical ecology through some state-of-the-art *intervention*. We are lucky to have a man called Hollingbroke on our staff. He has a way with drugs. If it weren't all so scientific,' he laughed, 'you'd almost call it *instinct*.'

I laughed too. He had certainly cheered me up, with his oceanic metaphor. He said he'd contact me again as soon as there was enough improvement in Ma's state of mind to allow further visits.

'Thank you so much, Doctor,' I said. 'You've been very kind.'

'Not at all,' he said. 'Schizophrenia is very stressful for the whole family. You all have to take it easy and above all *not feel responsible*.'

After I'd hung up I found myself awash in self-pity and relief, and ate five biscuits rather fast.

At seven o'clock Linda arrived with her new boy-friend: Duncan. It turned out she met him at the mental hospital. He was another regular visitor – the brother of someone autistic, or 'blocked', as Duncan put it. He had that sheepish, modest look that classified him as a Type One, according to the questionnaire, but puzzlingly, he wore a lot of aftershave, which is a Type Two characteristic. So tonight Linda had the best of both worlds.

'Why the fuck don't you ever have an ashtray in this place?' Linda accused me.

'Because we prefer people not to smoke here,' said Gregory in what I call his 'voice of authority'.

I could tell Linda was in the mood for a stand-off as she went and fetched an eggcup from the kitchen and lit up in front of him. An hour later Ruby Gonzalez showed up and plonked herself on the sofa. I poured her a huge sherry, but she said she was only drinking fruit juice. She attacked the peanuts with gusto. There was chatter about this and that. The snow, the catalepsy outbreak in Jutland, childcare, the Fish Wars, wallpapering. I had to dash in and out of the kitchen to check the dinner. Then just when we were giving up on him, Gregory's step-brother arrived. John lived locally and he and Greg only had each other left when it came to family, so he always filled in when we were one missing. As far as I could work out, this was what John was for. I saw no other purpose to him. A dinner-party man, with a range of ten after-dinner anecdotes and jokes, all of which I'd heard. They involved sex, farting and aeroplane journeys, mostly. It took courage for me even to look at Ruby Gonzalez. She gave me a bad feeling, like I was drowning.

'You're looking great, Ruby,' I said to her. 'Are you pregnant, by any chance?' (I had to know.)

'No, no,' she said with a big julie of a smile. 'I'm afraid I'm just fat.'

If you believe she's just fat, I said to Gregory later, then you're the one with the delusions. On a success scale of one to ten, the occasion ranked at about minus eight. There was Ruby, smiling and fecund, and Linda, neurotic in my mother's cast-offs, way too big but bunched together with a cheap belt. Her boyfriend (or her 'boyfriend substitute' as Gregory called him later) was silent, as Type Ones always are, and adoring. Linda called him 'darling' all the time, as if it was his name. John was his usual self. Over peanuts, he told Ruby the one about the arseless chicken. Later, in the kitchen, he winked at me and slapped my bottom.

'How's tricks, sister-in-law?'

'I'm fine, John. Can you put this casserole on the table, please, with a mat underneath?'

That was the extent of our conversation.

Ruby and Gregory had a lot to say to each other. She had one of those sexual foreign accents mixed in with the twang of Croydon. She was very flirtatious for a fat woman. Or perhaps just very fat for a flirtatious one. Either way, she had a lot of nerve. It wasn't just my husband she flirted with; it was everybody, male and female. She was nauseatingly charming, complimenting me on the food and cooing over photos of Billy and helping me take out the dishes, insinuating herself. Even the hard-nosed Linda allowed herself to be bewitched, as one professional woman sometimes is by another in a field that does not compete with hers. Perhaps I could have fallen for her too. But I held out, clinging on to a cold thing in my heart, a little shard of mistrust. My instincts rarely deceive me. We were discussing compost, of all things, when Linda decided to launch one of her attacks on Gregory – presumably to impress Duncan.

'Well, I think it's completely unethical, this Perfect Baby drug,' she said to Gregory, out of the blue.

'Isn't it?' she asked the room.

When nobody answered, Duncan chimed in, 'Yes, I mean, doesn't society need handicapped people?'

Which was brave of him.

'No to both questions,' Gregory replied, wiping his mouth on a napkin. 'By the way, Linda, I didn't realise that you were a devotee of Channel Praise.'

This was bound to sting Linda, who loathes religion in general, and evangelism in particular. She flashed him an acidic look and muttered, 'Of course I'm not a devotee. But the evangelicals haven't got it all wrong.'

She picked up her fork and began to drag it along the tablecloth like a teeny ploughshare.

'What's unethical,' asked Gregory, 'about wanting the best life for your child, and making sure he isn't disadvantaged from birth? And the idea of a society *needing* the handicapped is downright absurd and masochistic. Who needs problems? Who in this room would choose to have a handicapped child for the so-called good of the community? There are other ways of doing good than encouraging stray dogs and tramps, you know.'

Gregory was a firm believer in this. He was opposed to helping those in need directly, when they came knocking at the door. He would even turn away gypsies selling brushes, tea-towels and gardening gloves. But he wrote generous cheques twice a year to five charities.

'But if all babies were perfect babies,' said John, 'wouldn't the world be a pretty dull place, me old cock? Let's face it. Think about when they grow up. All the women would be a nubile twenty-year-old Mother Teresa with great tits and all the men would be Jesus Christ with a fat wallet and a huge dong. Personally I rather like being a flawed specimen of humankind.'

'Just as well,' muttered Linda. I helped everyone to more sauce.

'Not that there's anything undersized about my meat and two veg – don't get me wrong!' John added in the brief silence that followed, and he laughed, whizzing his eyes round the table. I could suddenly picture him at his software sales conferences.

'The Perfect Baby idea is a media distortion of the very serious work we're trying to do,' Gregory said tolerantly.

Of the two brothers, he was the one with the unspoken upper hand. When the boys were thrust together in a step-family, it was because Greg's dad had money, and John's mum had been frail. Ruby Gonzalez was smiling a faraway smile and nodding sagely.

'We're not trying to raise a generation of saints. We're just trying to eliminate some of the sinners.'

'So what's a sin then?' asked Linda sharply. 'Mental illness, for example?'

She and Duncan exchanged a look charged with pomposity and circumstance. All those visits to Manxheath had clearly had an effect.

'A sin, no. A major inconvenience to the families concerned in particular and to society as a whole, yes. Physical deformity and handicap likewise. Don't forget that it's already possible to abort a handicapped baby if it's diagnosed early enough. I've done thousands of abortions of malformed foetuses. All this drug is doing is to flush out – to *deselect* – the less competitive specimens, often before the woman even knows she's pregnant. Only the very highest-grade foetus will survive. We're talking about an intelligent drug – a sorting drug. That's why it can take years to have a baby using it. The woman may abort, in the very earliest stages, fifteen or twenty times before a foetus makes the grade. It has to pass a physical test but also an intelligence test, you see.'

'A bit like for the FBI?' asked John.

Linda and Duncan were exchanging disapproving looks, and muttering.

'By the way, Hazel,' John said through a mouthful, 'nice din-dins, not too salty at all, once you get accustomed.'

'Well, I still can't see anyone opting to use a drug which is going to cause miscarriages,' I said. This was my main objection to Gregory's research. 'I had three before I had Billy. It's the worst thing any woman can ever go through.'

There was a bit of a pause then, and Gregory and Ruby exchanged a professional glance.

'Well, that's one point of view,' Gregory said, 'but to

answer your point, and Linda's, there are a lot of very serious-minded people who believe that, in an already over-populated world, everyone should do their best not to create unnecessary or useless or negative life. Those are the people who are going to choose this drug. They're prepared to wait for that one child who's got that bit extra to offer, and I salute them for it.'

Gregory had that missionary light in his eyes, and he turned their beam on us all. No one could say my husband wasn't intelligent. Cleverer than all of us, that's for sure, I thought. Even Linda, who has a certificate in her loo proving she's in the top 2 per cent. I was feeling too hot, like something was about to explode. Gregory, who was toying with his glass, suddenly looked around the table and then across at me.

'Is there any more of that Sancerre, darling?'

When I came back with a fresh bottle, I thought I saw Gregory move his leg away from Ruby's under the table. I couldn't be sure, but the idea of it set my heart mashing with grief and hate.

'We're living on a threatened planet, you know,' Gregory was saying. 'I'm proud to think that I'm doing my bit.'

The threatened planet. The cliché of the decade. Call me selfish, but *what about my threatened marriage?* My heart was thumping too hard, the way it does when I think of those babies I lost, and the way Gregory dismisses it like it's nothing. The way it's as if they're attached to me by a string, and the way it doesn't make sense in words.

But Linda stood up, her face red.

'Come on, Duncan,' she said, jerking her head towards the door. The gesture tugged him up from his seat. 'We're going.'

There was a pause as this sunk in. Linda likes scenes,

or rather she likes to make a show of her principles by boycotting this and that. She's a crusader by nature; a splinter group of one. ('I *oppose* cabbage,' she told Ma when she was six.) She nagged me for years about buying factory-farmed meat and not bothering to put my empty bottles in the bottle bank. 'Can't you see it's political?' she'd say, smashing them in. She had clearly impressed Duncan; he'd gone the sickly fawn colour of wheatgerm.

'I take it that you two won't be queuing up at Greg's clinic for a Perfect Baby then,' said John, but the joke cracked on silence. We watched while they bustled about with coats and Linda put on her Leningrad hat.

Gregory called out rudely as they were leaving, 'You could always stay and argue it through rationally, you know, Linda. Or is that too taxing for your intellect?'

Linda slammed the door behind them both, and Gregory laughed. Ruby Gonzalez smiled a smug smile and patted his arm.

'There will always be people who take that view,' she said. 'They have a right to it. I respect that.'

Then she leaned across the table and patted my arm, too, so that I wouldn't get jealous.

'What a pity for them,' she said. 'They'll miss out on a second helping of your really most delicious lemon mousse. I know I ought to be on a diet, but do you think I could have some more?'

Which John took as his cue for the bulimia joke.

When Ruby and John had finally gone I didn't even bother clearing away.

'You do it,' I told Greg. 'I did the cooking. That was my contribution.'

To my surprise, he didn't say anything, but started collecting the dirty plates and glasses.

I went to the living-room and slumped in front of

the television. They were showing a re-run of one of the Reverend Carmichael's shows. *Holy Hour,* it's called. Channel Praise repeats them throughout the day, with Christian game shows and competitions and Church-approved chart music in between.

'Meddle ye not in the will of the Lord,' the Reverend Carmichael's voice buzzed. 'And the Lord's will tonight is that ye all phone in our special dial-a-prayer number with a loyalty pledge to our saviour.'

He fell to his knees and began speaking in tongues, repeating a word that sounded a bit like 'taramasalata' over and over again, with little hiccups for punctuation. He was everywhere – on billboards outside Jaycote's Park, on chat shows, in newspaper photo-features and on the front cover of his book, *God Alone Knows,* launched to coincide with the opening of Channel Praise. *Holy Hour* had only been going six months, but the Reverend's sweaty face and poppy eyes already felt like an institution. The tabloid press adored him because he was happy to provide stunts: Vernon bungee-jumping off the Severn Bridge, Vernon rowing a canoe down rapids to help children with cancer, Vernon weeping at the funeral of a grandmother raped and murdered by hooligans. Vernon at Easter, sporting bleeding stigmata on his hands. He quickly became known as 'the Raving Rev', and a poll among women showed that we found him supremely attractive. 'Vernon the Turn-On' was the headline verdict – and he obliged by posing shirtless, his hairy pot-belly in unashamed profile, to raise money for Sheep in Need. I don't know why I was watching him. Perhaps because I knew how much Gregory hated his show. There was something mesmeric about it. The money was pouring in. Glorene from Winchester pledged £1,000, with a prayer asking the Lord to help her with her financial troubles. Slowly, I drank gin. An hour later Greg put his head round the door and asked if I was coming to bed.

'No,' I told him. 'I'm thinking.'

'I didn't think watching Channel Praise was conducive to that,' he said, seeing the Reverend Carmichael's moon face filling the TV screen. He hadn't realised the state I was in. I was choking on a wodge of misery.

'Just go away!' I yelled at him.

I *had* been thinking. Horrible thoughts that couldn't be suppressed. Gregory looked shocked. He wasn't used to bad behaviour. Nor was I. We'd always been polite.

'Darling Hazel, you must calm down.'

He said it with the sort of gentle and reasonable voice police negotiators use to stop crazed people jumping off high buildings.

'Your menstrual chart tells me this isn't a great time of the month for –'

He ducked as I flung my half-empty glass of gin at him, missing his ear by inches.

THREE

Snip, snip.

High in the glass and steel tower that is the administrative headquarters of the Ministry's Edible Fats Policy Division, the Assistant Manager (Butter Sub-Unit) is enthroned behind a broad desk in an office with carpet-tiles the colour of dried blood and walls the colour of powdered coffee whitener. She is clipping her nails. Linda Sugden finishes her right hand, the trickiest, and starts on the left, her tongue protruding slightly as she concentrates on obtaining a blunt, business-like oval. Her profile is framed in the light from the window behind her, which shows only the grimy blanket of air that the weatherman on *Good Morning Gridiron* has been cheerily referring to as 'our old friend, that depressing, unshiftable bit of cloud cover'. It's been stuck there for days. Far below, Gridiron hums its city tune, while above the swathe of grey cumulo-nimbus, an aeroplane scrapes a chalky path, and fades to a dot.

It is nine o'clock, and Linda, normally a powerhouse of activity, has neither sorted her in-tray nor drunk her first cup of terrible Ministry tea. All she has done so far is to smoke three cigarettes. Like wedding-day rice, the nail-clippings lie scattered at her feet. She straightens her back, adjusts her focus and continues methodically. Two snips for the thumb. *Snip, snip.* The index. *Snip.*

41

The middle finger. *Snip*. The ringless ring finger. There is a quick knock at the door, and before Linda has time to answer, it opens, letting in a harsh blast of fluorescent light from the corridor. A figure flits in and closes the door softly. Linda tightens her jaw and does not look up. *Snip*. The little finger. Finished.

Linda believes in short nails.

'Morning, Miss Sugden,' murmurs Tish, her PA, who believes in long vampy ones, red-varnished acrylic extensions, and special glues for emergency mending. Trish who has small muscular legs clad in oyster Lycra, and who now wafts gusts of Opium from her tart little cleavage. Trish who owns no fewer than six leotards and who for two years was an air stewardess and is therefore used to heights such as this, the twenty-first floor, a work environment on stilts.

'Nice night last night then?' she asks routinely.

'No,' Linda scowls, still not looking up, knowing she won't like what she will see. 'I had a row with my brother-in-law over this genetic drug he's working on.'

She does not mention that the evening was finished off with a second row, this one with Duncan, whose sexual incompetence is hitting a strangely familiar sea-bed of hopelessness.

'I'm not a *charity*,' she had hissed at him this morning after yet another failure.

'It takes two,' he had said, as usual.

'That's the tango, not sex,' she had snapped. 'I don't *have* four hours.'

She'd slept badly, too. There'd been terrible dreams, culminating in a vile, half-waking nightmare about stirring a cauldron of boiling water and charcoal lumps, preparing a grey 'vitamin stew' for a herd of wildebeest from the Gridiron Environment Centre to eat for its midday meal. She had been put in charge of the project, and a deadline was involved. She had woken in a pitch of anxiety, with the dream clambering across her skin. She had stormed out to work, forgetting to apply underarm deodorant, and accidentally-on-purpose smashing a milk bottle on the doorstep, which she had left for Duncan to clear up.

Now, with controlled violence, she pokes at a cuticle with the claw end of the nail file, while Trish slaps sheets of paper in and out of trays. A minute later, thinking aloud, and unable to stop herself, Linda blurts, 'Which is worse, a man who starts but can't for the life of him finish, or one who finishes before he's started?'

And realises immediately that she's said the wrong thing, and it'll be round the whole of Ag and Fish by coffee break.

'I'm not sure I'm getting your drift,' replies Trish. 'Started what?' And her pencilled-in eyebrows vault to questioning arcs high in her forehead.

'Well, you know. *It*,' says Linda, unable to find a way of reversing the conversation, her face hidden as she stows away the manicure equipment in the bottom drawer of her desk.

'It?'

Linda's voice, still invisible and somewhere close to floor level, articulates, '*It*. The sexual act. Intercourse. So-called lovemaking. Sexual congress, physical union.' And then, with distaste, 'Bonking.'

'Oh, *that*,' replies Trish, catching sight of a Boeing 747. There'd been Mile Highs, foreign hotels, flight captains called Jim or Roger, and the friendly clink of G and T in her flying days. Cabin crew, doors to manual.

'Dunno, really. Depends how long you want it to last, I s'pose. Depends on your attitude to it.'

(Miss Sugden, she tells Chrissie later, looked like she needed a bit of help. There are some people, aren't there,

43

who you just can't imagine *a.* in the nude, *b.* showing their body to a person of the opposite persuasion, and *c.* actually doing *that*.)

'Go on,' says Linda, lighting her fourth cigarette with relief.

'Well to be quite frank I just let them get on with it at their own pace, myself,' Trish says, perching herself on the arm of a chair and gyrating her pretty ankle to reveal delicate bones. 'I like to turn a man on, don't get me wrong, but at the end of the day I can take it or leave it, because I'm big-hearted.'

The left ankle stops revolving and the right one starts. Linda watches, fascinated.

'I don't care what he does or how he does it,' Trish is saying, 'as long as I get the champagne before and the cuddles afterwards, and a bit of respect in the morning. I'm a Libra, I think I told you, so fair's fair's my motto.'

Linda's eyes widen in disbelief, then narrow in smoke, as Trish's little goldfish mouth clarifies, 'It's all in the stars, isn't it?'

Linda is a galaxy away. For a moment, there are no words she can reach. Then, with a small brain wave, she musters, 'I'm an Aries.'

'Well,' says Trish triumphantly. 'There you go then. Ambition and stubbornness. Setting your sights too high. Typical.'

Linda's jaw tightens, padlocking her face shut. Past embarrassment, they both shuffle papers about for a minute, and search the sky for relief. In the distance, a fire alarm rings. Then Linda stubs out her cigarette, reaches for her biro and lets out a sigh.

'Get me a cup of tea, please,' she says briskly. 'And could you tell Norma in Phase Two Marg. that I'm fed up with her memos. Her spelling is appalling, especially in view of her much-vaunted degree in English Language and Literature.'

Trish skims out on her sexy little legs, flinging the *Gridiron Echo* on Linda's desk. Trish has already asked for a transfer. Nothing against Miss Sugden *in herself*, she'd explained to the personnel officer, her mascara gaze frank. It's just that I prefer men. Even if they're wankers, you know. I just know how to handle them. I can't deal with Miss Sugden. I think she may have Mercury in her Ascendant or something.

'Champagne,' Linda mutters, attacking her in-tray with venom. 'Cuddles afterwards. That girl comes from fucking Mars.'

She rips open letters, crushes and hurls the envelopes at the bin, signs memos in threatening black ink. Writes a sarcastic letter to deal with a long-standing débâcle in Polyunsaturated. Makes a brief but effective phone call to Jonathan Higgins *vis-à-vis* his sorry performance at Wednesday's Rancidity Forum planning meeting. Writes a list. Sits back, breathes in deeply, exhales, waits for her tea, reaches for the newspaper. And freezes suddenly in concentration. The photograph on the front page is of a man with a moon face, wearing a peaked cap inscribed with the words 'God's Gift'.

'CULT REV IN TOWN', says the headline.

Linda stares at the photograph. The eyes are shaded by the cap, but the smile is the same fat-lipped Mummy's-boy smile she has seen on television, and more recently on billboards around Gridiron City. Inside, on page five, is a full-page ad inviting worshippers to join the Reverend Carmichael in Jaycote's Park tonight. Glancing up to check the door, Linda speed-reads the 'Message to the Lonely', doodles a moustache on the evangelist's upper lip, and gives what Hazel calls 'one of her snorts'.

Miles up, outside, the atmosphere spins and waits, while beneath, below ozone, like a bottom on a seat, the weather shifts uneasily. The cloud sinks and broods over Gridiron. The flattened city hugs the planet, a chemical trap.

At midday, Linda is in the supermarket. She is buying eggs.

'Seen the size threes anywhere, luv?' asks a wind-cheatered blob next to her in the aisle.

The smell of furniture polish seems to leak from his glands.

'Between size four and size two,' snaps Linda, spurning the attempted pick-up. 'Confusing, isn't it?'

And turns her back. Linda has selected five packets of free range. She checks the date-stamp and her mouth twists bleakly. LAID ON JANUARY 20TH. Call it a 'project'.

At the checkout, she helps herself to a packet of Love Hearts from the sweetie counter. Call it 'the greed of emptiness and the emptiness of greed'.

That evening, sitting on a plastic seat in the auditorium, Leningrad hat resting on her lap heavy as a dead cat, knitting needles devouring a ball of mohair, another dream comes back to Linda. It's the one before the one about the wildebeest. The one she'd forgotten. She and Ma and Hazel are walking along a bumpy road looking for a giant rock which is somehow extremely significant, but there are no signposts. The rain begins to wash away the road, and Hazel's husband Gregory appears naked with a platter of offal he's cooked, but he refuses to say whether it's factory-farmed. Only Hazel eats any, and with such a look of smugness it makes you puke. The dream ends in something sexual and disturbing, which sets Linda off knitting even more furiously. She does not notice people squeezing past her as the auditorium fills, or Carmichael entering. Or even that, suddenly, everyone except her is cheering – until the woman sitting next to her, who has a bad case of eczema, gives Linda a violent nudge.

'Someone else could have had your seat if you're not interested. They're turning them away at the gate, you know.'

'I can do what I like,' hisses Linda. But she puts down her knitting (Ma called it her 'habit with wool') and reaches for something from her briefcase, before fixing a long hard gaze on the preacher.

Words are plopping from his mouth in dollops.

'Welcome tonight, my children. Everyone got a seat now? Everyone comfy?'

Linda recoils. From where she is sitting, the evangelist is the height and breadth of a patio shrub. As he paces about the stage, his purple robes flap in the breeze, showing white trainers beneath. He has a tiny microphone clipped to his dog-collar and carries a silver tambourine.

'Is this your first time, sir? Yes? Ah, so you're a virgin, so to speak! Yo! Almighty Alrightey!'

He jingles his tambourine at a man in the audience. A giggle scutters through the crowd, and the woman next to Linda nudges her and whispers, 'Quite racy, isn't he?'

Linda gives a dead smile that shows teeth.

'Welcome children, welcome all of you. Hallelujah.'

The accent is transatlantic, and there is a faint reverberation on the microphone as he speaks. Charisma loads his words like extra ketchup.

'God's with us today, right?' (A cheer.) 'I didn't hear you, boys and girls! Is God with us today?'

'Yeah!' roars the crowd, and the eczematous woman next to Linda adds, 'Alrightey!'

Linda shifts in her seat and nestles something in the belly of the hat.

'Who wants a miracle today?' yells the Reverend Carmichael.

'We do!' chants the crowd, and the woman next to Linda begins to call, 'MI-RA-CLE, MI-RA-CLE!'

Others near by take up the cry, and soon the whole of Jaycote's Park is ringing with pantomime yells. A chorus of gobbledegook sets up at the back, mixed in with Hallelujahs and Praise-the-Lords.

'Yo, ye! Yeah!' comes Carmichael's voice, booming with juicy reverb. 'Me too! And God's gonna make us one today, for sure, because the big threesome is here tonight, I'm talking about God the Father (Lord be praised), Jesus his one and only son, and the third member of the Big and Awesome Threesome, Mr X the Holy Ghost. Here in Jaycote's Park, Gridiron. Let's hear it for Gridiron City!'

'Weigh! Woy!' yells the crowd. 'Weigh, wey-heigh!'

They punch the air, applaud, pop open cans of diet drinks. Then the purple-clad figure on the platform swivels himself round so that his back is to the crowd. When the cheers die down, he spins round and faces the expectant silence. He waits, immobile, for what seems like minutes. Tension buzzes and crackles across the auditorium. When he speaks, the smile has gone, and the voice has changed.

'Hey, you know what, folks. Jesus is telling me he might be doing a bit of healing tonight, for any of you folks with back pain. He's telling me he's focusing on back pain this week. And loneliness. Yup, I said it. That big L word. And you responded. Yeah. Yo. Wow, it hurts. Loneliness. Ouch. And don't you just hate to admit you're lonely?'

A sympathetic murmur spreads through the throng.

'A lot of lonely people here tonight? Don't be afraid of it. We're all lonely. Jesus was lonely. You can be lonely in families too, sir. Yes, madam, I can feel that loneliness coming through. And that back pain. Don't deny your loneliness tonight, folks. Don't pretend you haven't got that back pain. There's a cure, and it's Jesus speaking to me about it. Hands up, you back sufferers.'

A field of hands sprouts and sways in the air.

'Hands up, you lonely people.'

More hands blossom.

'A lot of loneliness in Gridiron City tonight. And a lot of back pain. I see a lot of you with two hands up. Now Jesus is telling me that your loneliness and your back pain may be connected.'

A few sobs float up from the crowd, and the hands begin to sway in the night air. Suddenly, high, high, high above them, a thing they take to be a strange bird soars in a celestially perfect and unpretentious arc to land with a splatter of yolk at the feet of the preacher. There is a shallow silence, the silence of a pan just before boiling-point, and then the crowd's murmur breaks in shock at the sharp yellow guk of treachery in their midst.

Carmichael's voice changes. 'Lots of lonely people,' he murmurs. He is gravel and honey now. 'And one very tormented soul.'

The outraged murmur rises an octave. Panic spreads. Hands shoot down to check wallets and handbags, then seek further reassurance in mints and hankies. Necks strain to catch a glimpse of the infidel. The woman next to Linda wheels round and hisses something at her, then straightens her back and calls out in a confident, teacher's voice that pierces the night air, 'Hey, Reverend! The lady with the egg! She's here!'

From nowhere, a spotlight swings to the aisle seat

of row sixteen, where Linda sits defiantly upright, her hands fondling another missile. On the ground next to her, in the aisle, is her open briefcase and the packets of free-range size fours she bought during her lunch hour. A hiss goes up from the crowd, but Carmichael, raising a stubby index finger, silences them.

'A tormented soul,' his breathy whisper reverberates. 'In need of love.'

The tambourine rattles ominously.

Linda stands up. Yells, 'You're a fraud! Religion is the opium of the people!'

And hurls another egg, which skims the evangelist's cassock and lands with a splat on a footlight beside him, where it quickly fries, blackens, and smokes with a brief whiff of bed-and-breakfast. Linda reaches for another, but Carmichael strides on his trainers to the middle of the stage and raises a hand in the stop gesture of a lollipop man.

'Wait,' he commands. He pulls himself to his full height of five foot six and faces Linda. The folds of his cassock spread behind him like the wings of a giant bluebottle. A man in the audience begins to cheer, and from a corner of the auditorium a slow hand-clap spreads across the crowd. Linda hesitates, but only for a second. She is just taking aim with another egg when the preacher speaks. His lips are soft pillows of flesh, and the voice he pours into the microphone is ineffably gentle, like oil.

'Come here, my child, and throw your eggs.' A gasp comes from the audience. 'Yes, young woman. Come here. Hurl eggs. Hurl abuse. Show the folks here all that pain that's inside you. Get that devil out.' He gestures to Linda to mount the stage. 'Come on up.'

Blinded by the glare of the spotlight, Linda stands

motionless for a moment until the excitable woman gives her a shove.

'Off you go then, you pathetic bloody attention-seeker,' she hisses through clamped teeth. 'And take your eggs with you.'

Linda can't believe her luck.

'Just watch this then,' she mutters.

She strides towards the stage clutching two packets of a dozen, and mounts the steps to the sound of hoots and jeers.

Who would have thought that such a small woman could contain such oceans of hate, they said afterwards. All those eggs. Such suffering. Ten omelettes' worth, at least. The next day it was the talk of Christian Gridiron. Those who had seen the spectacle boasted of it to their friends, who wished they had been there and in some cases pretended they had.

Conscious of the eyes on her, Linda took careful aim with her first egg. Carmichael stood with his arms outstretched, his eyes closed, a human coconut shy. Linda savoured the moment, sizing him up, weighing the egg in her palm, ignoring the jeers and taunts from the crowd. And then she threw. She aimed for the centre of his torso, and as the missile whizzed towards him, there was a sharp collective intake of breath. It seemed destined for a hit, but by some quirk, it fell short by a couple of inches and landed with a soft crunch at his feet. There was a murmur and a cheer from the crowd. Carmichael opened his eyes, but his face remained impassive.

'More!' he commanded.

Linda couldn't see him properly through the glare of the lights, although by now he was only a few yards away. His face was as bland and amorphous as pastry.

'No problem!' she screamed.

She wasn't going to allow one missed shot to deter her. She reached down for another egg, and took another step forward. The crowd hissed again. A man at the back yelled out, 'Communist!' and a snigger went up. The crowd brayed louder. Her heart was thumping.

'Bastards!' she yelled. 'You're all bastards!'

'Lesbian!' shrieked a woman's voice.

Another egg. Aiming, she focuses. This one is for Kenneth, who told me he loved me while he was getting that girl from the anthropology faculty pregnant. And hurls. It misses by a yard, and splats on to the stage, a streak of sticky yolk. Never mind. Have another go. Plenty of ammunition. This one's for Fergus who kept porn mags under his bed and once – Linda exhales in a tennis champ's grunt as she projects the egg high, high into the placid cow's belly of night. The crowd holds its breath as the egg lands with a candid little plop on the grass verge behind the stage. Fergus, who once called her Susie by accident, right at the moment of –

'More,' breathes Carmichael into his microphone. 'There's more anger in there, my poor child. Get it out. Get those devils out.'

SPLAT! A near miss, that one. Very near.

'Again, my child,' exhales the Reverend. 'Again!'

So here's one for Bobby, who was married and wouldn't tell her he loved her because that was something you only told your wife and four kids, and that day she'd bumped into them in the park, practically walked straight into them here in Jaycote's Park, a sunny smirky family, and he'd walked straight by, not even noticed, and she'd just crumpled then and there behind a laurel bush that smelt of air freshener and bawled her eyes out – there. That's for you, you self-satisfied, lousy, selfish –

It lands at the far side of the stage, but Linda doesn't see, because her eyes are streaming. Another, and another, and another. Jamie. Pete. Douglas. John One. John Two. John Three. Derek. More, more, more. More than the heart can stand. Finally, after a dozen eggs, she's getting up to date. This is for Duncan last night, and the humiliating spectacle of – splotch. A feeble shot. Now family. Hazel first. Cowardly Hazel. Brainless Hazel. Ma always preferred you deep down, Hazel. Nice pine furniture Hazel, married to a man who serves up offal in the nude and – fuck you, Hazel.

'Hey! A double-yolker!' someone yells from the crowd, but Linda doesn't hear.

Ma's turn. Ma, Ma. Can't forget Ma. Linda is sobbing now, deep racking sobs that strafe the crowd like the random light of a wild search-lamp. Ma, who tried to wreck my life, Ma who –

Linda almost dislocates her arm with the force of the throw, and she's past caring about targets. The throwing is all. It lands she knows not where. The crowd is in a frenzy now – cheering, booing, singing snatches of hymns, ordering french fries and frankfurters from the hospitality vans, clapping, speaking in tongues.

'Shhh! One left,' murmurs the preacher through the bubble of voices. 'Throw the last egg, my child. You know who it's for.'

A soft voice. Gentle, fatherly, loving. The voice of healing balm. Ah, the peace of it.

'Be brave, my child. Release the devil and let Jesus in.'

She clasps the egg so fiercely she can feel the physics of its shell resist her. She heaves her breath in and lifts her arm slowly to throw, but it's trapped. Can't move, won't move. Dad, Dad, Dad. Oh Dad. This one's for you. Two diseased goldfish and a broken heart are all you left me. She's weeping and sliding about in a slippery mass of yolk and white; the stage is a puddle of grief with a man standing in the middle whose arms are outstretched like the crucified Christ. I can't throw it. I can't, I can't. Dad. She staggers forward, slips, stumbles and falls, crashes down, hardly noticing the shell break like a mouse's skull and the trickle of egg through her fingers, and she's on the floor, slithering and helpless in a pool of slurp, her face up against a pair of white trainers flecked with yellow and the wet hem of a purple robe, and she's grasping for it now, grabbing wildly at air, and there's a hum in her ears which is the bleating and cheering of a hysterical crowd, distant as foreign radio, and she is choking, and begging the trainers: God help me, God help me, God help me.

'Rise, my child!' says the steady voice of conviction, and a hand, short-fingered and thick as iron, pulls her to her feet, and forces her arm aloft in a gesture of triumph.

Suddenly, no longer gentle but hard-edged, and with ruthless victory in his voice, 'Praise the Lord, a miracle!' shouts Carmichael, the reverberation knocking Linda flat again as she weeps and weeps, flooding out her heart's ocean, and offers him her frail and battered soul.

FOUR

My day had been less 'successful'.

I should have put two and two together a long time before, but I just didn't get round to thinking about it. About Greg, and Ruby, and that weird psychic remark of my mother's about voluptuousness. And their work together on that drug that obsesses him so. I'd always had a bad instinct about that drug. But I thought about it a lot that night of the miserable dinner party with the lemon mousse. I don't think I slept a single minute. At the beginning of the night, my head was reeling from the dinner party and those gins I'd downed to take the edge off it, but as the hours wore on things became clearer. By about five-thirty I was pretty sure. I got up and showered and warmed Billy's bottle, with *Good Morning Gridiron* on the radio, and the cold shard still jabbing at my insides.

At breakfast, I poured two bowls of cornflakes, and mixed some Fiba-mash for Billy.

'I know you're having an affair with Ruby Gonzalez,' I said.

Gregory lifted his eyes from his coffee and looked at me steadily.

'What?'

'I said I know you're having an affair with Ruby Gonzalez.'

He put down his coffee and smiled condescendingly.

'Really, Hazel – '

'Shut up. Don't bother denying it. Is it because she looks like the Virgin Mary, or just because she's pregnant?'

I hadn't expected it to come out quite like that, so obviously loaded with bitterness, but I hadn't slept, had I. He raised his eyebrows higher and higher, then laughed. Just laughed.

'First you're invisible, and now I'm committing adultery with the Mother of God. These are some pretty severe delusions, Hazel. Are you serious?'

He laughed, but there was anxiety in it. With fake nonchalance, he added, 'And by the way, Ruby isn't pregnant. As she said to you last night, she's just a bit overweight.'

I felt flattened. A night of sleeplessness for this. Gregory squinted at me sideways, as if he were puzzling over a diagnosis. Then he gave me his serious, doctor's look.

'Two things, Hazel. First of all, I don't think this is the kind of discussion we should be having in front of our son.'

Billy was chomping his way through his bowl of Fiba-mash, apparently oblivious, but I was nevertheless stung by my old friend, guilt.

'Secondly, can I suggest you go and have a chat with someone?'

It wasn't the first time he'd suggested this, but I played the innocent.

'What d'you mean, a chat with someone?'

'A *chat*. With *someone*. A *specialist*. How about that psychiatrist at Manxheath? You said he seemed like an excellent doctor. You're under a lot of stress with your mother, and it might help to talk it through with someone.'

'You. *You're* a doctor. I could talk it through with you, couldn't I?'

'But I'm your husband.'

'Exactly. That's why I'd like to discuss your infatuation with Ruby Gonzalez with you, and not my mother's *shrink*, who has nothing to *do* with it.'

'*Shwink*,' echoed Billy. '*Do* widdit.'

I remembered the rattle of my mother's swinging bag and the inexorably erotic handshake Dr Stern had given me. I imagined his slightly puzzled, sympathetic expression as I explained my husband's infidelity.

'Listen, Hazel, I'm sorry, but I really must go to work. I'm operating in an hour. Please calm down. Let me get you something.'

In a moment, or perhaps in half an hour, my husband came back with the post and two small white pills.

'Here, take these,' he said. 'They'll help you relax.'

After he left, I ripped open the post mechanically, then sat and stared into a white space, while in my side vision, Billy's fat hand reached forwards and closed like a sea anemone around a fistful of Fiba-mash.

'Shwink,' he said again, and applied it to his face.

Manxheath Institute of Challenged Stability
Dear Hazel,

Strange to see you the other day, after such a long absence. I am trying to work out why you came. Did your guilt build up to unacceptable levels? They say that's the way with visitors. Especially relatives. It's practically a recognised syndrome. Do bring my grandson next time: I would like to see him in the flesh, as it is also *my* flesh. I don't hold with this modern view that grandparenthood is something one can ignore because one's had nothing to do with the creation of the child. Of course one has. 'The chicken

57

is merely the means by which the egg reproduces itself,' remember? You're the chicken in this case: the halfway house. Billy and I have a bond that you ignore at your peril.

I'm concerned about him. He's been sending me rather disturbed telepathic signals, which tell me he may be constipated. You can't be feeding him properly. Call yourself a mother? When did you last have a good look at his stool?

That wee sexual *frisson* that passed between you and Dr Stern, by the way, didn't go unnoticed. I thought it in very poor taste. I'm surprised you had the nerve to try it on. It is the kind of thing that used to happen sometimes in the library when I was Deputy Chief Librarian, usually in the natural history section, of all places. I made a point of disrupting it. Told them they could take their libido outside and do it in the street like dogs. It has to be said you were looking quite dreadful. Thin, but not in an attractive way, and completely washed out. You had 'poached-egg eyes'.

Not much news to report this end. In Group we've been sitting round *en silence absolu* half the time. Keith has recovered from that fight you saw him have with Mrs Murphy, who is now on enhanced Largactil. Scrabble is her whole life, and she panics when someone cheats or comes up with a word she doesn't know. It was 'Spud-u-like' that did it. Keith's a genius.

Oh yes – Isabella's so-called phantom pregnancy is all of a sudden progressing rather rapidly, so perhaps you could bring a few maternity supplies with you when you next get an attack of 'guilty relative syndrome'. I am also short of fresh compost in the greenhouse so please recycle a few household scraps, but don't bother with eggshells, they take too long to rot down, despite what that ridiculous woman pundit with the frizzy hair and no proper nose says on TV.

Today is the anniversary of your father's death, so spare him a thought, silly bugger though he was. I wonder whether that Texaco woman Bernice remembers him. I expect not. I expect the erotic young creature (who is probably pushing fifty, now I think of it), I expect she has moved on to fresher and more available pastures. Thanks to art therapy, I now have a good likeness of her in effigy, but haven't decided on the most —

Must go. Collection time. Get your son's hair cut. Yours sincerely,
Your Ma,
Moira Sugden

It was an average kind of letter to get from my mother. Recently she'd reverted to writing her letters on paper, which meant I was more likely to read them. There was a time when everything was in black ink on scraps of cardboard in her tall, loopy handwriting. Then there were the sheaves of stained Kleenex, which I assumed had writing on them. For about six months her missives came written on old-fashioned waxed toilet paper of the kind I remembered from the municipal public conveniences of my childhood — paper which Linda used to complain 'doesn't so much wipe anything, as move it around'. There was a time when she'd written on what looked like banana leaves. I chucked them straight in the bin. Sometimes, I chose not to read the legible ones anyway. They had a bad effect on me. The one she'd written after I married Gregory left my neck rigid. It felt like rheumatism, but my GP diagnosed rage, known in the trade as anxiety. This morning's letter I'd opened distractedly, my mind still on the conversation with Gregory. The mild annoyance it stirred in me ('poached-egg eyes') seemed an irrelevance after the night I'd just been through. But I had to admit she was right about Billy's constipation, despite all the Fiba-mash. His hair was also very long; I'd never had the heart to cut his curls. It was slightly uncanny, the way she seemed to have an instinct about him. She'd faxed Gregory at work one time to say Billy was coming down with chickenpox. And three days later he did. When Linda and I were younger, and the three of us were all living at home in the Cheeseways, the house was a cauldron of psychic surveillance. Outright spying, too. One day Ma boasted to me that she'd read my diary systematically over the years. And my letters from boyfriends. A red cloud flew in front of my eyes. Then came the dreams about hitting Ma, but she was made of rubber, or sometimes jelly.

I threw the letter in the kitchen drawer, on top of a hundred other of her epistles from the State of Absolute Delusion and, clutching my two white pills, headed for the toilet.

We had two in our house. The downstairs was a white porcelain Armitage Shanks, with a black plastic seat. It was next to the utility room, where we kept the washing machine and the dryer and a cupboard with the Hoover and various brooms and dustpans in it. The upstairs was more fancy, with a low-slung bowl in oyster grey and a wooden pine seat. I hesitated about which to choose, and then decided on the downstairs. It was more toilet-like. I flushed the pills away and watched the last gurgle of water disappear before the bowl refilled. Then I bundled Billy up warm in his buggy and took him to the Busy Bee Playgroup. He gave me a wet goodbye kiss and toddled across to the sandpit to join a potato-faced girl with plaits wielding a plastic spade.

'I'm digging to Australia,' she told him, 'and I'll do a wee-wee when I get there.'

'And I'll do a poo,' said Billy, grabbing a purple rake.

I looked at my watch; it was nine-thirty. I had nearly three hours. As I walked home, down Woolcott Road, past the small park, the post office, B and Q, the betting shop and Tesco's, the shard inside me grew colder and colder. I thought about my husband and realised he was a perfect stranger to me. It was a short walk home, but on the way I decided something.

Some men are their work. Gregory was one of them. The fact that I knew rather little about what he did — the bare minimum, in fact — had seemed an advantage. Until now. I'd only visited the clinic a couple of times. It was Gregory's private territory, like the loft full of Airfix. It made me slightly nervous. It was the kind of small, intimate private clinic that sprouted in the late eighties and early nineties for specialised 'luxury' problems. Babies, in this case. Either too many or not enough. Gregory liked to call his business 'fertility management', because that covered both the creation and the destruction side. The clinic had the hushed, neutral ambience you'd expect in a bank or an insurance office — the abiding calm of a place designed to welcome mature women who'd taken calm and rational decisions about what to do with their wombs, and the contents or vacancy thereof. The nurses wore pastel uniforms that matched the wallpaper, and they ushered clients into a waiting-room where frazzled nerves were soothed by Dire Straits at low volume, the *Economist*, home decoration magazines and glossy, well-fed pot-plants. Every day a stream of elegant heels crossed the threshold. Not just Gridiron heels: heels from all around the country. Like the Reverend Carmichael, but on a smaller, more discreet scale, my husband Gregory had something of a following.

I had been there for the inauguration of the Fertility Management Centre, of course, as the Principal Scientist's wife, but the first time I saw it as a working clinic was when I'd locked myself out of the house, and had gone round for Gregory's key. I hadn't bothered phoning first; I knew he'd be there. All the women glared at me — it must have been my trainers. Or the baby in his pram, bawling for milk. When Greg arrived, I could see from his face he was furious. He practically threw the key at me. He wouldn't let me breast-feed in the waiting-room, and bundled me into a specimen room to do it. It smelt of ointment and urine and I asked myself why I'd married him and I couldn't remember.

'It's bad for morale to bring a baby into a clinic like this,' he hissed at me as I wrestled with the hydraulics of my maternity bra. 'You fool.'

He was right. It was bad for morale. Mine. As the tears juddered in my eyes, he ordered me a taxi home. He must have felt guilty about it though, because that night we made unscheduled love, and he said sorry, sorry, sorry, sorry, sorry, I was so awful. Sorry, sorry, sorry, sorry, he went on, sorry, sorry, and I was swept off to sleep on a wave of his ghastly remorse. Looking back, perhaps the extra sorriness was for other things. Anyway, he was himself again in the morning.

I only went to the clinic twice after that, but never with Billy, and I made sure to phone first. I thought the whole thing was crazy — those women in the waiting-room, I mean. Half of them desperately wanting a baby, the other half wanting to get rid of one — why didn't they all show some sisterhood and just swap about? That's how calf embryos are transported to Australia — in the wombs of rabbits. I read it in the *Reader's Digest*. I made the mistake of telling Greg this. He told me it was one of the most stupid things he'd ever heard me say. So after a while I stopped asking questions about the clinic, and Greg's work, and the drug called Genetic Choice. But now I was regretting it. Now I wished I knew more. That remark he'd made about making Ruby a member of the team: I couldn't get it out of my head. Greg isn't a team person. He hates teams. He likes sex, though, sort of. And he likes Ruby, who looks pregnant, and who is working with him on the Perfect Baby drug. You can see my line of thought. Deluded, Gregory would have said, shaking his head.

I'd always known that Gregory kept a backup copy of the Genetic Choice document on floppy disc in his study. I could hardly not have known, the amount of time he spent on it. Most evenings, after dinner, he'd go and work on it while I caught up on some ironing and watched tired old movies with Anthony Holden or Lee Remick on television. But it had never crossed my mind, until now, to read it. It had never seemed like it might contain any great secret. It was just there. We lived with it. Gregory talked about his research a lot, but he'd been doing it ever since we were married and I'd learned to switch off. I understood a few rudiments of science, but Gregory never learned the knack of explaining ideas simply, and the things he got passionate about were what seemed to me minutiae — the vagaries of quality evaluation and gene selection processes and clone perfection indexes. I sometimes worried that he got so bogged down in the detail that he lost sight of the whole thing. I never said so — though Linda, being Linda, did.

'Aren't you worried you're going to overlook something very simple?' I remember her asking him once, with the eager, dangerous shine her eyes have when she disapproves.

'Ah, the wood and the trees argument,' he'd said. 'No. You need to see the trees individually first. They make up the wood. When you've counted all the trees, you have your wood.'

I couldn't help laughing at that.

'Oh Greg, you're so pedantical,' I teased.

'Pedantic, you mean,' he corrected me sternly.

See what I mean?

I saw a pregnant woman on my walk home from the Busy Bee, and I took it as a sign. She was floating along in the drunken, milky trance of the third trimester, and I hated her. I decided that, when I got back, I would become a spy, like Ma. Just once. And I felt the blood drain from my innards, as though a plug had been pulled very suddenly, and the future was being sucked out.

I didn't go into his study much, even to hoover and dust. It wasn't my territory, and I felt like an intruder. A huge and terrible feeling of doubt rose inside me like vomit. The study smelt of marker pens and other stationery, and a thin light filtered through the drawn blinds. There were files on every shelf, marked neatly along their spines: 'IVF', 'Amniocentesis', 'Chronic Infertility', 'Over-fertility', 'Genetic Systems', 'Genetic Patterning'. There was a box of discs, and I spent a while hunting through until I found the one marked 'Genetic Choice'. It's a funny word, choice. It seems to have changed since I was a kid. You can have anything you like, Ma said, doling out tea. Fish pie or fish pie. You choose. Now Gregory has created another choice, that has nothing to do with fish pie. That's progress.

The body is 80 per cent water. Mine felt like it then, with just my skin holding it in. I didn't want to know. So what, if my husband and Ruby Gonzalez were cooking something together? And so what, if the thing they were cooking was, for example, a perfect baby? Never, since Ma had been certified, had I felt so close to the State of Absolute Delusion myself. And there in my mind's eye was Greg, telling a psychiatrist (Dr Stern, perhaps) about Hazel's 'unfortunate delusions' and about her needing treatment like her Ma, all the stress she's been under, thinking she's invisible, thinking Dr Gonzalez is the Virgin Mary . . .

I'd done a computer course once, as part of business studies, but my knowledge was out of date and it took me a long time to get into Greg's system, and, once in, to find my way to the right document. Scrolling through, there was a lot I didn't understand; graphs and charts and genetic maps. The text in between was written in the impersonal, ponderous language of science that I remembered from school. (A bull's retina was dissected. A Bunsen burner was placed beneath. A current was passed through. A scalpel was applied to.) There was a whole rat section, which concluded that 'the difficulties involved in assessing the vagaries of rat personality rendered the results impossible to quantify in a satisfactory manner'. Perfect-looking rats had been bred, it seemed, but Gregory couldn't tell whether or not they had 'low-grade', 'average', 'promising', or 'class one' personalities. I laughed at that. Poor Greg, trying to create a Jesus Christ rat. That bit was dated three Christmases ago. I remembered him being gloomy then, about rats. Obsessed. He even thought my Yule log tasted of rats. He'd been up to his ears in them.

Then I got to the bit about 'Baby B'. I understood that bit. It was quite simple. Not just the language of it, but the idea. It was too obvious, and I should have guessed. Because you can't live with a man like Greg, all bottled up like a specimen, without there being a secret sickness in one of you, can you? A regular guy, you think, just a bit introverted, but then they all are, aren't they, scientists? They have that reputation. I've seen them together sometimes, at conferences, standing in little groups stabbing at mushroom quiche on paper plates, their heads angled questioningly. They want to understand things, to know how things work. When my sewing machine broke down, Greg took it apart. Hundreds of tiny cogs, all ranged on the pine table, and screws and nuts and little pieces that probably don't even have names. And he worked out what was wrong and fixed it and put it all back together again, and when he'd finished and the sewing machine worked he had a look of joy more profound than on our wedding day. I realised then that they need to master a thing, to get at its insides and see how it works and then modify it so that maybe it works better. Maybe perfectly. A sewing machine, a body, a mind. They want to do it better than the manufacturer.

What I'm getting at is, it turned out that Greg had already used the drug on a woman.

Me.

The mother was administered the drug – without her knowledge – over a period of thirty-nine months. During this time she experienced three mid-term miscarriages and an unknown number of early 'spontaneous' abortions (all, presumably, of low-grade foetuses) before a satisfactory conception in June 1996 resulting in the birth of a healthy baby, a boy, on 5 March 1997. The boy is known to the study as Baby B. Early post-natal tests showed a baby of over-average birth weight with no remarkable features.

That red cloud again: I recognised it from before. My

first thought was that it was absurd, ridiculous and almost funny that our son should be called 'Baby B'. Was I therefore Mother H? Was Gregory Father G? Or Father Gregory G? It was suitably Catholic-sounding. I actually giggled quite a lot, in a light-headed, shivering way, before I cried. Then, slowly, it began to sink in. Billy was an experiment, like any other, but he was not kept in a cage with rat-droppings. (*Sperm was introduced. An ovule was impregnated.*) The typescript danced in front of my eyes. My boy. I'd thought he was Baby Ordinary. I was proud of how normal he was. How, when he was born, everything was there. Having lost three embryos —

Gregory had used a medical term for them: 'blasted eggs'.

It turned out that they were part of the experiment too. The Genetic Choice Programme referred to my little ghosts on a string as 'natural fallout'. In hospital, where I'd had their remains scraped out by dilatation and curettage, they'd called them 'the products of conception'. (And I'd thought, in those early years, they were the fruits of passion.) I was lucky, it seemed, only to have lost three. It might have been ten, according to the projected wastage statistics.

There was more about Baby B, but I had dried up. I had to sit back and drink some water, half a glass, before I could read it.

Baby B was breast-fed for six months, and pursued an average growth and learning curve. Follow-ups at thirteen, fourteen and fifteen months showed no features that distinguish Baby B in any way, physically or mentally, from an average healthy male baby of his age. At this stage of the trial of GR218 it is therefore apparent that the drug has had no

*visible or measurable effect on the baby produced
by this type of positive screening, and we conclude
that stricter screening criteria be incorporated in the
drug in future testing. Furthermore, in a future trial,
a change of mother is recommended. Baby B's mother
has a satisfactory IQ level, but it is not higher than
average.*

So the breeding stock had not come up to the mark:
Gregory was going to have to identify another silly
goose to lay him a golden egg. And it's true I must
have a defective IQ, because if I'd been intelligent as,
say, Dr Ruby Gonzalez, I'd have seen all this coming.
I'd have guessed a long time ago.

I carried on reading. There were some more math-
ematical equations and a series of graphs with Baby
B's head measurements. I noticed my hand on the
plastic mouse that controlled the screen was sweating
and dead-looking, like in horror films set in catacombs.
This can't get any worse, I kept saying to myself. But it
did. At the very end of the document there was a short
paragraph in a different style. It was less scientific, less
balanced. It might have been written after a couple of
drinks, by an exhausted man. In it, Gregory had added
the sting. The bit I'll never forgive him for. The bit that,
as I swallowed the words, turned my tongue to ash.

*Of some concern. The possibility that GR218 has
nevertheless had some effect, other than that targeted.
No signs to indicate this is the case. As yet. Possible,
note possible, that GR218 has selected and enhanced
genetic features or functions not factored into the system. E.g. rogue gene, not physical as far aware, poss.
psychiatric? Suggest continued assessment of Baby
B. Attempt to determine whether this the case. Of*

*crucial importance to further trials of GR218. Also of
concern to parents of Baby B: maternal grandmother
diagnosed paranoid schizophrenic. Some apparent,
note apparent, evidence child–grandmother telepathic
link, one or two-way unclear: stress, hypothesis only.
Evidence rogue gene re-enhanced by process?*

And that was all. No word of remorse. The screen did
not explode. No blood poured from it. There was
nothing.

We'd both wanted a baby so much. Not when we
were first married, I suppose – not in the days when it
was a question of newspapers in bed till midday, trips
to Venice and Carpetland, frequent sex, tasteful, pricey
living-room curtains and glass coffee-table buying. All
the usual upwardly mobile newly-wed stuff. I was
working in the client charter section of customer services
at Lockwood's, and they'd recently made me a junior
manager, so I had self-esteem, as well. We bought the
house in Oakshott Road and held a party. I was a pretty
woman with a talented husband. We had money.

I realised that I didn't have to be a mother like Ma.
And with Gregory running the clinic, I was in the best
hands. Curiously, when it came to it, Gregory hadn't
taken the miscarriages as badly as I had. Given all the
monitoring he'd done, I'd expected him almost to see
them as a sort of failure on his part, but he was very
philosophical.

'It happens more than you think,' he'd said, consoling
me in my nil-by-mouth hospital bed.

His faith was quite unshaken.

Hindsight: why's it never there when you need it?

I remembered that, when I was pregnant with Billy,
and past the stage of worrying about another miscarriage, I'd been happy. I'd smelt pungently hormonal,

and I'd spent hours contemplating my inside-out navel, perched like a landmark on my huge belly. Gregory was excited but distanced at the same time. He became more fanatical than ever about my monitoring. He took weights and measurements every day. (And here they were now, in the file.) And then, when I pushed Billy out, shot into a mad orbit of pain and screaming with a dry throat, Gregory put him gently to my nipple and said, 'A perfect baby boy.'

I was allowed to hold him for ten minutes, a strange, bloody organ snuffling at my breast in the place where my heart used to be, before Gregory whisked him off for tests. They must have depressed him, those first results. He managed to hide it – or perhaps I was just too elated to notice.

Had he ever seen our son as anything other than a failed experiment? He was always a loving father, but I never understood the pity that seemed mixed in with the tenderness. And though I developed, early on, a gut feeling that Greg felt disappointed in Billy, I never voiced it. When he spoke to Billy harshly, it was with a reproach in his voice that was in no way justified by whatever misdemeanour Billy had perpetrated. I put that down to Gregory's high standards, his punishing work schedule. But now it was clear: Billy was living proof that Genetic Choice hadn't worked. 'Pig-ordinary', Greg called him once, when he was only a few weeks old.

'I'm glad he's pig-ordinary,' I'd said. 'Isn't that all any mother has the right to hope for? That her child has a head, two arms and two legs? And all the right organs in the right places? And can smile?'

'Yes, of course,' Greg said, ruffling the baby's head in a crude sort of way.

And he cleared his throat and gave a tight, bright, horrible smile which made me flinch. I was about to say something about it when Billy vomited down my back and matters moved on.

My head was reeling as I gulped more water, this time straight from the tap, in the bathroom next to the study. Billy. Baby B. Me. 'The mother'. For the first time in my life I drank all the water I wanted. Little more than a pint, I suppose, but it felt like three gallons. I'll get intoxicated like my father, I thought. Drown from the inside. But finally I couldn't swallow any more, and as the cold water splashed in my face I felt my brain swivel into a strange mode. With hands that were still shaking, I took out the disc and put it back neatly, exactly where I'd found it. It was a quarter to eleven, so I had just under forty-five minutes left before I had to fetch Billy from the Busy Bee.

I'm not proud of what I did next, but I did it. What else was there to do? In the worst extremities, I've always resorted to hooliganistic violence – a small souvenir of behaviour I'd been party to in the State of Absolute Delusion. Driven by an instinct that seemed to come from somewhere you retch from, I began to smash up the house.

I started in the kitchen. Bottles, jars. Oil and kidney beans and rice and apple-and-ginger barbecue sauce. I even found the bicarbonate of soda – I'd been looking for it for months – but I smashed the jar on the floor anyway. Months. It was strangely satisfying. Anyway.

My heart was pounding and I could hear myself shouting, but couldn't make out the words. I got more inventive in the living-room. I took a whole fistful of Billy's wax crayons and wrote, 'YOU BASTARD' on the pristine white wall. ('White is the only colour for an internal wall,' Gregory's mother had told him on her deathbed. The hospital walls had been a liverish green.) I emptied two packets of mustard and cress seeds on

71

the carpet and watered them. Then I wrote, 'FRY IN HELL, RUBY GONZALEZ' on the door and set fire to Greg's favourite childhood memento: a church he'd built from matchsticks at the age of fourteen, before he lost his faith. It burnt beautifully, but I doused it with water just before the end, so he could see what the ashes consisted of. I'd get to the Airfix later. With relish I smashed the photograph of his dead mother who had left me, in her will, the two gallstones she'd had removed in 1989. It was the only photo of her he had. They say that no one should do that, destroy mementos of loved ones. But I was almost enjoying myself, killing his past, killing mine, killing our present. I found a tube of tomato purée and wrote, 'OUR LIFE IS A LIE' on the pale blue Persian rug which had been a wedding present from Don and Jade. Then I remembered the Black and Decker power saw that Gregory kept in the cupboard under the stairs. I'd always wanted a go with it. It made a hell of a noise as I got to work on all the pine. I amputated two and a half table legs, so the whole thing crashed into a slope like a Dali. I went to work on the chairs next. Legs, back seats. Little pieces, big pieces. The dresser. In half. I swear, I cut it dead in half. And crashing down it all came, with all those carefully chosen bits of china, all those nicky-nackies that tell you you've been places and done things on holiday. Have you ever sawn pine? God, the smell. Pure heaven. It was worth it for the smell alone, and the hellish noise that hurt so much it was like I was actually sawing my own head off. There was something savage and free about wrecking that home I'd worked for. It was like a primitive rite, in which you create one part of yourself by destroying another. I was just starting on the bathroom, emptying bottles of pills and smashing up all the mirrors (I gashed my hand and wrist on some glass, but didn't notice till later) when Jane-next-door rushed in and grabbed me by the hair and dragged me out of the bathroom. She must have used the spare key we'd given her.

'Christ Almighty, I thought you were being raped and tortured by a sociopath,' she said in a choked voice.

She forced me down on the sofa and pinned me there, looking about her wildly.

'Jesus, Hazel, have you gone completely crazy?'

'Yes! Yes! Yes!' I breathed.

It felt so free. Suddenly I went faint, and grabbed her arm. She made me do some respiratory exercises which reminded me of childbirth classes, then picked her way through the mess to make me a cup of tea in what was left of the kitchen, while I bled on to the sofa. When she came back she had the face of a prison warden, and handed me a steaming mug.

'Drink this,' she said, as though it were the antidote to snake-bite.

I sipped and scalded my tongue and gums.

'I'm going to phone Gregory right away,' Jane said, after she'd picked most of the glass out of my wrist.

I let her go through the palaver of phoning the clinic and getting transferred from extension to extension before a nurse told her he was busy on a Caesarean and he'd call back if it was urgent.

'Tell him his wife is extremely ill,' said Jane frostily, and put down the receiver.

I could see she was close to tears from the shock of having a madwoman on her hands. It's not something that occupational aromatherapists usually have to cope with. She drove me to casualty at St Mary's hospital. I watched her mouthing something to the receptionist, her eyes darting to and fro, a twisted look on her face.

'I'm sorry, Hazel, but I just can't handle blood. I'll fetch Billy for you,' she called as she ran like a bat out of hell through the opaque vinyl swing doors. I waited on a moulded plastic seat, slightly sticky, to be stitched up and bandaged. The man next to me had dislocated both his shoulders at the fitness club, he told me, doing an exercise called the Reverse Pec Strut. There was an old woman with two carrier bags which she kept her life in, I'd say. She had stinking, suppurating sores on both legs. I wanted her to die. It took a long time before they saw to me, but I was off floating in my own murk, a fish that had strayed too deep and beyond direction.

They stitched me up in a room with a poster on the wall that said in gothic writing:

It's nice to be important –
But it's more important to be nice!

It hurt like crazy, but after you have given birth all pain is relative. The nurse, labelled Ward Sister Fagin, wore orange foundation but she was cold as stainless steel. Staff in casualty wards don't take kindly to self-inflicted injuries. Afterwards I waited on a bench. An hour later Jane came back, without Billy.

'I've left him at my mum's,' she said breathlessly. 'She's looking after my niece, so he's got a playmate there. He's quite happy, by the look of it. I didn't think he should see you in this state.'

'Thank you, Jane, God, thank you. So much. Now please, please take me home,' I begged her. 'I have to pack my things. I have to leave my husband. He comes from hell.'

'All husbands come from hell,' snapped Jane, as though it were obvious, and we drove back to Oakshott Road in her white Renault 5. She dropped me at my door.

'Call me if you need me. I'll bring Billy back around four.'

I had to know if my son was going to go strange and turn into Ma. If, or when. Or could he be touched by the rogue gene already? He did unusual things sometimes – things I'd taken to be 'boy behaviour': squashing woodlice, hitting objects inexplicably with a stick, impersonating emergency vehicles. In a way, it all fitted together. Where I come from, the bus to misery arrives promptly and drives fast. I'm not a resourceful woman. So I sat down on our marriage bed and cried like a four year old. Who could I turn to? My family were useless – a loony mother, a father dead from water poisoning and a sister whose hobby was *Schadenfreude*. As for friends – well, I didn't have many, when I came to think of it – just mothers, really, people to discuss potty training with over coffee and custard creams. Jane, who'd just proved herself adequate in a crisis, wasn't someone I could confide in. It would have to be someone in a position to help. Someone to whom Genetic Choice already meant something. Someone with power, who knew the system – who would know how to stop Gregory. If it wasn't already too late. And I thought of Ruby, with her smug smile and her robust tits, and her bloody nerve. I needed someone on my side. A stranger who would take my story seriously, and who could help me find out whether my son was born with an unrefundable ticket to la-la land. The 'rogue gene'. One particular tree Gregory had failed to count in his nightmare wood of factors and indices. I pictured myself collaborating with my saviour, the two of us working over a sheaf of documentation, heads bowed, the light burning late in his office, preparing the case against Greg for the General Medical Council. Or the police. It was a noble and heroic portrait.

And yes, I admit it, there were other things too, about Dr Stern. His sympathetic ear. His dependability and assurance. His eyes. And the handshake that squeezed my heart. On the phone to him I was shaking, but I spoke very coldly and clearly. Yes, he said, he'd heard about Dr Stevenson's Genetic Choice work. Very interesting, very, er, contro*ver*sial. Hadn't had the pleasure of meeting him *personally*, as far as he *knew*, though their paths may have *crossed*, once or twice . . .

'Meeting him personally is no pleasure, Dr Stern,' I said. 'I'm regretting it by the minute.'

I told him everything. The pills. The miscarriages. Ruby, and the fact that she might already be pregnant. The possibility of Billy having a thing. You know, a hereditary factor. A rogue gene, something telepathic which meant they could talk even if they weren't together. A time-bomb of dangerous psychology. What Greg called somewhere in his report a 'variable'.

'I have to know about Billy,' I said. 'Then I can decide what to do.'

'These are very *serious allegations*,' said Dr Stern.

'I know,' I said. There was a silence.

'Can you, er, *back them up* in any way? Provide some kind of *paperwork* on this?'

When I told him all about the disc, and what sort of things were on it, he became excited and intrigued. He asked me a lot about what I'd understood. How familiar was I with scientific terminology? Very, I told him. It's my muzak. Then there were quite a lot of questions about me 'as a *person*', since we hadn't had a chance to get to know each other when I'd visited my mother. He spoke gently, picking his words very carefully, like flowers for an important bouquet. He was clearly trying to work out whether I was telling the truth or whether I'd gone mad, like Ma. I didn't blame him.

'Is there any way you can bring me the disc?' he asked eventually.

'Not without Greg noticing it's gone,' I told him. 'It's too risky.'

In the end, we agreed that I should leave without it, but go back to the house in a couple of days, while Gregory was out at work, and copy it or print it out.

'I'll contact your husband,' he said. 'I'll tell him I've taken you into my care at your own request.'

'I'm not coming to Manxheath,' I said quickly, picturing Ma's bulky silhouette in the doorway.

'Of course not, Mrs Stevenson. But it might be better for your *husband* to think that. I'll convince him that it's best to keep your *son* with you while you're . . . *ill*. Have you got somewhere to go?'

'I'll book into a hotel. With Billy.'

'Good idea,' he said. 'Somewhere like the Hopeworth?'

The Hopeworth. The pride of Gridiron City. The brightest star in its small firmament. A sign that Gridiron is on the up and up. Executives stay there on business. It's the venue for Lion's Club lunches, multi-charity dinner-dances, the Gridiron Floral Experience, Gala Nites. It's across the park from Manxheath, but a whole world away. It has a coffee shop that serves the best whipped *cappuccino* in the North. It has little racks of postcards depicting views of Gridiron: Gridiron by night, Gridiron at dawn, and a little pie-chart showing panoramas of Gridiron with fireworks and a cartoon Mickey Mouse doing cartwheels in the foreground. It is a haven of sanity.

'Yes. I'll be at the Hopeworth – under Sugden.'

My maiden name. It always reminded me of a blocked sink. I'd been happy to get rid of it, once upon a time.

'Have you, er . . . ?'

'It's all right, I have money,' I said, recalling the

American Express card that carried my other name: Mrs Hazel Stevenson. My card, Greg's money.

'Tell my husband I've smashed up a few things in the house,' I said. 'But I found the bicarbonate of soda.' I felt unnaturally calm and collected. 'And give my regards to Ma.'

I could have told Greg about what I'd done to the house myself, as it happened, because as soon as I'd put down the phone, it rang. I knew it would be him. I let it ring for ten rings while I decided what to tell him. I'd keep it brief.

'Hello?' I said coolly.

'What's going on?' he asked, not even trying to hide his annoyance. 'I got some garbled message from Jane saying you were ill.'

'I'm OK,' I told him. 'But I had a sort of turn. I think you were right about the stress. I've just spoken to Dr Stern at Manxheath, and he's going to give you a call. He thinks I might need some kind of rest. I'm going over there now, and he might keep me in. He says Billy can stay with me, and go to the hospital crèche.'

'My God,' said Greg, sounding genuinely concerned. 'What do you mean, a turn?'

'Well, it all started last night,' I said. 'I had a lot of things churning round in my head, and this morning after you left, after we had that row about Ruby, I just sort of snapped.'

There was a sound like a stifled groan from the other end of the line.

'What?' I said.

'I'll be on my way as soon as I've tidied up this post-op patient,' he said.

'No,' I told him. 'Don't bother. I'm OK. I don't much want to see you, in fact.'

'I'll call Dr Stern right away,' he said. 'I'll put him in the picture.'

'I've done that,' I said. 'I told him you think I'm having delusions. And he knows about Ma already, remember?'

'I'll talk to him anyway,' said Gregory.

His voice sounded very faint, like he might be wondering something. I hung up.

Having Dr Stern on my side made me feel strangely powerful. It was the same feeling I have had sometimes during sex.

FIVE

Today's the day
The time is now
Let Jesus in
It's *Holy Hour*!

'Welcome folks!' The televangelist rolls up purple sleeves and rubs together chunky, do-it-yourself hands. 'A pleasure and a privilege to be here today, folks. It really is.'

'Amen,' murmurs the audience. Those without concessions have paid £30 a head.

'Amen,' croaks Linda, and stubs out her cigarette into a foil ashtray.

She is watching the show on TV in the Ministry canteen. Across the formica, Hervé Démaret, her French visitor from the Commission du Beurre Congelé, stirs his bright pink raspberry yoghurt with distaste and observes the absurd Mademoiselle Sugden, stern dominatrix of the Edible Fats Policy Division (Butter Sub-Unit), with baleful eyes. Back in Lille, such shocking dress sense would warrant a memo.

'You English, you put too much false colouration in your *nourriture*,' he reproaches her, by way of conversation, inspecting a lump of vermilion fruit with the mistrust it deserved.

'Shhh! D'you mind? Can't you see I'm having lunch and watching television?'

Colleagues within earshot exchange did-you-ever smirks, and shrug their shoulders. Trish, at the next table, points out Linda to Chrissie and makes a circular gesture next to her head, indicating a screw loose.

'You call zat lunch?' snorts the Frenchman, inspecting Linda's plate as though it were an animal dropping. And jerks his head in the direction of the gesticulating televangelist.

'You call zat television?'

Linda pretends to notice neither the exaggerated scrape of Herve's chair as he leaves, muttering, *'Elle est dingue, cette nénette,'* nor his whispered conversation with Mr Foley, her boss, who is sipping unsweetened espresso in a corner seat. His face indicates he would be happier with poison.

'Not the first complaint I've had,' says Mr Foley. Linda feels the sting of two pairs of eyes, one blue, one green, on her back as she returns the television's stare.

The Reverend's hands cleave together and knead, as though attempting to mate.

'And a privilege and a pleasure – a *great* pleasure, Hallelujah – to be able to share a joy and a hope here with you on this special day.'

The TV picture cuts to a section of the studio audience, where a family of five with the faces of bloodhounds are nudging each other and grinning in anticipation, then swoops along the front row, taking in the tans, jewellery, and pastel tracksuits of women empowered by hormone replacement and the Lord.

'And the message is this, folks.' The preacher's face forms itself into a benign tumour of intimacy.

'The message is this.' Master of the pause, he waits. Waits, and then waits some more, until a murmur sets up in the audience and the Third Age jangles its bracelets. Finally, he raises a finger for silence.

'The good-news message is this. The money that's been pouring in, which you special people have dug deep in your pocket and your heart for, is now ready to start working for the glory of GOD! PRAISE JESUS!' The preacher smites the air with his fist, and a cheer erupts, whipped to a froth by tambourines and a drum-roll.

In the Ministry canteen, Linda gulps fizzy water and winces as her nose pricks with gas.

'We've been talking a lot about the House of God here on *Holy Hour* in the last months,' the Reverend is saying. Linda feels his eyes on her, and as they burrow electronically to her soul, she becomes aware of a spreading flush. She stabs a haricot bean.

'A divine project to glorify his name,' exults the preacher. 'He died on the cross for us. So now we're going to do something for him. You too, sir, and you, madam, and you junior faithful too. Help create this cathedral in his glory. Help *design* it.'

Linda cuts into a mushroom pie and releases a steaming dribble of black liquid, which she mashes into her potato and rakes into a cowpat shape to cool. She wishes she had not worn such thick woollen tights.

The Reverend is explaining that the design of the cathedral is not a competition, as the Lord loves us all equally, even the morally abominated, such as homosexuals and lesbians. God likes team things, and God likes communities, and God likes families, because prayers-together are stayers-together.

Tortured by wool, Linda wiggles in her seat and scrapes at a forkful of grey matter, as the preacher paces the stage, jabbing a finger at members of the audience to emphasise the point that he who buildeth his house upon a rock – the rock of faith, the almighty rock of faith, the almighty, blessed, holy, powerful and empowering rock, praise Jesus – shall be for ever blessed. Today, tomorrow *and* yesterday. Yo.

'Yo!' squeals the Third Age, and drums its trainers on the studio floor.

'Now let's get practical,' continues the evangelist. 'We want your ideas, diagrams and plans, people. However lowly. For he careth not for the quality, he careth only for the act of faith. Your ideas, folks, will be combined, streamlined and amalgamated by technology to create a cathedral in the glory of the one great architect. Perhaps you'll send a photo of a building you particularly like – be it the Taj Mahal or your local leisure centre. Or something your child has drawn.' (Linda's face tightens, then forces itself into a tolerant smile.)

'Perhaps you'll just send a donation. And remember, think interior as well as exterior, so you ladies can dazzle us with your design and furnishing ideas.

'Spill out your heart to us. Let's hear what you want. And then what we're going to do, with God's help and a bit of computer technology and Ron, our architect, we're going to incorporate all of that into one magnificent building. Yo! Alrighty!'

Hoots of glee from the studio audience, as the man called Ron demonstrates his computer software, which draws three-dimensional architectural plans in Virtual Reality. A structure that looks like a melted candelabra erupts on to Ron's screen, and the audience breathes a great 'Whooo!' of admiration.

'Help build the House of God,' Linda hears the Reverend murmur to her alone. Mummified in wool, her overheated thighs ignite. Suddenly, from nowhere, a picture emerges in her head like a Polaroid snap: a chair, its velveteen upholstery heaving to an ancient rhythm, with herself on it, naked, callisthenically squirming, astride –

She witnesses her own sallow buttocks juddering and the Reverend's triumphal groan.

* * *

Name: Sugden, Moira Janet
Age: Fifty-nine (a dangerous age)
Marital status: Single. Also separated and widowed
Children: Linda and Hazel, ungrateful
Weight: 16 stone 11 pounds
Bust: 50 in. approx
Waist: None (ha ha)
Education: Librarian's Higher Diploma, Inverness
Hips: 2 yds approx., large chairs only.
IQ: Well above average
Friends: Signora Isabella Pimento and Mr Keith Proutt
Guru: Dr Stern
Enemies: Dr Stern? Dr Sarah McAuley. Linda and Hazel.
Medication: Lithium et al.
Personal therapist: Dr Sarah McAuley
Hobbies: Gardening. Reference books. Iris Murdoch. Virginia Woolf
Expectations: Few

Yes, late husband, it is I. And you thought there might be an escape beyond the grave. My decision to write to the dead, i.e. you, is perfectly rational (though try explaining that to the likes of Dr McAuley) because I will not be disappointed when you fail to reply. Pessimism pays, in the long run. 'You can put hope in one hand, and spit into the other,' say the Danes. 'Then take a look and see which hand holds the most.'

Useful places, libraries.

Look at the facts: despite the hundreds of letters I

have written to them over the years, our daughters never answer – unless you count Linda's 'pull yourself together' postcards from Brussels, sent because she likes me to know that, despite her bulldozed ego, foreign travel is an 'integral part' of her important career at the Butter Mountain. (A slippery slope, I told her.) Hazel just coddles herself in domesticity, on the other hand. A clever-dick doctor husband with a face as memorable as a cardboard box (he is some kind of fertility hero), a curly-haired, constipated boy, Billy, to whom I am denied access, a 'nice house' in Oakshott Road, Le Creuset casseroles: the usual capitulation.

You may have been wondering where I've been all these years. What has been occupying my time since you left me with that witch from the flyover. I would put money on it that she has re-aligned herself to a hapless New Zealander by now, and chucked your ashes in the Whirlpool Spa. My life since you left has been normal-ish. Like most people's, it has been a bit of this and a bit of that. I have been up and I have been down. I have been in, and I have been out. This time, I've been in for two years. Quite a stretch. I have no plans to leave, having no home to go to, as your daughters sold the Cheeseways house and put the money in a 'trust', which is an odd word for it, as they don't.

Time. I have had a lot of it on my hands, one way and another. I have spent it, passed it, and sometimes killed it. And time, in turn, has been killing me. A fact spelt out for me by others, younger than myself and more in the know about the human body and its frailties.

'Unfortunately, Mrs Sugden . . .' they say.

'I'm sorry to have to tell you this, but . . .'

'Bad news, I'm afraid, Mrs S . . .'

The doctors tell me that, if I cannot reduce my weight, I will drastically decrease my life expectancy.

'But I never expected much of life in the first place,' I tell them. 'You only have to look at my CV.'

They point to charts that map my folly, to graphs on whose most dangerous matrices I am a lone statistic, to catastrophe scenarios of which I form the epicentre, and thence to a medical pale which I am far and hopelessly beyond.

'I don't want redemption,' I tell them. 'Leave me in peace.'

But they want to help. They want to explain. So they tell me there is a risk of internal breakdown. Your body is full of organs which you have abused over a lifetime with your excessive dietary habits, Mrs Sugden. Spleens, livers, pancreases, tracheas, bile ducts, upper and lower bowels, phlegm systems, aortae. There will be a build-up of 'undesirable matter' which will cause a blockage in an internal lift shaft, a log-jam in a tube of gristle, a failure of the heart to hoik the sphincter muscles into gear. And pop will go the weasel. My fat will squash me.

'Eat less,' they say. 'Prolong your life.'

'Why?' I ask. Silence. They shuffle my notes.

'What for?' I repeat. More silence, as though I had not spoken.

'Any reason?' I query again. Taboo, taboo, taboo. But I persist: '*Pourquoi*?'

And they have nothing to say. They pack away their doomy stethoscopes. They cannot claim that I enhance the world as they know it.

'Cheer up, Mrs Sugden,' they prescribe as they leave.

But Mrs Sugden does not need to 'cheer up'. It may fly in the face of reason, but Mrs Sugden is already cheerful. How? A woman of my age, a mountain of lard with a poor medical prognosis? Full of bright thoughts, and plans for her future? Impossible! A po-faced librarian, you thought, sad doler-out of 50p fines and public humiliator of those who leave snot, a panty-liner or a rasher of bacon between the pages, a woman with no inner resources who, when it all got too much, retreated to an institute for the out of kilter where they mop the floors twice a day and teach grandmothers to suck eggs. But, Brendan. But, but, but. Miracles do happen. And some pigs *can* fly.

Let's just say it happened. One day there was nothing but a flat expanse of lawn, and the next, its white Jurassic skeleton towering above the trees, its glass a-dazzle, its plant life astounding the unwary – the greenhouse. It has changed our lives. But its sudden appearance aroused no interest in the staff here. In fact, they were quite oblivious. A failure of perception, I suppose. Or mass hysteria. Our daughter Hazel walked past it on her last visit without a glance: her loss.

Gardening is a never-ending task, but we are reaping the fruits. Yesterday, kiwis: today, rhubarb. Tomorrow – who knows? – runner beans, gladioli, water lilies and pomegranate. Everything is possible. I am a happy woman. And you, Brendan, are a dead man.

My successes to date: last summer I supervised the planting of four miniature tangerine trees of a variety found in only twelve of China's thirty-six provinces, and we dealt with the potato blight by applying cigarette butts to the root area. In September, Isabella Pimento and I stayed up all night to watch the blooming of a Tibetan plant which flowers only once every fifteen years. It was marvellous: yellow with red stripes, and it positively sang, but by dawn it was stone dead. November saw the sprouting of a new variety of fig tree, and a bumper crop of radish, and I organised the drainage and re-planting of the tropical pond. There were a few mishaps while the fauna were transferred; one angel fish went down the plughole in the sink, and three blue Lapu-Lapu died inexplicably. I fed them to the Venus' fly-traps in the carnivorous corner. I'd have eaten them myself, but the fly-traps were looking poorly. Three days later they died too.

In December, I went public with my enterprise, and invited Dr Stern and Dr McAuley (or 'Sarah' as we are urged to call her in Group) for a conducted tour. They seemed impressed, and spent a while with their heads together over it, but they caused so much damage that the invitation will not be repeated. They trampled all over the plants, crashing into trees, walking right through them even, regardless. It struck me as surprising how little basic biology doctors seem to know. When I quizzed them about it, I found they had no conception of the delicate balance of carbon dioxide and oxygen in this essentially artificial environment, nor of the vagaries of the food chain, or the alchemic process by which plants convert light into chlorophyll. I explained that a return visit was out of the question, and walked away. We are urged, in Group, to walk away from situations we find 'uncomfortable'. Hence I do a lot of walking. Keith pointed out to me the other day that I ricochet like a ballbearing in a bagatelle machine from one catastrophic encounter to the next. Later Dr McAuley asked me to talk about it in Group ('What does the word "greenhouse" signify to you, Moira?') but my lips were firmly sealed. I am no fool.

So, *Monsieur Complètement Mort*. Are you impressed by my endeavours? Are you jealous of my boundless energy? Yes, I have had some hard times since you left. No, I have not been quite the standard mother to those two girls – but they survived. I think of you sometimes, Brendan Sugden, though I never dwell on you for long. My art therapist has been encouraging me to express you in clay, but all I can come up with is a phallic sausage shape. It seems to be what she's after. (Simple things, eh?) I appear to be turning into something of a 'people pleaser' after all.

Yours sincerely,
Moira Sugden

PS: In case you were wondering: *Non, je ne regrette pratiquement rien.*

*   *   *

Less is more. On TV I have seen them, the rich women with perfect figures in St Tropez, who wear nothing but a Lycra G-string, a bit of gold jewellery, and round their insect waist a sequinned pochette containing an American Express card and a single condom. Having always admired the luxury and elegance of travelling light, I tried to keep my luggage down to essentials when I packed to leave my husband: two suitcases of clothes, a box of junior nappies, three dummies, Billy's buggy, sixteen plastic dinosaurs, a spare hanky and a Lego garage. The rest could come later.

I had always wanted to see the rooms in the Hopeworth. Ours was Number 308, double with cot, reached via a pinging lift and a runway of carpeted corridor, and entered by means of a key to which a brass hand grenade was attached. It was elegantly neutral, with a small but cleverly designed bathroom containing sachets of mauve shower gel, white towels in six sizes, and a shining toilet, the seat of which wore a beauty queen's ribbon emblazoned 'Disinfected for your hygiene protection'. The mood of the main living space was beige, with some understated chintz, and from the corner of the ceiling, the giant eye of a television gazed down on the double bed. Billy jumped up and down on the tight-sprung mattress and shouted for an hour while I unpacked, and then we squatted on the floor and laid out the brontosaurus, the stegosaurus, the triceratops, the pachycephalosaurus and the tyrannosaurus rex in a row to graze on the thick pile carpet. Billy managed to eat some of it too, and after I had cleared up his sick as best I could, I told him, 'This is a hotel. It's a nice place. We're on holiday, darling.'

'Yes, Mummy,' he said, picking up the triceratops and inserting its horny beak into his nostril. 'Wiv sand and ice-cream.'

And was sick again, all over the pachycephalosaurus.

You couldn't see the Manxheath Institute of Challenged Stability from the window, which made me glad I'd asked for west-facing. Instead we had a view of the play area in Jaycote's Park, featuring a frightening maze from which wafted the screams of lost children, and a giant maggot made of old tyres. Twin toddlers crawled into its mouth and emerged a minute later from its arse, minus their anoraks. Their mother slumped on a bench, surrounded by child paraphernalia, gazing on her offspring with drained eyes. Other children rocked violently to and fro on the backs of Disney-type sea-creatures on huge springs, and crowded for a go on the giant frog slide.

I ordered toasted tuna sandwiches and grapes from room service and we picnicked on the floor. Then I bathed Billy, sang him 'A Partridge in a Pear Tree' as far as seven maids a-milking, and put him to bed. I wasn't in the habit of drinking heavily, because of Gregory's monitoring, but I was free of all that now – and free to explore my 'thing' with alcohol. When I was born, Ma's cousin Dodie told her I would be a 'dipsomaniac' by the time I was forty. Ma latched on to this idea, and as early as five I knew I was going to grow into a raggedy, prastuphulic woman, dependent on alcohol. I had only eight years left to fulfil this family prophesy. So as soon as Billy was asleep, I lay on the bed and watched an Australian road movie starring a zany, devil-may-care platypus, while experimenting my way through the contents of the fridge mini-bar.

The next morning, after breakfast (croissants for Billy, aspirin for me) and ten goes on the frog slide, I drove Billy across town to the Busy Bee playgroup and then went straight to Manxheath. I spent fifteen minutes in the car-park applying make-up to powder over any evidence of debauchery that might make Dr Stern doubt my word, but as it turned out, he didn't. Far from it.

This time I took in more: the halogen lamp that shone light on to Gorgonzola green walls, the rows of books by Jung, Freud and R. D. Laing, the Modern Art calendar featuring a turd-like bronze sculpture on a lawn, the framed degree certificates. The lack of wife-and-kiddies photograph. And Dr Stern himself at his desk, a fountain pen in his breast pocket, licking an envelope. I saw his eyes take in my bandaged wrist, but he didn't mention it. Instead, he smiled at me genially, and expressed surprise that I hadn't brought Billy. He repeated that there was a *place* for him, whenever it was *needed,* in the hospital *crèche.* That it would be a huge *advantage* to have him at Manxheath during the day, whenever that was *feasible.* I thanked him, and said we'd give it a try, if there was a sandpit, as we were sort of on holiday, and Billy was expecting some sand. I asked after Ma.

'She's doing much better,' he told me. 'Though the fantasies are still quite florid. It's an expansive disease that tends to, er, *unbridle* the imagination. And the imagination can be one's *own worst enemy.* Some people's is best kept in check.'

'She's back to her letter-writing,' I said, remembering the last one ('sexual *frisson*').

91

'Not in itself a *bad sign*,' he said, and gestured me to sit down.

He took out his pen and laid it on the table, where he rolled it with his palm like a tiny rolling-pin. Looking up, his zoomy eyes clutched me. He must have been forty-five, but at that moment his excitement made him look like a boy of ten who has stumbled on frogspawn.

'I'd like you and Billy to come for *tests*,' he said. 'But occasionally, later on, I may also need to involve your mother in sessions with Billy. The telepathy thesis needs *verification*.'

He hesitated when he saw me stiffen.

'Any *problems* with that?' he asked gingerly.

'Yes. I'm not at all keen on the idea,' I said. 'I've managed to avoid any contact between them so far, and I want to keep it that way.'

It came out rather bluntly, as I wasn't used to expressing an opinion. Dr Stern's eyebrows lifted and disappeared behind a shock of dark hair.

'May I ask why?' he said.

A strange question, I thought, trying not to drown in his eyes.

'Well, for a start,' I told the psychiatrist, 'my mother is mad.'

'Mad is a word we prefer not to use here. Our clients are *differently oriented*. Their stability is – '

'Challenged,' I interrupted. 'I know, Dr Stern. But she's my Ma and to me she's a loony pure and simple. I grew up with her in the community, remember?'

My head twanged.

Dr Stern smiled generously and inspected the pristine cuffs of his yellow shirt. His wrists, covered in black hair, were shockingly sexual. I wondered if he realised.

'Challenged stability isn't catching, Mrs Stevenson.'

He was still smiling, and for one excruciating nano-second I had a paranoid thought: He's laughing at me.

'I understand what you're saying, but try to see the benefits. In view of the allegations you're making, it's essential that we get some evidence, and her involvement is crucial. We'll try to work on your *problem reflex* in our next session, shall we?' and his smile broadened to reveal his impeccable teeth, causing my insides to cinch up. I didn't want to argue with him. I knew he was right. It's just that I didn't want Ma –

'Don't worry,' said Dr Stern, reading my thoughts. 'It'll all be perfectly well *supervised*. We have excellent staff here. And your *mother's* relationship with your *son* could turn out to be more *fruitful* and *positive* than you think. We'll get going this week, and then as soon as I've got my hands on that GR218 file, I'll have a *clearer picture*.'

He looked at me quizzically, as though he wasn't sure what to make of me. He was wearing a red-and-green tie today. It had a subtle, swirling design.

'We don't want to waste each other's time, do we?' he went on.

He had spoken to Gregory *at length* on the phone. Not only had he convinced my husband I was ill (which took little doing, apparently, on account of the so-called delusions), but he had ordered him not to visit until I was 'a great deal better'. Part of Manxheath's policy where relatives are concerned. The clients come first. No exceptions. It *might precipitate a mental emergency* is how he put it. The phrase rang a distant bell.

'So there's no question of your husband suspecting you've seen the incriminating evidence,' Dr Stern concluded with a reassuring smile.

I felt my back and shoulders relax. The man was a rock of sanity. Thanks to him, the plan had worked, so far: Gregory thought Billy and I were staying at the Manxheath Institute of Challenged Stability at the State's expense, rather than at the four-star Gridiron Hopeworth, at his. In the meantime, Jane-next-door would by now have assaulted Gregory with her own feminist interpretation of my breakdown. I had been tipped over the edge, the way women are by men. Centuries of oppression, exploitation and manipulation. Nineteen stitches, the Sister said, and just missed the vein. Hazel was breakdown material all right. And who wouldn't be, with a young child, and none of the fiscal independence that forms the bedrock of a woman's self-esteem? Did you know the poor creature believed she had become literally transparent?

So that was how I began my revenge. My head was so cold you could store ice in it. Dr Stern would find out the facts about GR218, and my miscarriages, and Billy. We would analyse them, prepare a dossier, call a press conference, hold hands, step back, and watch the thing explode.

Five days went by. I picked out the stitches in my wrist, leaving a puckered pink scar that was to itch for a month. The Hopeworth Hotel saw to the daily needs of a toilet roll, BLT sandwiches, laundry and television, so I only went out shopping for essential items unavailable from room service: plastic helicopters and rubber glo-in-the-dark monsters for Billy, Facial Creme and women's magazines for me.

It's only when you read the agony pages that you discover to what extent other people are worse off:

Dear Ruth, my husband is no longer interested in sexual intercourse. Ever since I had an abortion sixteen years ago, I have spent every waking minute

thinking I am possessed by the devil. I drink a bottle
of wine a day, sometimes more if I go out . . .

Dear Ruth, my boyfriend says my intimate parts
taste of parsnips. Is there anything I can do to remedy
this, as he is not keen on the vegetable?

Dear Ruth, do foreskins matter?

Dear Ruth, my ex-friend Lulette says I am a
'disgusting slag'. Help!

I devoured these magazines, with their glossy photographs of mistresses (I saw one advertising nail varnish
who looked a little bit like Ruby Gonzalez; I stuck
her on the wall with a drawing pin through her eye),
and opposite those same photographs of perfection the
tragic stories of the imperfect, those women like me
whose man or whose life has let them down. Hungrily,
I ingested their lives as a vampire bat sucks blood. The
woman who finds out that her husband is a transvestite.
The women whose daughter is such a kleptomaniac
she steals things from herself. The woman whose baby
twins starved to death inexplicably. The woman who
has 'never knowingly had an orgasm'. Oh the pity of
it. I even started to write my own letter to Ruth.

Dear Ruth, I have been depressed ever since I discovered my husband genetically engineered our baby.
Now that his mistress is pregnant, I feel as if morsels of
me were breaking off and floating away downstream
like a waterlogged loaf made from the wrong ingredients. Is there a cure for disintegration? A type of
glue, perhaps? I read somewhere, or did I dream, that
there is a new spray on the market called Domestic
Bliss, to waft happiness into the home, attacking the
chemicals that cause bad blood. You know, Ruth, I
could do with a friend . . .

But here I stopped, scrunched the letter in a ball and flung it in the bin: I had no need to write to Ruth now that I was seeing Dr Stern on a daily basis. He was most attentive. His brain was an Alka Seltzer of energy, his intellectual deftness mirrored in quick little physical movements which quite disrupted me. He was forever interrogating me, during those professional yet extraordinarily intimate sessions, about Gregory and our relationship. He would sit in his swivel chair by the window, and I would face him. The light behind him often resembled a halo.

'How often do you have *sex*, would you say, on *average*? Once, twice a week?'

Really quite personal questions. I explained about our fertility chart.

'And how would you describe your *role* during intercourse? Active or passive? Are you more a physical or more a romantic person, would you say? Or a *mixture*, perhaps?'

Questions that left me quite embarrassed, and inexplicably aroused, though I'm sure they were necessary for the research.

Then: 'Tell me about your childhood, Hazel. Were you a little girl who was *loved*?'

And: 'When your father died, Hazel, can you remember how you, um, *felt*?'

Easy questions, really, but the answers are always rather difficult. Dr Stern, who must spend a fortune on dry-cleaning, and who does not wear a wedding-ring, says he is pursuing 'two separate lines of approach' with me, whatever that means.

So as you see, Ruth, I am being looked after better than I could have dared to hope, and thanks to Dr Stern I shall not be weighing down your postbag!

SIX

When I'd been loading the car to leave the marital home, Jane had yelled something to me over the fence about my sister, which disturbed me. I hoped she'd got it wrong, and it was another woman with a bizarre fur hat she was talking about. But it needed checking out, so on that Sunday morning I turned Billy into a sort of chrysalis consisting of duffel coat, balaclava, scarf, gloves and furry boots, heaved him into the buggy, and wheeled us off to Linda's flat in Bollingate View Terrace, opposite St Manfred's Church. The bells were clanging furiously, never quite hitting any tune.

'Terrorists!' Linda shrieked as she slammed the door shut behind us, and continued in a shout, 'Why do I have to move into a neighbourhood where the only social group is a cell of fucking bell-ringers?'

'Some of them might be Mensa members,' I ventured.

'I've invested in earplugs,' she decibelled.

Billy woke up and began to cry; I shoved the silicone nipple of his dummy back in the balaclava and he fell asleep again. I left him in the hall in his buggy and followed Linda through to the lounge, a red velveteen womb with high-backed chairs and fussy footstools.

My sister turned, sized me up, then shouted accusingly, 'You're taller than me again!'

'Heels,' I mouthed. 'And no need to shout.'

I waited while she removed her earplugs with two swift magician's movements of the little finger, and laid them in a perspex box on the coffee table. I noticed that my face, reflected in its dark wood varnish, was as calm as a fish's.

'Worth every penny,' Linda was saying at normal volume.

The air in her flat was sour with stale cigarettes.

'And useful for meetings. This type of earplug is the Rolls Royce of acoustic minimisers.' Then looking me up and down again, 'Even taking the heels into account.'

'Linda, you're obsessed.'

'Off with them.'

'Linda – '

'Off with them!' she bossed, leaning on the back of a chair and wrenching off her own suede Hush Puppies.

Sometimes there's no point arguing with Linda. It's a question of energy levels. We went through to the bathroom, where we stood barefoot next to each other in front of the mirror, levelling our big toes along a line of grouting. Linda put a copy of *Assertiveness and You* on her head to confirm she was the taller.

'By a good five centimetres,' I reassured her.

'I'm one metre sixty.'

'And I'm one fifty-five, just like I've always been.'

'Not always, you haven't,' she said, full of mistrust. 'You've always been up and down. At Florrie's wedding you were a midget, then last October, that time with John when he got cautioned at the Pizza Hut, your pendant was level with my earrings.'

'Sitting down's different,' I calmed her. 'Body length. You have a short body, and mine's long. And your earrings go on for ever, if you're talking about those turquoise Sri Lankan ones.'

Linda grunted, still suspicious, but finally let it drop.

Billy must have woken up while we were drinking tea, and performed a silent Houdini act to escape from his clothes: he tottered into the living-room naked except for his socks.

'The boy is father of the man,' commented Linda.

Billy and I began a game of hide and seek. From the kitchen came the crashing of plates as my sister loaded her mini-dishwasher. I closed my eyes and counted to ten, then hid with Billy. I was about to say something about the eggs when Linda, emerging from the kitchen with a plastic basket of ironing, said bluntly, 'I hear you've left your husband.'

I watched her from behind a chair. I was glad she couldn't see my face.

'Who told you I'd left Gregory?' I called as nonchalantly as I could under the circumstances.

When Billy turned a questioning face to me I hugged him so tight I felt his little goose-fleshed ribs might crack.

'The bastard himself. I phoned your house to tell you some good news, but he answered. In quite a state. Said you were having a nervous breakdown, and that you'd turned the furniture to sawdust with some kind of power tool. I said I hoped that pseudo-Regency lampstand had been one of the victims.'

She paused.

'Well? Is it true?'

'About the lampstand?'

'No, about Gregory.'

To gain some thinking time, I popped up from behind the velveteen and played my surprise card.

'Well, *I* hear the Reverend Carmichael has a new convert. Was that the good news you were going to tell me?'

Linda flushed with angry pride.

'How did you hear about that?'

'You know Gridiron. News travels fast. Jane-next-door told me. Her physiotherapist friend was there, with the St John's Ambulance.'

'Naa-nah, naa-nah!' sang Billy happily, recognising a word from his vocabulary.

'So it's all go,' I went on, dressing Billy again as Linda, all elbows, dashed away energetically with her smoothing-iron. 'Come on, Lin, let's hear it from the horse's mouth. Jane just yelled it to me over the fence when I was loading my car to leave Gregory, but everything she says is garbled, so I didn't know whether she'd got it right.'

I had been in such a state myself that when Jane told me about the eggs I was past being surprised by anything. Though given the extent of Linda's perversity and fanaticism, I had reflected later over the whisky, it somehow figured.

But Linda wasn't to be drawn.

'Well? Is it true you've left your husband at last?'

'What d'you mean, "at last"? Were you *expecting* me to?' I asked her.

Linda returned my stare with a glare.

'Does Dr Stern know you're here? Gregory said he was treating you in Manxheath.'

'I'm not actually a patient,' I explained, anxious to keep my cover but riled at being categorised as a loony alongside Ma. 'Billy and I are staying in the Hopeworth, though I'd rather you didn't tell Gregory that for now, as it's ferociously expensive.'

'All right for some,' grunted Linda.

'So I'm just visiting Manxheath daily to help Dr Stern with some research.'

'Yes, of course,' said Linda, mustering some tact as she adjusted the heat to woollens. 'I phoned Dr Stern when I heard. He's filled me in, up to a point.'

'What did he tell you?' I asked.

Linda began to fold a shirt, paying great attention to the sleeves.

'Well?' I insisted.

Linda blushed.

'Just that you . . . needed a rest.'

She looked at me like I was a dangerous soufflé that might explode in her face.

'Well,' I said, 'he's right. I do.'

Dr Stern must have spun Linda the same line he'd spun Gregory. It was Dr Stern's suggestion that I tell nobody about what Gregory had done until we had all the facts. That suited me: I wasn't ready for Linda's I-told-you-sos, and her organising of demos, and God knows, probably roping in the Reverend Carmichael as well. Let her think I had cracked, if she wanted. Let her think I had joined Ma in the State of Absolute Delusion. Which she clearly did.

'Everyone needs a good rest from time to time,' said Linda with effort. She was unused to being nice to me, but she soldiered on. 'And it's good, this new policy of bringing the community into the care environment. Dr Stern said it means Billy can spend time in Manxheath, and get to know Ma.'

'Yes,' I said vaguely.

I wasn't sure I liked that bit, but there was no avoiding it, if I wanted to discover what Gregory had planted in my son's genes.

'It's certainly better than the care-in-the-community thing they had.' I was keen to make the conversation sound normal. 'Remember that time they let Ma out of Coxcomb and she hijacked that City Hoppa?'

We reminisced for a while about some of Ma's depressing escapades; her famous death threat to the Minister of State for Education, her trip to Bali – then lapsed into silence. Billy and I sat on the floor gazing at Linda ironing. There was something abnormal about her steam button; every time she pressed it, an enormous cloud of vapour emerged, and she would disappear behind it in the manner of a high priestess. When the church bells clanged eleven, Linda shook herself out her housework-induced trance.

'Mind if I catch *Holy Hour*?'

'No, go ahead,' I replied.

My turn to be tactful. She pressed the remote control and there knelt the Reverend Carmichael before us, his face shiny with faith.

We watched for a while as Carmichael chewed his way through a rambling prayer full of thees and thous about catalepsy, adultery, and bullying in old people's homes. After the Amen, he wiped the sweat from his brow with a tiny olive-green handkerchief and gave the signal for the hymn. The silver band orchestra began a smooth, catchy tune and the voices of a choir sprang from nowhere. Next to me, the soft sound of Linda's slippered foot tapping in time to the music.

'So, Linda, is it really true you've been converted by him – in person?'

'I've found the Lord, yes,' muttered Linda, her face all fixed-over as if she had applied a cleansing gel masque that mustn't crack.

'But you were an atheist,' I said cautiously.

'Well, now I'm a Christian,' she snapped. 'And it's none of your business. So if you want to take the piss you can bugger off.'

Tests: personality, intelligence, co-ordination, Rorschach. I had them coming out of my ears. Joining dots, saying why such-and-such a word (billiard ball, pathos, handbrake, flying fish, Neptune) was the odd one out, talking to Billy and being recorded on video playing with educational toys. He thought it was all a game, which increased the pressure on me: I knew just how serious it all was. My son's brain was at stake.

Meanwhile Ma's crisis had 'resolved', according to Dr Stern, and she was looking quite perky and less mottled about the mouth, though she still shuffled. I caught sight of her sometimes in corridors, and avoided her when I could. She joined Billy for the sessions that concerned 'hereditary factors', while I shopped or went over for a swim in the hotel pool. I bumped into her in the Day Room after we had been coming to Manxheath for about a week, and it emerged she had developed an uncanny rapport with Billy: she seemed to know everything about him: the origin of every little scar on his knee, the names of his playmates, his aversion to broccoli, his conviction that a policeman would kill him. Yet he could barely talk.

'I'm surprised Linda should have remembered so much about him, and then told you in such detail,' I said.

I meant it, because Linda always tried to ignore Billy as if he were some buzzing fly. She must have been scraping around for things to say on her visits, I supposed.

'Oh no, it wasn't Linda,' said my mother. 'I told you before, Billy was sending me messages.'

Oh well, I thought. They had put her on a new drug.

'Slow-release capsules,' she whispered to me conspiratorially. 'I'm going to take a leaf out of Keith's book and insist on suppositories. It drives the psychiatrists mad. I'm trying to convert the whole Group, but Monica's holding out; she says her arms aren't long enough.'

Dr Stern was the go-between when it came to arrangements with my husband over Billy. Gregory no doubt thought the psychiatrist was on his side: one's wife has nutted up, dear colleague. Your syringe or mine?

Gregory and Dr Stern had agreed that Billy should spend the weekends at home, but Gregory wasn't insisting. Better things to do, I suppose. He took Billy to McDonald's one Saturday, acting like a typical male divorcé before he'd even got divorced. Then took him home and let Billy watch him play with a remotely-controlled fighter plane in the garden all afternoon. At least that's what Ma said, with great firmness, when I bumped into her in the Day Room.

The day we went to print out the disc, Dr Stern seemed very calm, but I could sense his excitement under the surface. I chose a time when I knew Jane was at her karate morning. Dr Stern waited outside in the car, wearing his scarf round his mouth and hiding behind the *British Medical Journal* – though I said to him later that's a sure way to stand out from the crowd in Oakshott Road, we're staunch *Telegraph* readers. The house was still a wreck. Part of me yearned to get out my mop, and another part rejoiced in the disorder I had wreaked. Gregory hadn't even put the shelves back, though he, or Ruby Gonzalez, had sponged the floor quite efficiently. There was a slimy smell, and I noted with interest that the mustard and cress had taken root in the living-room carpet. My messages of hate, although smeared, were still decipherable. I was glad I'd left Dr Stern in the car. He might have made something of it. I noticed Gregory's portable phone lying on the floor; I hesitated for a moment, then put it in my handbag.

While the file was printing out, I checked the bathroom for unfamiliar toiletries and then hunted through Gregory's drawers looking for other tell-tale signs of Ruby Gonzalez's presence – perfume, knickers, a doctoral thesis bearing her name. But there was nothing –

just his maroon socks. All Gregory's socks were the same colour, because I had insisted on it. It saved sorting them after I'd done a wash. He resented that. Perhaps he had moved in with her. Perhaps he had a whole drawerful of exciting, multi-coloured socks at Ruby's place, and just came back every now and then for a supply of shirts, and to remember how unreasonable I'd been over the sock thing.

Back in the study, watching the paper emerge from the plastic feeder, I pictured my saviour in the car, reading about cardiovascular disease, and my heart pounded in great kerthumps of gratitude.

When I slammed the door shut on my home, I didn't look back.

'Here you are, Dr Stern,' I said proudly, handing him a sheaf of papers through the car window.

Dr Stern couldn't wait to read the document, you could tell; he was all over it like a sniffer dog, riffling through it and grunting. Once I'd settled into the passenger seat he turned to me and said, 'Call me Ishmael.'

It sounded familiar, which was surprising. Ishmael must be quite an uncommon name.

'OK, Ishmael,' I said, feeling shy.

Dr Ishmael Stern.

Oh well, I thought. I'm not the only one with a strange ma. He drove with great intensity, as one does when taking a driving test; every small movement super-accurate and slightly exaggerated. When we got back to the Institute he excused himself. We were standing outside his office.

'I have to read this document, and make some notes,' he said.

We said goodbye, and as I turned away from his closing door I felt a strange sensation. It was as if a shroud were being peeled away from my soul. As I turned, I almost glimpsed it, from the corner of my eye, as it furled up in a transcendental spiral and wafted down the corridor. If it hadn't been invisible, this shroud, I'd have seen it. Don't tell me I wouldn't.

SEVEN

Filthy February skies disgorge themselves on the North. On tarmac, on corrugated iron and on patio tiles, on superstores and charity shops and bottle banks, and into a thousand ornamental ponds in the back gardens of Gridiron City, a liquidised grit hammers down. In the city centre, gutters gargle on coagulated silt, giving a desperate feel to the streets.

By eleven, the air in Bulger's parfumerie and accessories department hangs sour with clashing toilet waters and the damp clothes of Saturday shoppers. On the escalator on the way up to the third floor (soft furnishings and lingerie), sandwiched between two women of indeterminate age, Linda does violence on her umbrella.

'Ouch!'

'Sorry.'

Fuck it.

'Look, it's my wedding, Mum,' says the woman on the stair above Linda. Her pink placcy mac makes her look like an upright frankfurter.

'And it's my money, and your dad's,' the other fires back through Linda's head. 'I'm not having you wear some rubbish.'

'*Fold*, you bastard!' Linda performs a karate-chopping gesture on the flapping umbrella and snaps two ribs.

'It's a Designer, Mum.'

'It doesn't flatter you, Cindy, is all I'm saying. It just doesn't flatter you, that type of romantic-style bodice. Not with those what-d'you-call-them-ruched leg-o'-mutton sleeves.'

'You said I could spend two hundred and twenty-five pound. On my choice of wedding-dress, you said.'

'Two hundred and twenty, I said, maximum, and I did specify, Cindy, that it had to be white, or whitish.'

Linda stuffs the broken-ribbed umbrella into her bag and checks her list:

1. Antimacassars.
2. Bra.
3. Mouthwash, etc.
4. Doo-da for washing machine.

'Excuse me, we need a referee here.'

The frankfurter is tapping her on the hand.

'Wouldn't you say that cream was whitish?'

'Jesus Christ!' yells Linda, whipping round. 'D'you think I give a toss?'

That's done it. Mother and daughter exchange a look.

'Don't you use language with my daughter, young madam,' threatens the mother. 'There's places for people like you, you know.'

'Yeah,' agrees the frankfurter. 'Who rattled your cage?'

Linda carries with her at all times an imaginary Kalashnikov rifle, loaded and cocked, but before there is time to gun them down, mother and daughter have glided off the escalator and wheeled arm in arm towards an archway marked 'Bridal'. A pair of twins in a double buggy get it instead, their brains splattering all over a row of naked mannequins.

Bra first. Padded bras do not come in as many shapes and sizes as bosoms themselves, for who would choose, reason the manufacturers, to have big overblown operatic ones, more akin to udders than breasts – or one even smaller than another, or a pair that would fail the famous 'pencil test'? Linda is particular about her mammary glands. They are past their brief heyday, and have taken quite an emotional pasting over the years. They deserve a break. The enhancement of existing assets, she reasons, is not politically incorrect, as long as it stops short of optical illusion.

Prussian Rose, Lolita, Gypsy Doll, Proud Princess. 34B, 34C, under-wiring or cushion fit – all statements, but which one to make?

So engrossed is she that when a husky voice that comes from somewhere between Caracas and Croydon asks the assistant for maternity lingerie 'for the already fuller figure, if you know what I mean', Linda doesn't register.

It's only while wriggling before the cruel omni-directional mirrors of the changing cubicle, some fourteen bras later, reflecting on the injustice of breast size, and how you can only please some of the people some of the time, and that the Lord had obviously designed her tits as a cross for her to bear, that Linda suddenly recalls with shock the night she heard that voice before.

'Are you pregnant, Ruby?' Hazel had asked.

'No, I'm afraid I'm just fat.'

Now *she* had had what men would call 'knockers'.

Linda's high-powered job has trained her in swift, creative management, and the decision-making skills that have won her status at the Butter Mountain do not desert her now. Without a moment's hesitation, she lets drop the Midnight Blue 34C and, a naked breast clutched in each hand, stalks the length of the narrow changing corridor. She'll recognise the shoes. Career-woman shoes, low-heeled and navy blue, or perhaps cream. There is little movement behind the curtains; just the guttural sounds of emotional pain and the cloying emanation of sweat. At floor level, there are tights with holes, slouch socks, boots, bunions, trainers, something orthopaedic-looking.

Up the far end, one curtain is barely pulled across. Linda tiptoes up to it, peers in, and draws a sudden breath. There is something unmistakable about the sloping shoulders and bulbous back, and the plait of dark hair that runs down the length of the spine to cleft-of-buttock level. The faceted mirrors stare back, and reveal the front, side and three-quarters view of a woman. A woman in fecund splendour, admiring in the mirrors a gigantic moonish belly atop a triangular bird's nest of pubic hair.

If Dr Ruby Gonzalez were naked and heavily pregnant, this is what she would look like.

For three lurching seconds, Linda bears silent witness, then drops her tits in shock and rushes back to her cubicle as though stung by a bee.

* * *

While Linda was shopping that Saturday, I was swimming.

I am a good swimmer, thanks to the Tadpole Club. Linda and I learned to swim there as children. Ma would sit in the spectators', her glasses all steamed up, crocheting something crooked or reading from the *Pocket Floral Encyclopedia,* which she always carried in her handbag. 'A positive minefield of information', she called it. Our friends at school and at the Tadpole Club would always snigger at the way she looked, planted there in the third row like an absurd obelisk, but in fact Ma was almost normal in those days. Afterwards we'd go to the sweet shop: Rolos and marshmallows for Ma, sherbert and a Wagon Wheel for me, wine gums and Love Hearts for Linda. Linda always read out the inscriptions: 'Kiss Me', 'Sweetiepie', 'Yours Forever', 'Be Mine'. Fodder for the soured dreams of later life.

'Sue the manufacturer,' I told her once, after another evening of Kleenex and comfort eating. But she didn't laugh.

The Tadpole Club taught me to swim, and swimming taught me that the brain can sort swiftly and painlessly through the ghastly bric-à-brac of its contents if the body is occupied by a banal enough activity. Hence my attraction, in times of stress, to the gormless rhythm of breast-stroke. Now, every morning, I would do fifty lengths, bubbles swilling past my mouth, my muscles going through their routine. And I would empty myself of Greg, of Ruby Gonzalez, of my time-bomb son, and of Ma. After the fiftieth length I would take a deep breath and dive down to the chlorine depths of the pool where I would stay until my ears buzzed and my mind burst into a realm of white clarity.

In the two weeks I'd been at Hopeworth, I'd established what you might call a routine. Billy and I crossed the park in the mornings to Manxheath, where I would drop him off at the crèche with a mixture of guilt and relief. I think he felt it too, because he'd cry until I was out of the door, and then stop abruptly, and head for the trike park. I saw him, as I passed a small window on the way out, the only parent to dawdle. Most of them were mums, nurses, wearing the sky-blue Institute uniform with a black elastic belt fastened by a big buckle. They bustled with small anoraks and lunchboxes, and looked harassed.

Then I'd go for my swim, see Dr Stern for my session

at eleven, and go back to the hotel for lunch. I'd order my room service, and watch soap operas on TV. Around three I'd walk back to Manxheath through the park to fetch Billy. Then mother-and-child activities until bedtime: playing on the swings, feeding the ducks, watching cartoons, reading, wiping away tears, tickling. It suited me, this new life. No home to run, no supermarket shopping to do, no dry-cleaning to fetch, no pans to scrub, no husband to –

No husband.

One day stood out from the others. It was partly out of a sense of duty that I had paid another formal visit to the State of Absolute Delusion. I regretted it as soon as I arrived. Ma gave me a guided tour of the grounds. The light was bright as a camera flash on the trees and grass, but alarmingly, the sky was almost black. It was murderously, frozenly beautiful, and I could feel the cold through my thermal underwear. That's the tragedy of things you order from a catalogue.

We went round the garden. Ma walked faster than before, but she still dragged her feet. As we walked along, she named the plants, but there seemed to be more names than plants, as though she were seeing something I couldn't. She thought the silver birch trees were mangoes, and warned me to 'watch out or you'll fall in the pond'. Then she started to mutter angrily about 'deliveries' not arriving on time. Her voice became so hoarse and rasping I thought something in her larynx might give out, and the words repeated themselves on a loop: 'The bananas should be planted this month, they're delicate, they need their roots soaked for a week. They need their roots soaked for a week, they need their roots soaked for a week!'

I backed away from her, ashamed of my fear. She stood in profile on the iced lawn, a lone plastic bride on a vast wedding-cake. It was frightening, because I thought I'd seen the whole bag of tricks. Dr Stern hadn't quite prepared me for this, with that light-hearted word, 'cavalier'. Finally she moved, and I started to follow, but suddenly she was yelling at me again at an intense pitch.

'You're walking on the ferns! Get off the ferns, you wee idiot! Get off! Get off! Get off!'

I could see nothing but the spikes of frosted grass beneath my feet. Ma's face had gone bluish in places, and she licked her lips every few seconds. Cavalier. I followed in her footsteps out of wherever we were.

'What did you think of the greenhouse?' she said afterwards.

We were sitting in the Day Room, drinking tea from styrofoam cups. Patients wandered in and out aimlessly, or sat smoking in front of the huge aquarium-sized TV. It was as though nothing monstrous had happened.

'Oh,' I said, trying to find a word. 'Gorgeous.'

I didn't know what she was talking about. I wanted to run away. A young man with staring eyes edged up to me and said, 'If that's your mother you're in a lot of trouble,' and he shuffled off, trailing a length of string behind him to which an empty cotton reel was attached. I watched it bounce along the lino after him and thought: Tell me something I don't know. Ma ignored him, and licked her lips to speak again.

'I call it Project Eden. What d'you think of that for a name? Your father would have approved.'

'Project Eden sounds fine, Ma.'

I shut my eyes. If Linda had been here, we could have exchanged the glance that said: Abandon Hope. I missed Linda now, for all her obnoxiousness. I missed her suddenly and violently. She would have understood. We have danced the same highway of eggs.

'Linda tells me you've left that antiseptic husband of yours,' she said. 'And now you're living it up in the Hopeworth at vast expense to the taxpayer. You always were vainglorious.'

Her eyes were fencing about behind the greasy lenses of her glasses, but I intercepted the attack.

'The fact is,' I said, as levelly as I could, 'Gregory and I have had some marriage problems, and I've moved out of Oakshott Road.'

'And I also understand you've joined the club.'

That look again. Never think the mad are powerless. 'What club?'

She laughed. 'The loony club, hen. Is there any other? Your stability's been challenged.' She smoothed her skirt with an exaggerated wiping movement. 'You're one of us now, like it or lump it.'

I wanted to punch her in the belly, but stopped myself. She licked her lips again.

'D'you think I haven't noticed that you're seeing Dr Stern on a doctor-to-patient basis?'

I caught a whiff of her; she smelt of wallpaper paste and Roquefort cheese.

'I'm seeing him on business,' I said.

It was the first thing I could think of. Her glasses flashed in the light. She put back her head and laughed pantomimically.

'Business!' she said loudly, so that the other patients steered round to look. 'Business, my farting arse. Did you hear that, everyone? My daughter here thinks she's seeing the doctor on business!'

A tall man barked something unintelligible and stomped out. The fat boy I'd seen before playing Scrabble, who'd been attacked by the old lady, was now playing chess. He was looking at me with an unnervingly cold stare, like I was a tacky ornament not worth the money. Between

114

his thumb and forefinger he held the pointed head of a black bishop.

'Bishop to H4, knight to G7, queen to F8 and checkmate in four,' he said. I had heard that voice before, from Martians in films, and Directory Enquiries.

'That's Keith,' said my mother. 'He's only twenty, and he's a Grandmaster. His dad showed me the cuttings. But he'll only talk about chess, the rest is in sign language,' she said, smiling towards him and nodding encouragement. 'Anyway, why d'you think you'd be seeing Dr Stern if you weren't suffering from psychological disorder of some kind? What makes you the big exception?'

I sipped at my greyish Institute tea, said nothing. Did I perhaps mention that, once upon a time, she had worn a pinny, rolled dough, made us cheese and pickle sandwiches for packed lunch, explained pi and tectonic plates, taken us to the Tadpole Club? So don't talk to me about betrayal. When I'd finished my tea I would go.

'You remind me of Signora Pimento, you know, my friend who's expecting her ninth,' my mother was saying.

I knew Mrs Pimento by sight. I had watched her and Ma together the previous day when I was out on a walk. I'd hidden behind a conifer and spied on them reciting the Latin names of shrubs to one another. Mrs Pimento was a heavy woman, placid as a giant aubergine, swollen to bursting with a phantom pregnancy. Indoors, she occupied a wicker throne in the Day Room, and knitted baby clothes in garish acrylic.

'Hysteria, they used to call it when I was a wee one. Don't know what it's called now, but some of the drugs are similar to mine,' Ma is saying. 'My diagnosis is that you're just a bit hysterical, like her. You've sailed through umpteen pregnancies, I tell her, so why worry about this one? The older you get, the longer you gestate. But there's no convincing her.'

She was in one of her animated moods, and her cheeks were the kind of pink that comes from fever or a sharp slap. I had always feared her like this. Anything could happen. But suddenly she was smiling at me generously, her face askew.

'Don't worry hen – I'm sure Dr Stern's looking after you.'

I was shocked to find that I needed to lick my lips before I spoke.

'Yes,' I said. 'Dr Stern's being ever so supportive.'

Her glasses had quite cleared. A change of mood. Sometimes on television they show the speeded-up movements of clouds. They seem to be about to do one thing and then they do another. They swirl one way, and then a ridge of unexpected, inexplicable high pressure sends them whirling off to do damage in another corner of the map. My Ma is like that, only there is no map.

'Do you know whose brother Keith is?' she's asking me brightly, winking at Mrs Pimento, who has just walked in. I tell my mother no, I don't know whose brother Keith is. I don't want even to look at Keith.

'Go on, ask him who his brother is,' urges Ma.

'Do you have a brother?' I ask him in a too-loud voice, as though he's deaf.

He replies in a complex choreography of the hands. They are butcher's hands, too raucous for elegance. When he finishes, he folds them on his lap with finality. His face shows no expression.

'He wants to know if you play chess,' translates my mother, and before I can reply she turns back to Keith.

'No, course she doesn't. She's not very intelligent, this

116

daughter. Try Linda, she'll give you a game.' And she announces loudly to the room, 'My other daughter's a civil servant, you know.'

'Anyway, I was going to tell you who Keith's brother is,' she tells me. 'It's Duncan! Have you met Duncan? A very nice young man – blond, he doesn't look at all like Keith, but that's today's gene pool for you, he's Linda's new boyfriend. Now isn't that an amazing coincidence?'

'Holy Mary be praze,' says Mrs Pimento, crunching into an apple and staring through the window into the frosty garden.

'Apropos of nothing – ' says my mother, but Mrs Pimento interrupts with a strange cry:

'*Aaaw*!'

It could be misery or pleasure, or the two combined. As it turns out, it is just that. Both.

'I see two beautiful magpie out there in garden. First I just see one, and I think sorrow, then I see second one, for joy.'

'For every depressive a manic,' says my mother, not looking. 'Anyway, Keith, apropos of nothing, to tell you the truth, Hazel and her husband are getting divorced.' She says it so matter-of-factly that to begin with I don't take it in. Then I try to laugh.

'We're doing nothing of the sort.' I mean to sound scoffing, but the words come out all smashed up.

Keith, to whom all this is addressed, is lining up his pawns for a fresh game, and takes no notice of either of us. I try to laugh again.

'What a ridiculous idea,' I say, although of course it isn't ridiculous, and has been on my mind incessantly. In my mouth, the sudden taste of brine. I am aware that the argument is a public one, even though the audience is indifferent.

117

'The lady doth bang on too much, methinks,' says my mother, catching Keith's eye and winking at him.

He makes an impatient gesture with one hand, as though to brush away a fly, and looks the other way. Ma begins picking at a loose thread in her tweed skirt. I catch her glancing across at me to test my reaction, her mouth already working, chewing on silence, to form another sentence.

'It's not a coincidence at all,' I say quickly, switching back to the subject of Linda and Duncan. 'Duncan and Linda first met here.'

'Even more of a coincidence,' retorts my mother triumphantly, to infuriate me, then reaches for the tea tray and inserts an entire rock cake into her mouth.

'I can't speak now,' she manages through it. 'I'm chock-a-block.'

A raisin flies out and hits Mrs Pimento on the forearm. She snaps out of her trance and swings the big canon of her belly around to accuse us. Her bright skirt, straining its elastic waistband, falls over the great mound in a bulging waterfall of fabric.

'That's some pregnancy you've got there, Mrs Pimento,' I tell her, marvelling despite myself at the concrete form delusion can take. The phantom appears to shift about.

'Yes, my dear,' she says sweetly. 'The doctors take photographs, use camcorder and all that, zoom, profile, close-up. I will star in a book about challenge.'

Then suddenly childlike, swinging back her greying locks, she makes a hook of her index finger and gestures with it for my mother to come hither. For a frozen moment she is the exact replica of Demis Roussos.

'We go look at plants in garden, Moira, my fren'?' she asks lovingly, in a whisper. 'Look at *Chimonanthus, Jasminum nudiflorum*, see if that 'Soleil d'Or' *Narcissus* bloomin' yet? Come on, Moira, my fren'.'

Then louder, 'An' you, Keith, you lookin' pale, you need breath fresh air, bit of movin' about, good for your alimenti canal, boy.'

But Keith is engrossed in his game. He is playing both sides of the board, and I wonder who he's rooting for.

'King pawn F3, rook G5, pawn takes knight, and check,' comes the voice, through lips that are barely parted.

'You coming, Mr Kasparov?' calls my mother gaily.

Keith does not lift his eyes from the board, but he raises a hand and waves in the direction of the two departing women, who sail arm in arm through the french windows and out into the open sea of the lawn.

I am left indoors with the loonies.

An article in the paper the next morning sent a despairing chill through me.

The baby-care, stationery and frozen vegetable conglomerate Hooper plc is rumoured to have made a £4m. offer to the Fertility Management Centre in return for a 51 per cent share of the 'Perfect Baby' trial drug GR218. Last night, Hooper spokesmen were refusing to confirm or deny the sum involved, but conceded that merger talks were at an advanced stage. The news was greeted with dismay by ecologists and church leaders. The Reverend Carmichael denounced it as a 'devil's pact' and urged an all-out boycott of Hooper products on his influential satellite television programme, Holy Hour.

There was more, but I put the paper down, my heart tightening in a lonely spasm. Hooper had finally delivered. Gregory and Root Hooper had been doing a complicated merger dance for the last year, which involved me driving out to the Savacentre to buy ingredients for elegant soirées for the millionaire and his entourage. Much whisky was downed during these evenings, but none of it ever seemed to go to anybody's head. Root Hooper would always present me with a waxy-looking white orchid in a plastic box with 'Sincerely Yours' on a card, and kiss my hand elaborately while staring at my tits with his yellow herring's eyes.

'If I can clinch that deal,' Gregory always said afterwards, without fail, 'I'll be free for pure science.'

But somehow the deal had never got past the orchid and lumpfish canapé stage – until now. Coincidence, or was something up? That 'breakthrough' Gregory had been so excited about, perhaps. Was Ruby's baby due? She'd looked a good seven months gone to me, that night of our loathsome dinner party. Or might Gregory have guessed that my 'nervous breakdown' was a cover, and that the guinea-pig mother had read the file and passed it on? I cut out the article carefully with nail scissors and wrote at the top, 'Ishmael: Swift action???'

Later that morning, I slipped it under his door. There was no floor covering on the other side, thank goodness, so there would be no tragic misunderstanding, like in *Tess of the d'Urbervilles*, which we'd done at school. She wrote Angel a letter, didn't she, saying she wasn't a virgin but he never got it because the mat was in the way.

The article got me thinking. Greg wasn't stupid. If he ever suspected I knew what was in the file, he would panic. He would realise that he was treading on thin ice, and that he might have to try shutting me up.

Strangely, Ishmael didn't contact me about the cutting. The next day I was heading for his office for my session when I bumped into my mother and Billy. She said straight away, 'I borrowed him from the crèche.

Now listen, Billy wants me to read him the story about the Magic Train. But I can't find it. Did you bring it with you?'

Billy's fat little hand disappeared inside her huge one, and the rest of him was buried in the folds of her skirt. I caught sight of the grey petticoat, and for a brief moment, felt unable to breathe.

'You've no right to take him out of that crèche without asking me!'

But I saw Billy look crestfallen, and I let it drop.

'How d'you know he wants the Magic Train?' I asked her. 'He can't even say the words.'

But she just snorted in disgust.

'Honestly Linda,' she said.

'I'm Hazel.'

'Well, honestly, Hazel, or Linda, what's the difference, two wrongs don't make a right. It's obvious he wants the Magic Train. What kind of a mother are you? Come on, wee poppet,' she said to Billy and she veered off, her man's slippers flapping on the linoleum.

Billy gave me a smile, and was pulled along after her.

'This is no place for a child,' I called out at Ma's retreating back.

'Och, bollocks it isn't,' she foghorned, not bothering to turn. 'Dr McAuley says I can provide him with some positive input on a semi-permanent supervised one-to-one basis, and Dr Stern agrees!'

'Do you resent that?' Stern asked when I crashed into his office and poured all this out.

'Yes. I can't see how Billy can like her.'

'Well, there's no accounting for children's taste. They don't have the *same prejudices* we do.' He stopped and smiled. 'Take *advantage* of it. Get her to babysit. You need a bit of time to *be yourself.*'

Be myself? I didn't quite understand what this meant, but he said it with his usual gentle tact and sympathy. There was a generosity about him that was almost spiritual. It was in that moment that I realised something: Dr Ishmael Stern actually cared for me. When I looked back into his dark eyes I felt the vertigo of a weird epiphany.

'I don't have plans to go out,' I said.

'Well, maybe you should.'

There was a pause.

'Who with?' I finally asked.

An unfamiliar flush swamped my thighs, and a voice sang high in my head. The psychiatrist smiled.

'Me.'

I smiled back, aware of my teeth.

There was a huge gaping silence, and then he said, 'Hazel, can I tempt you?'

Doctor Ishmael Stern. I noticed he always wore Italian suits, good shoes, a tie that complemented his shirt – a rare thing in a British man. At the Institute he was the calm heart of a perpetually busy machine, in which phones rang, secretaries rushed in and out, and nurses hovered. And there is always something about dark men that makes them seem extraordinary powerful, like they stalk the earth outlined in black felt-tipped pen. You could say I was in love with him. Or you could say I'd been reading too many women's magazines. Or you could say this always happens: women and shrinks, sex and God.

'I want to take you out to dinner,' he was saying. He had his hand on my arm now, and his grip was firm. 'We both need to get out of here. It's been too intensive. And I need to talk to you about a few things.'

Funny, that word 'need'. Its power; its mesmeric insistence. I need you.

'About Billy? Is he going to be all right? And the cutting? Did you get it?'

I found myself speaking fast, but in a way that passed for normal. Couldn't the man see that he had fried my heart?

'Wednesday evening OK?' he asked, as though I hadn't said anything.

'I'll pick you up at eight.'

'Yes,' I said.

Yes, Ishmael. Yes, yes, yes.

*   *   *

The light is on in the window of Flat 17, Bollingate View Terrace, and through it a spiky form can be seen darting to and fro, wielding cutlery and an ashtray. In her small kitchen with its artificial oak units, Linda Sugden is microwaving her TV dinner. When the machine pings, she slides the meal on to a plate, moves into the lounge and settles in a red velveteen chair to watch the news. A mug of Nescafé sits before her, planted on a cork-and-melamine place-mat depicting a Thai flower-market scene. She lifts the cardboard lid from the aluminium meal tray and the exotic vapours of Ham, Aubergine and Coriander Bake burst forth.

'Comfort and joy,' murmurs Linda to herself, releasing a pneumatic fart and lighting a cigarette.

Comfort and joy, and a packet of Love Hearts for afters. The Rancidity Forum has come to a close, and Linda feels exhausted but fulfilled. This week has proved to be something of a watershed in Storage Policy. Her eyes glaze over as the latest figures from the Fish Wars appear in a complex graphic, and the Energy Minister launches a nationwide compost appeal.

'Life's a bitch and then you die,' she sighs five minutes later, stubs out her cigarette, and farts again.

She's halfway through the Bake when suddenly a familiar figure pops up on the screen, clad in a yellow anorak with a red crucifix logo, and wielding a banner declaring 'WE ARE ALL PERFECT BABIES'. A group of a thousand demonstrators, the reporter is saying, many of them physically challenged. There are shots of the guide dogs, hearing-aids, and wheelchairs of the halt and the lame. The controversial trial drug GR218; controversial merger plans of the Fertility Management Centre and Hooper plc, headquartered in London; the charismatic and controversial babywear, stationery and frozen-food magnate Root Hooper (shot of Root Hooper banging his fist on a table); controversy; heated argument; debate; moral dilemma; outrage; crusade; practicalities; uncertainty.

Now the Reverend Carmichael is addressing the throng through a green megaphone: 'Big business has put itself behind Frankenstein. Together they will create monsters. The wages of sin is death, saith the Lord! Boycott Hooper products, folks, and show the Big One you're on the side of righteousness!'

And replacing the megaphone with a pair of giant garden shears, he begins to cut to pieces a miniature towelling Babygro to the sound of frenzied cheering.

'Whatever the outcome of this dispute,' the po-faced reporter concludes, 'one thing's for certain: the Perfect Baby issue will be on the social agenda for some time to come.'

'Good on you, Reverend,' murmurs Linda. 'As ye sow, Gregory Stevenson, so shall ye fucking reap.'

And opening the packet of Love Hearts, she reads the inscription on the first. It is pink, on a lemon background.

It says: 'My One True Love'.

*   *   *

124

You don't feel like a woman any more after you've had a baby. Not a real woman, a sexy one. What mother has time to wax her legs properly and stay awake long enough to get aroused by something which is after all old hat – her husband? What mother of a young child feels an overwhelming sexual desire for the father of her infant, after that infant has vomited milk on her shoulder all day? Give me her name and address. I will write to her and tell her she's a liar.

I saw the loss of my libido as part of being invisible. Men don't look at women who push buggies, except in Italy, where as an ensemble you become, momentarily, the manifestation of the Madonna and child, a sort of street icon. (On a trip to Padua, I was a goddess.) But Gridiron isn't Italy, and no one looked at me, and I became part of that sub-species of womanhood known as the mum, an underclass that forms the great marshmallow cushion on which other lives, more interesting and worthy than ours, are sustained and serviced.

So when, over dinner with Dr Stern, I felt the unmistakable urge for sex, I was as sweatily pole-axed as an adolescent. It all started with a sugarlump. We had driven out to an Italian restaurant in Mutton Acre, the sort of charm-packed village that advertises itself on brochures as a 'hidey-hole'. I liked being someone who went to dinner there. All the clients of its chic restaurants were professional couples, who either had no children (they drank more, had more fun) or had left their offspring with baby-sitters who lived where I once did, in the Cheeseways near the Works. Baby-sitters whose ambition it was, as mine had been when I baby-sat, making use of their telephones and investigating their larders and their loft conversions, to marry one day and have dinner in Mutton Acre. ('You're so conventional,' Ma always told me. 'Even the dipsomania.')

When we had sat down at our table, and the waiter had fussed over us and taken our order and planted a giant pepperpot on the table between us, we clinked glasses and then Ishmael did something strange: he told me to close my eyes and open my mouth. I did what he said, and was shocked to feel a violent sweetness on my tongue. I opened my eyes, crunched and swallowed. The psychiatrist had fed me a sugarlump, like I was a horse. He offered no explanation, and carried on talking about his autism research as though nothing had happened. I was too dumbfounded to mention it. We drank. The salt of the margarita tasted painful and exquisite after the sugar.

And then I felt it, a tingling flush that crept all over my body. Desire. I was surely leaking hormones on the tablecloth, and I wondered whether Ishmael had noticed.

He was looking elegant, as usual. He wore a pink shirt and I felt his eyes flit over me, stirring up rogue elements in groiny places. Suddenly he smiled and put down his knife and fork carefully and touched my hand. His voice was slow and reasonable.

'I except you're wondering where things *stand*, Hazel,' he said. 'Where *you* stand.'

I was expecting him to say something about the attraction between us, so I was almost disappointed when he began to talk about Gregory's file.

'My diagnosis is that although you're upset – disturbed even – by all this, you're coping very well. I've got some one-a-day *vitamins* for you, by the way, because we need to keep you as well and alert as possible while this is going on.'

He reached in his pocket and slipped out a plastic bottle of pills.

'You can start them now,' he murmured.

He opened the child-proof top for me, took one out, and popped it in my mouth.

I swallowed in a reflex.

'Here,' he said gently. 'Wash it down, love. Now, one a day. Don't forget.' He screwed back the top and handed me the bottle.

He had called me 'love'.

'You chose to do the *right thing* about this information,' he went on. 'It's a hot potato, and you picked the right person to handle it for you. I'm *aware* of the Hooper merger but I still need more time on it. A week should do it. I've gone through the file. It's not really my field but I know enough. Now it's just a question of completing those *tests* on your *son* –'

'And?'

'There are some exciting things going on, Hazel,' he said. 'Things your husband didn't think about, because he's not a *psychologist*. He should really have – ' and then he stopped abruptly.

A shadow passed over me, but I shooed it off. He was grasping my hand tightly now.

'What I'm saying is that he's on to something very *exciting*, but he has no idea how to *harness* it. I need to know more. And I'll find out,' he said.

He forked a morsel and posted it in his mouth. For some reason I couldn't eat. He smiled at me while chewing, and I played with the giant pepperpot.

Swallowing, he sipped at his water and pronounced, 'Your husband is a good scientist. His records are methodical and his study is elegant – ' but here he broke off again, and stopped smiling. He took a little stick of bread and dipped it in his seafood sauce. His face was serious now.

'Elegant,' he said in a different, censorious tone, 'but totally unethical. Quite against the *code of conduct*.'

'Immoral,' I said, gulping air.

The vitamins had done something to my system. I felt strange.

'Yes, if you want to use that word,' he agreed. 'In fact, Gregory's personality is one I'd be interested in exploring out of professional interest one day.'

'Do you think he could be unbalanced?' I asked. 'Clinically speaking, I mean?'

'Unbalanced – no. It's just that the scientific spirit got out of hand, and triumphed over the checks and balances. In any case, as I see it, it's actually a delicate ethical issue. One which you *could* argue a case for. I'm not saying I think he's *right*. I'm just saying that the scientist in me can understand while the man of ethics – the *moralist*, if you like – disapproves almost entirely of the principle.'

'And of the result? If everyone were born perfect,' I said, 'it would put you out of a job.'

'That's right,' he said thoughtfully. 'An end to mental suffering. That would be quite an *achievement*.'

'And Billy? Is he OK?'

'Fundamentally, yes. Some interesting *results* have emerged, though. He does seem to be capable of tele-pathic communication of a *limited nature* with your *mother*' – he raised his palm to stop me – 'but, as your husband *suspected*, it's only a one-way thing. He can communicate with her, but she's only a *recep-tor*.'

'Thank God for that. She won't be filling his head with junk, at least.'

'No. He seems to have been busy filling hers with his own little concerns, though. You do have to realise, Hazel, that they *are very close*.'

'I suppose they are,' I said, realising suddenly the significance of the constipation, the McDonalds, the remotely-controlled aeroplane, and the Magic Train, and feeling like an idiot not to have spotted it before.

'So,' he concluded, 'the success of the Baby B experiment was limited to this example of telepathy, with the wrong generation and in the wrong direction.'

'How do you mean?'

'Well, according to the *file*,' Dr Stern said, 'one of the aims of Genetic Choice is for the baby to intercept the wishes of parents and act *accordingly*.'

'And that's perfection? I'd never thought of it like that.'

There was a certain Gregory-type logic to it which might make sense on graph paper.

'It's part of it,' he answered. 'But only a very *small* part. There's lot's more. Other things. It's a fascinating *dynamic*, Hazel. Completely fascinating.' He stroked my arm gently. There was a pause, and then he said, 'You know, Hazel, in a funny sort of way, I'm jealous of your husband.'

Which was absurd. Gregory was at a gene conference with Ruby in Miami. He was probably probing her 'birth canal' even as we spoke.

Dr Stern dropped me off at reception, saying he 'had to get back'. In the car, he kissed me on the cheek. I could feel the imprint of his lips for a long time afterwards. I knew he had wanted me.

I had a dream that night. He pinned me down on the floor of his office. Its surface was mushy, and soon began to deliquesce to a soup-like liquid. Ishmael's chest was bare, I remember, and matted with dark hair. We were having sex, in a motion that was tortuously slow and swimming-poolish. We were weightless, and octopus-like, and I have a memory of my legs round his neck and he had one hand on each breast while, miraculously, a third slowly, slowly massaged what Ma always referred to as one's 'front bottom', and then suddenly the pace changed and he was thrusting inside me like a madman with a vision, and I was being food-mixed, my soul and my bum aflame. It was exquisite, but also excruciating, because Gregory was watching us from a corner of the room. He was laughing at me and calling out various taunts, but Ishmael, who couldn't see or hear him, just kept shrieking in my ear, 'Hazel, are you safe?' and I couldn't remember, because I couldn't see the chart and had forgotten the dates, and didn't care, and then I burst and became ectoplasm, and floated out of the room.

EIGHT

M *anxheath Institute of Challenged Stability*
Dear Late Husband,
  Something I forgot to ask about your current 'lifestyle':
is it a question of fluffy clouds, cherubs wielding cornu-
copias, and Earl Grey tea with a thousand vicars? Or is
it more a question of keeping your end up in a sea of
faeces? I am curious. One of these days, I shall come
and check. Here, apart from some 'special sessions' with
our grandson, it's purgatory as usual. Can you see us
down here, from your celestial vantage-point? See the
bitter-looking female who moves like an eel? She's Dr
'Sarah' McAuley, mine hostess. In charge.
  Once a day we sit in a semi-circle, with our ashtrays,
our balls of wool and our psychoses, and mouth off
about what beached us here, far from our beloved
suburbia, with its mortgage and two veg.
  Here we are: the Group. Take Max. Look at him with
his cunning badger's face, and then tell me there is no
justice in the world, and no God. He's tall because he was
a brigadier. He served in the Falklands and performed
secret missions in Beijing, though a blond man of that
height in a Chinese community is hard to keep a secret.
Lay him end to end and he'd be six foot four, but see
the giveaway stoop? That's guilt at work. They say that
if he hadn't been caught in a series of peccadilloes –

whippings, acts of violent buggery with junior officers, obscene phone calls to the high and mighty (that's what did it) – he'd have been in for a generalship. I don't know. 'They' is only his room-mate, David, who believes everything he's told.

David's the one next to Max. He of the horn-rimmed glasses, the seventies sideburns and the eternal Silk Cut. He's talking now, about leather. You are looking, incidentally, at a man broken by circumstances. As evidenced by his bitten fingernails. Nail-biters are to be pitied; they are like Jesus, suffering on the cross that we may be spared. Anyway, when David's marriage fell apart, so did he. The day his wife walked out, his sanity upped and left with her. He's obsessed with the legal side of it. The Bar Association conspired to wreck his life, forcing his innocent wife to run off with his company's accountant. The couple ran a business together, manufacturing inner soles for shoes. They dominated the market in the Midlands, and had trade links with Portugal, fending off the Taiwanese threat when lesser operations went under. Anyway, Wifey and the accountant are running the shoe business now, and there are letters flying about between their lawyers and Dr Stern on the question of 'incompetence due to insanity'. Wifey visits sometimes, small, tarty, pert, like a wee sweetie in a fancy wrapper, different shoes on each occasion, and calling him 'darling', while he looks up at her doggily from his armchair, waiting for her to throw a poisoned bone. I presume the accountant and the legal team wait in the car-park. When the staff aren't looking, Sweetie pushes papers under his nose, and hands him a pen. He reads them and writes mechanically – but it's not a signature; it's a message to the lawyers. 'Fuck You' on every document. Wifey reads it and smiles in a pained way.

132

'You should watch out, David,' I warned him once. 'Those lawyers will change your name to Fuck You by deed poll, and you'll have signed away your life.'

So he agreed to alternate it with 'Bollocks'.

Dr McAuley thinks the lawyers are a fantasy, but she's never seen Sweetie's antics. The way these doctors put so much faith in people who are supposedly sane, and turn a blind eye to the fact that they're cunning cut-throats who'd sell their children's kidneys for a go on a one-armed bandit. No case notes, no case to answer. That's doctors for you: pedantic. Look at our son-in-law, Greg Stevenson. Carries a tape measure everywhere, in case someone says 'How long is a piece of string?' Hazel always lacked imagination herself. She just wanted a nice life, I suppose – and she has one, if hideous curtains from John Lewis, a designer-splotched thing in pastel, at £21.75 a metre are proof of it.

Can you see how we're sitting? How the semi-circle is arranged around Dr McAuley to make her feel useful and in control? We are encouraged not to sit in the same place each time, so we do. I'm there in the middle, with Keith to my left and Isabella to my right. Next to Isabella, an emaciated, desperate wee figure, with bulging eyes. Is it a dragonfly? Is it a cricket? No, it's an anorexic, a creature defined by the medical dictionary as an 'ossature' – that's Latinate for bag of bones – who squeezes in where she can. And there's Monica Fletcher. Over there, in the navy Popsox, all scrunched up in a ball. She crouches on the floor when she's feeling low. She's very geographical; the day we find her perched on a high shelf, we'll know they've found the right drug combination – but no chance of that, I fear. You'd be surprised at the sheer volume of water that comes out of her. She takes the world very personally. Every starving baby is one she has given birth to, every torture victim and every murderer on Death Row is her husband or son, every rape victim is her sister or best friend, every hunted fox, drowned dog, or sexually abused tortoise, her pet. Frankly, her selflessness ends up being rather invasive, bless her.

The doctors have been experimenting with hormone therapy, the theory being that she's too feminine, too inclined to self-sacrifice and frailty. They assume this is a purely physical phenomenon – a question of oestrogen balance. So they give her doses of testosterone, and she grows a fetching crop of facial hair, and she carries on, all lace and dimples and wee seed-pearls of tears trickling forever down her pink-and-white face, forever writing billets-doux to her husband saying sorry, sorry, sorry. I found one and read it: darling this and darling that, sorry, sorry, are you OK, my love, oh I'm so looking forward to another honeymoon in Clermont-Ferrand, sorry, sorry, I love you etc, your loving wife Monica. Clermont-Ferrand!!?? That made me laugh. An industrial metropolis of rusting iron and belching smoke, if I remember rightly. He should be the one apologising.

Keith is playing chess in his head again. You can tell from the way his eyes flicker. He doesn't participate in the Group, being indifferent to humans on the whole, and not speaking. Right from the start, I took a liking to him. He makes me think of how our son might have turned out, if I hadn't sat on him. I remember, years ago, Hazel came home from school one day with a whole load of jokes about dead babies. I made her tell me each of them at least three times, standing on the kitchen table. I laughed till the tears ran down my face.

Look, Brendan: Isabella's talking now, about her cervix dilation, waving her arms in that operatic Latin way, fecundity and motherhood written all over her. Born to breed. She's had so many, she tells me, whole litters of them, she's lost count. All given up joyously for adoption, in that spirit of altruism I so much admire in her. Breast-fed and vaccinated, and then off into the wide world. But this latest offspring – how long has she been carrying this creature? Eighteen months? Two years? (Dr McAuley, who is childless herself, said once she reckoned the swelling was wind. If that's the case, I told her, may you be the first to be blown to kingdom come when Signora P. lets loose *that* fart.)

'It's usually nine months with me,' Isabella told me yesterday. 'Sometimes ten. Eleven maximum. But never this long before. I try not to worry.'

Best friends we may be, but she won't tell me who the father is.

Now Dr McAuley's turning to David: 'Shall we carry on with your story, now? We'd just got to your marriage, I think.'

Watch. Max puts his head in his hands, and Monica has her just-finished-crying-but-just-about-to-cry-again look. David is a very precise man.

'10 June 1976. The happiest day of my life. We spent our honeymoon on the Greek islands of Paros and Antiparos. It was – ' but he's started to make strangled noises, which is his way of crying, and fumbles for a cigarette.

'Blissful?' asks Isabella Pimento, helpfully.

My turn to pipe up: 'Nice weather?'

'Romantic!' That comes from Monica Fletcher. Look at her, Kleenexing for all she's worth.

Max lifts his badger's face out of his hands, and looks up, as if dazzled by the light. He barks, 'All a horrendous farce?'

Silence. Keith will come up with something. Yes, look, he's gesturing with his hands. I translate for him.

'The beginning of the end.' David nods, takes a shaky

135

drag of his fag, and wipes his nose on his sleeve, Monica being too self-obsessed to think of sharing her paper hanky.

'Yes, it was the beginning of the end, I suppose. Though I didn't know it then. You see, I'm not very – empowered' – see us all smile; this is an Institute sort of word – 'I'm not very empowered sexually.'

'You mean you're impotent!' crows Max.

David shudders and recoils into his cloud of smoke. Dr McAuley's role is to make sure the big ones don't throw sand in the little ones' eyes, to punish and reward, to stir up wee McNuggets of insight in our dumbfounded minds.

'It sounds like *you* might have something to share there, Max,' she suggests helpfully. 'This is an issue I think we might find ourselves talking around later, but I'd like David to complete first.'

That's the trouble with communicating with psychiatrists. You have to learn their language.

'Now, David, you were sharing with us around your feelings of disempowerment.'

'No,' says David. He's addressing himself to Max, like the fool he is. 'I don't mean impotent. I mean I was overwhelmed by the way she seemed so experienced for a virgin.'

What's the betting Max is going to say something about 'virgin on the ridiculous'?

'Virgin on the ridiculous, was it, the idea that she was a virgin?' he guffaws on cue.

'You could say that,' replies David. 'In any case, it made me wonder if I really knew her after all. And it made me have – problems of a sexual nature.'

Now they're discussing premature ejaculation and expectations of sex. Time for Isabella and me to get out our knitting: no point getting involved in *that* kind of discussion, though Isabella murmurs that she's never had any sexual problems with *her* men. See Keith, off in another world, and the Ossature, in her yogi's starvation trance, her bony knees clamped together. And look how Monica Fletcher is blushing and looking uncomfortable, and whimpering a little when the language gets explicit. Whoops! She's in tears and crying out in her poor quavery voice, 'Are you all mad? I don't understand how you can talk like this! No one's saying anything about *love*!'

Watch us all look up sharply. It's not like her to be so vehement, even with the beard.

'Surely if a woman *loves* a man,' she's saying, 'she's not going to start criticising how he makes love to her, is she? She's just going to *take* everything he wants to give her, and be *joyful* about it. Love should be unconditional. There you are, talking about – ' but here she stops for the ugly word will not pass her pretty moustached lips.

'Orgasms.' That's Dr McAuley. Matter-of-fact as a toilet brush, when it comes down to it.

'Yes, well, there's no need to, is there. They're not – they're not – they're not – *everything*!' and she's in fresh tears, shocked at her own ferocity, and scrabbling for a fresh Man-Size pack of Kleenex in her bag.

'Get out your mops, Group,' says Max gaily. 'We're in for a flood, and it's looking Bangladeshi.'

Note Dr McAuley's patronising smile.

'Progress,' she says. 'My feeling is that Monica is starting to experience some unexpected growth. But growth is painful.' She sweeps kindly eyes around the circle.

'Thank you all. I'd like to complete with you now, and we'll share again tomorrow.'

A putting away of knitting, a scraping of chairs.

Now look, Brendan! Quick, over there! The Ossature

has risen from her seat too fast and collapsed, crashing down like a hat-stand! There's the gallant David going to the rescue, and there's Monica quickly unloosing a second, emergency floodgate in her heart. Max is having a good laugh, like he's sicking something up. Ah, she's reviving. And she's up! And she's yelling something about Daddy! And she's down again! That's right, Dr McAuley, give her a slap around the chops and do the biz with your buzzer.

There's nothing we like better here than a bit of *Sturm und Drang*. You may well ask what your ex-wife is doing amidst all this commotion. I am singing an old nursery song from days of yore, with Isabella on backing vocals:

> There was an old man called Michael Finnegan
> First grew fat and then grew thin again
> Then he died and had to begin again
> Poor old Michael Finnegan begin-again!

Meanwhile see our arses getting smaller, late beloved? That's us leaving.

*　　*　　*

Manxheath, 14 February
Dear Greg,

Happy Valentine's Day! Roses are red, violets are blue, I'd like a divorce, and so would you. Please write to me confirming this, care of Dr Stern at Manxheath; meanwhile you will be hearing from my lawyer before the end of the month. I assume you will not be contesting my full custody of Billy, since you are about to become a father again. I shall be upholding my right to half of all your assets, including your share of the Fertility Management Centre, and your continued maintenance of myself and Billy until I can support us financially, if Lockwood's will have me, or perhaps I could go back into travel agenting. Billy and I will be moving back into Oakshott Road as soon as I have recovered from the delusion thing, so you and Ruby had better start flat-hunting.

Hazel

What does it mean, to know a person? There are facts. I am thirty-two, he is thirty-eight. He is a doctor, I have tended to 'work at home', which involves a certain amount of dusting and ironing, daily childcare, and an addiction to a soap opera called *The Young and the Restless*. We have a Fiat, a Volvo and a two-year-old son. Did he keep my three dead foetuses pickled in a jar? I picture them sometimes, their chameleons' padded fingers pressing against the glass, their faces turned to furious bloated prunes.

Oakshott Road, 16 February
My dear Hazel,

I am sorry it has come to this. However, Dr Stern tells me you are not at all well, and certainly not in a fit state to make any major decisions about your life. We clearly need to talk, but I will respect Dr Stern's judgement that you are not yet ready for this. He will tell me when you are.

You are quite mistaken about my relationship with Dr Gonzalez. We are simply professional colleagues, and good friends, collaborating on a research project. You know I was never attracted to overweight women. When you are better, we will talk it all through, but in the meantime, there is no question of divorce. I am sorry not to have seen more of Billy, but as you know, Dr Gonzalez and I have been on a fund-raising visit to Latin America and the United States.

Yours ever,

Gregory

PS: The living-room carpet has developed some kind of vegetable growth.

I showed Greg's letter to Dr Stern. I couldn't think straight. Ever since my hyper-realistic sex session with Ishmael, I felt groggy all the time. Crazed with love. Yes; love. I recognised it as a form of madness; something clean and pure, that pushes personality out to the chaotic fringes of being. Here, anything can happen. There are no patrols.

'Leave it at that,' he said. 'We need him to believe you're ill. He mustn't suspect you've seen the file. You'll get your divorce' (his hands were on my shoulders now; did he realise what he was doing?) 'but be patient about it.'

'But what he's doing needs to be exposed, Ishmael, before it goes any further. You saw the cutting I gave you. He's got Hooper behind him now. The money's huge. I keep feeling we can't have much time left.'

'Trust me,' he said.

Has a woman ever drowned, I wondered, in the oil wells of a man's eyes?

'We won't let him get away with it, Hazel. We'll stop him. When the *time is right*. I'm preparing a dossier.'

Did I imagine it, or did he then kiss me on the lips, and pull me down with him on to the floor of his office, strip off my tights and knickers with a practised hand, and within seconds, have us doing it on the floor like frenzied beasts?

The next day I woke at six, and reached out for Ishmael beside me in the bed. I reckoned I could still feel his

140

flesh on mine, but he wasn't there. My heart hurt. The vitamins he'd given me the other night were next to the bed, in a plastic container. He'd been right to prescribe them: looking in the mirror, I noticed how careworn my face looked. I reckoned that my whole system could probably do with a boost, now that I had something to live for. So when I finally got the lid off, I took five.

Love was a violent, heavy animal. A bull that crashed into me head-on, impaled me on its horn, tossed me in the sky. When I landed, I had bruises on my soul. I planned to deck Ishmael in jewels, like a king. I would. Like a king.

'Just done a wee-wee,' said Billy, waking up and removing his sodden nappy.

Staring closer in the mirror, I realised I owed it to myself to get my act together. Today I would spend some time and some money on it. I wanted to be a new woman.

I watched Billy eating cornflakes at breakfast, and cooed over him, ridden with guilt. But he seemed older, and less interested in baby talk. Leaving home seemed to have coincided with a development spurt. Or caused one.

'Gwanny,' he said. 'Wanna see Gwanny.'

'You will, darling,' I promised. 'After the crèche.'

'Take me there, Mummy,' he said, his face squashed into a bright little smile. For a brief instant there was something of Greg about his eyes, and I recoiled.

'Off we go then,' I said, wiping his face. 'Mummy will come to fetch you later.'

'And Gwanny?' he asked. (Bugger 'Gwanny'. What does he see in her?)

'And Granny, if you like.'

'Good,' said Billy, getting down from the table and into his buggy. 'I love my Gwanny.'

Those pills; was it them that made my heart soar like Concorde in the face of such depressing news?

It was early, and I was the only customer in the Hopeworth's *Soins Intensifs* Beauty Clinic. Three white-coated beauticians stood behind me in a semi-circle and we gazed into the mirror together.

'Trust me,' said the man. His name was Bobby. 'I'm an artist.'

'I will,' I said.

'I'm Sherine and this is Mabs,' said Sherine. 'I'll get you a coffee.'

'Transform me,' I told them, feeling the potent rectangle of Gregory's credit card in the pocket of my ski-pants. Mabs went and got some thin rubber gloves. The beauticians turned out to be quite a trio.

First Bobby waxed my legs and depilated my bikini line while Sherine and Mabs massaged my body with coconut oil.

'Milk and Hermesetas?' asked Sherine.

'Or are you artificially sweet enough already?' joked Bobby.

Then the three of them put me in a tub to steam and went off for a cigarette.

Twenty minutes later, when I was itching and tingling all over, they threw me in a pool of freezing water. When they'd pulled me out, Sherine covered me in something called Galilee Mud. She applied it as though she were icing a cake. She was left with a great smear of it on one cheek, but I didn't say anything.

After it had set, and cracks began to develop, Bobby came and hosed me down with warm foamy water.

Mabs laid me on a giant paper cloth and applied Miracle Body Cream in a slapping motion. It smelt of floor-cleaner. Sherine set to work tinting my eyebrows and lashes deep black, while Bobby did my nails. Sherine spilt the dye all over Mabs's coat. It made a stain whose shape was reminiscent of a pair of Fallopian tubes.

Then we all had more coffee, and Mabs washed my hair.

Bobby dyed it, which involved more chemicals and some strangely folded aluminium foil.

Sherine cut and re-styled it. That took an hour.

Bobby, who had been to drama school, applied daring new make-up. That took another hour.

Then they all said together, 'There.' And smiled.

I smiled too. My mirror image, a bright, sassy woman with clipped chestnut hair and a bold red mouth, smiled back. God, she was beautiful. I didn't recognise her as me.

I didn't read the bill. I just signed.

'Bye,' called out Bobby, Mabs and Sherine as I left. 'Don't do anything we wouldn't do!'

'Buy yourself some frocks!' Mabs's voice called after me faintly as the door closed to.

'Yeah!' echoed Bobby. 'Go mad!'

My body buzzed all over, and my mind quivered on the edge of things. There was a brightness and newness to the world. I knew how new-born babies must feel. I phoned my mother and asked her if she could fetch Billy from the crèche and take care of him until I got back.

'I've fetched him already,' she replied. 'We've been in with Dr Stern for tests. Billy isn't missing you at all. In fact, he's forgotten you exist. So don't worry.'

Rather than stinging me, this heightened my jubilation. I decided to follow Mabs's advice, and took a taxi into town and spent £558.99 on clothes, including some lacy underwear. As I looked at myself over the course of that afternoon, in various mirrors, and from different angles, I marvelled at the beauty of my reflection. Walking down the street I passed myself in more mirrors, and only recognised myself minutes later, so unfamiliar was this new woman. She was beautiful, happy and in love.

When Ma saw me, she shook her head.

'Don't see what was wrong with your hair the colour it was,' she remarked. 'Too much eyeliner, too much colour in your cheeks. The overall effect is that of a cup-cake. Billy thinks so too, don't you, pet?'

And it was true that he seemed to be shrinking away from me. He hid in Ma's skirt, then popped out his little face, shocked, aghast, and shouted, 'Mummy!' as if to warn me of something I couldn't see. But a few hugs and smiles set him right, and I let him try on my new Bloody Hell lipstick. A streak of it transformed his lips into a clownish gash, and I laughed. In fact I couldn't stop laughing.

'What's got into you, Hazel?' asked my mother, looking at me strangely. 'What sort of pills are you taking?'

'Red ones,' I said. 'Dr Stern gave me some, just in case.'

I was still laughing at Billy, who was smearing lipstick on his teddy bear's nose.

'Just in case of what?' she asked, her face all twisty.

'Athletes use them, Ma. Multi-vitamins, to perk you up. Don't you realise how run-down you get coping with a small child?'

Ma said, 'Did I hear you say *coping*?'

She was looking pissed-off, which was fairly typical of the way she reacted to any shred of happiness in my life, so I just gave her my new, gorgeous smile. My Bloody Hell smile, which at that moment began to stretch independently across my face until it hurt.

I suppose, looking back, it was a sort of defection. I'd always known there was a place I could go if ever I needed to – a corner of my mind that was waiting for me. It wasn't frightening. It was somewhere I almost knew; I'd grown up with a view of it, and a free pass. It was just across the way, and I had family there.

I used to like the story of Alice in Wonderland. She fell down that rabbit-hole, didn't she, into a world where things were at the same time unusual and familiar. The important thing was, I was in control.

'Hazel!' murmured Stern when I swung into his office in a satin bomber jacket, a tight pencil-skirt and three-inch heels.

'I – hardly recognised you. What have you done?'

He looked aghast, but then, as his eyes took me in, the shock turned to –

It must have been love, because suddenly he was looking like he had to wrestle with something, to rein it in.

'I've stopped being invisible,' I said. 'Don't you think I'm beautiful?'

I was breathless with ecstasy, and my heart was pounding in a way I hadn't felt since I was fifteen, when a boy at school put his hand inside my knickers.

'You're incredible,' he said.

He was talking in a low voice and steering me back towards the door like I was some kind of shopping trolley.

'Just incredible. Look, I'm so sorry, but I can't see you right now. Your *husband* is arriving any minute – and I think it would be best if you *weren't around*. He wants Billy this weekend. He told me on the phone – is that OK?'

Of course it is, I tell him, smiling wide and seeing the effect of it, my bright lipstick dazzling his eyes. I can see my whole face and body in his dark irises, bobbing in front of me like a little doll version of myself, in a glassy bubble. It feels good. Everything's good today – everything.

'Good,' he echoes aloud, looking me up and down again.

'Good,' he says again slowly, with that same look, which gives me a little dose of a funny feeling I can't name. But the thing about feelings is that you can kill them, as you might wring a chicken's neck out of mercy, if you found it in bad shape. *Insecurity is the curse of women*. Quote, sister Linda, *circa* 1983, over a plate of muesli at the Women's Cafeteria. I needn't be insecure. I am, after all, in charge.

'Your husband is coming to discuss you, Hazel,' Stern is saying.

There's a mustard-yellow file with my name on it on his desk. He sees me looking at it.

'Just some notes,' he says, and puts it away in the cupboard. He comes over to me smiling. When he puts his hand on my arm, I feel microwaved, dizzy with love.

It's a strange thing, love. You catch it unawares, like a disease. I hadn't remembered it like this. I had associated it with contentment, not unrest. My eyes slipped away from his and reached instead for comfort. They fastened on the glass paperweight with anemones inside – a little self-contained, unchanging world. I could see why Ishmael kept it on his desk. I wanted, in that moment, to crawl inside it and be a foetal shrimp, frozen in time and space. Something was going wrong. My mouth was dry and my heart was a frenzied chicken in a coop.

'Your husband is coming to discuss you,' Ishmael whispered urgently. 'But I won't let him visit you. I've been telling him you're *depressed*. Don't worry, I've told him you're quite capable of looking after Billy. And that it's all *for your own good*.'

I tore my eyes from the paperweight.

'Look, Hazel,' he was murmuring. (People were always saying 'Look, Hazel,' it struck me.) 'We still have to *play for time*. I don't yet have all the information I need. Go now. The last thing I want is for your husband to see you like this.'

'See me like what?' I asked.

He paused for a moment, his round eyes blank. The pause was a fraction of a second too long, and the monster doubt hatched.

'Beautiful and happy,' he said, kissing my cheek and gliding me gently out of the door. 'Gregory won't be expecting it.'

Remember last night, Ishmael, do you remember my dream last night? Here, he said, slipping two yellow pills in an envelope and pressing it into my hand. Take these at six o'clock. I shoved the packet into my handbag and left, with an unconnected image that stuck to the walls of my mind: when we were children, Linda and I had a game where you had to pick up as many sticks as you could from a tightly heaped pile, one by one, without moving any of the others. Spillikins. Leaving Dr Stern's office, I remembered this game called Spillikins as clearly as if it were yesterday.

As soon as I came out I saw my husband. He was walking straight towards me, carrying his briefcase. He looked distracted. His hair was greyer than I remembered it.

'Morning,' he said to me vaguely, and walked past stiffly, as though his joints were riveted. He hadn't recognised me. I felt drained and shaky, but I carried on up the corridor. Just as I turned the corner, I heard him knock on Dr Stern's door.

'Greg, come in,' I heard Dr Stern call in a hearty voice I didn't know.

'Ishmael,' said Greg's voice, loud and smooth.

First names.

Then there was another game we played called Categories. That was when we were older. The categories were things like cars, flowers, fruit-and-veg, boys' names, girls' names, animals. Someone chose a letter, and then you started filling in the columns on your paper, one word for each category: Ford, forsythia, fig, Frederick, Fanny, fox. Or Jaguar, jasmine, juniper berry, Julian, Jane, jaguar again, because there are very few animals that begin with J. Whoever finished first won. Ma used to win, always. She plays it with Keith now, using different categories: medical conditions, dead authors, flowering shrubs, foreign politicians, racehorses. Keith can't do flowering shrubs, and Ma makes up the racehorse names, but between them they fill whole sheets of paper. Psoriasis, Proust, *Pyrethrum* 'Brenda', Pasqua, Play Your Cards Right. Mammary inflammation, Milton, mimosa, Milosevic, Mummy's Boy. Botulism, Baudelaire, *Belladonna crassiflora*, Bhutto, Beginner's Luck.

Category: doctors. One begins with I, and one begins with G. Their names don't begin with the same letter so clearly they have nothing in common.

Did I really listen at the door? I must have done, because I saw myself reflected in the window opposite. There, in the corridor, crouching low, her head squashed up against the wood, was Hazel. The confident, laughing Hazel who spent all that money on her appearance. What is she doing? Hazel down on her knees now at the door, her bum squeezed like toothpaste in that pencil skirt, the poky heels splayed sideways, the head a chestnut mushroom of hair, the eyes screwed up, ear thrust against the wood of the door, intent on listening.

She couldn't make it all out, but she heard enough. Words like 'collaboration', 'research project', and 'pooling resources'. She heard something about 'delay the divorce proceedings', and then Ishmael's voice: 'Hazel's treatment', and 'de Cleranbault's syndrome', and then 'if the cap fits'.

'A delicate situation,' said Gregory. 'And this enormous bill from the Hopeworth . . .'

Then they had a drink. Hazel knew that because Gregory began talking about whiskies, Glenfiddich, Glenmorangie and Laphroaig, and their murmuring voices took on the reassuring ocean wash of shared comforts. Hazel stood up and smoothed her pencil skirt about her hips. Slim as a racehorse, she thought. Not a trace of cellulite, no unsightly varicose veins, no unwanted hair, plenty of muscle tone . . . My mind staggered. I reached in my handbag for a yellow peppermint, and swallowed it whole with an arid throat.

And for the first time since I was a small child, I fled, hell in my ears, to the fat and unaccommodating bosom of my Ma.

NINE

Paperwork, paperwork. The memo about the Poly-unsaturated schedule, with copies in triplicate. The briefing documents for this afternoon's policy brain-storming. The colour-coded priority sheets for Monday's development symposium. Trish is powering through them swiftly, one eye on the clock. She's off to lunchtime aerobics on the dot of one. You try and stop her. Linda, forcing open the vacu-pak of her sandwich with her car key, surveys Trish's competent little sorting movements and wonders how many hours of workout it takes to get one's bum looking like two crabapples in a bag. What sort of training equipment, what sort of inane compulsiveness, what degree of narcissism. Fancy turning one's body into a cause. Jealousy mingled with ideological distaste engulfs her, and she breathes in deep to avoid drowning.

Outside, ravens whirl like rags in a tumble-drier, black against sepia squirls of sky. March: the shittiest month, season of chilly sleet, emotional torment, and for Linda, chronic chilblains. Her birthday is on 24 March. She will be thirty-five. Thirty years ago, on her fifth birthday, she received a small plastic doll called Katie-Koo from Dad and Ma. You filled a little internal pouch with water so it could lachrymate and piss. Hazel had bitten off its head, and shortly afterwards Dad had left home. In

Linda's five-year-old consciousness the decapitation and the abandonment were connected. Lately on *Holy Hour* the Reverend Carmichael has been preaching about the season of renewal, but the only regenerative impulse Linda can summon concerns her Road Tax Disc.

Hoiking her feet on to the desk, she bites into the spongy triangle of a chicken tikka sandwich and counts her one blessing, which is that, work-wise, she can afford to relax. The Frozen Fats (Surplus) meeting has gone as planned, and a weight is off her mind: two million metric tonnes, to be precise. Even Mr Foley, who considers Linda Sugden a brilliant mind but a walking attitude problem, has had to admit she has pulled off something of a policy coup with Operation Fatberg, her Arctic 'sea burial' initiative.

But while work has eased off, family matters have been screaming for attention. In particular, Hazel's breakdown. It neither rhymes nor reasons, and Dr Stern's theory about 'nervous exhaustion' doesn't bear serious analysis. She's given him quite a grilling on the phone, and still has only insubstantial answers to some of the crucial questions, e.g. this: Why would Hazel massacre all those chairs when she was so fond of pine? It just didn't make sense. Or this: Why would she claim to be taking a winter 'bucket-and-spade holiday', when the Hopeworth Hotel was miles from the sea?

Something else jarred, too. A pair of twin elephantine thighs, a triangle of dark hair, an obscenely pregnant belly —

Bleugh.

'Beg pardon?' asks Trish, rolling a green leotard in a towel and flexing her buttocks individually.

'Only connect,' murmurs Linda thoughtfully, chewing on chicken tikka. 'Connect, connect.'

'You what?' asks Trish. 'Connecticut? My ex-boyfriend, he went out there and became a structural engineer. Got two kids now, four and one.'

'Five,' says Linda automatically.

'What, days in Connecticut? When you off then?'

'No, not Connecticut,' snaps Linda, throwing her crusts in the bin. 'I was thinking about my family.'

Katie-Koo had blue eyes. All dolls seemed to, back in the sixties.

'Oh. But they're local, aren't they?' questions Trish, briefly interested. They say Miss Sugden is from the Cheeseways – the shit end of town.

Linda says, 'Except my dad. He went to New Zealand and got poisoned.'

'Oh wow,' responds Trish, genuinely aghast. 'How horrific. We used to stop off in Wellington on the long hauls, but there was never much to do after eleven, except a bit of night-surfing. Nightmareville.'

'One of the goldfish he won me was called Ariadne, but I can't remember the name of the other one. I think it began with R.'

This galls Linda, who'd won Memory Badges at school, as well as the Tidy Desk medal.

'Richard? Rudolph? Ross?' Trish volunteers, but Linda is lighting a cigarette, lost in thought.

'Well, see you later, alligator,' smiles Trish, swinging a bright plastic beach bag over her shoulder, and heading for the gym.

'Goodbye, macaroon,' murmurs Linda and inhales deeply, getting that giddy feeling she loves, then letting the smoke dragon from her nostrils. Then, cigarette in her left hand, she reaches with her right for a large piece of paper, selects four coloured felt pens, and with a firm professional instinct that has never let her down, begins to draw a diagram.

The management guru Klaus G. Armstrong maintains that good, efficient management is fundamentally all about working with people. Working with people, using resources, making connections, doing A where a lesser thinker might choose option B, not ruling out C when D, E and F might offer superficially better prospects. Management is also an instinct, a flair, a magical knack like the laying-on of hands, a melding of inspiration, common sense, Olympian vision and a roll-up-your-sleeves, shit-or-get-off-the-pot practicality. It involves an almost biological feeling for structure, an eye for detail, a certain skill in pattern-recognition. Linda has learned a lot from Klaus G. Armstrong's practical ideas and methods. Who hasn't.

In a red circle she writes 'Hooper plc – Perfect Baby Drug'. She links this circle to another one, in yellow, in which she writes the name Gregory Stevenson, and to another, in green, labelled Dr Ruby Gonzalez. She draws a wiggly yellow line between the circles for Gregory and Ruby, then puts Hazel's name in blue in another circle, linked to Gregory's by a solid black line with an axe through it. In a smaller yellow circle below Hazel, she writes 'Billy' in blue, and in a smaller green circle below Ruby, draws a stick-figure with a huge head with two hairs sprouting from it, and surrounds it with yellow question marks. On the right-hand side of the page she writes 'Vernon Carmichael' in purple. Next to him, a huge cross of righteousness. And takes another huge and giddying drag on her cigarette.

Yes. It's all beginning to make sense.

*   *   *

Manxheath Institute of Challenged Stability,
Friday
Dear Brendan,

There's a story I tell Billy. Once upon a time there was a king with money and a car, and he married Hazel, and they had you. But a wicked witch in a Latin cabaret costume covered in sequins, and dangling a pink feather boa, came pirouetting into the picture, a spinning carousel of the erotic, and the king couldn't resist, because sex and scientific talent are potent ingredients, and your silly mother is an abhorrence to anyone in their right mind, with her low self-esteem and her nylon Welcome mat. So they set up house, the king and his Bird of Paradise, in a detached house with two bathrooms, and they made the beast with two backs whenever they pleased, and would have lived happily ever after, but for a great tragedy that befell them, whose cause they never discovered, but they blamed themselves, which was only right and proper, and they shrank, shrank, shrank until they were the smallest and least significant people on earth.

It's hardly surprising that Hazel is looking peaky these days. She's demonstrating some fairly florid manifestations of acute mania, and is clearly in more of a sexual pickle than I'd thought. Thank goodness the crèche is reliable, because she most certainly isn't. The other day I spotted no fewer than three paper-clips in her hair. Today I'd just started on the tiger-lilies in the greenhouse when she came rushing up screaming, dressed in her prostitute's outfit. I hauled her off to Signora Pimento's nest, which is near to completion, and poured half a hip-flask of brandy down her, which I'm afraid only aggravated the raving. I ransacked her handbag, and found a portable phone (which I pocketed) and her mysterious red pills, which I planted in the 'miscellaneous medications' bed. Then I sat on her. It was all I could think of to shut her up. She always had 'lungs'. The shock of it seemed to send her into a coma (as you know I am a heavy woman), so I left her there with her silly suspenders showing and got on with the business in hand. The business in hand is two babies to be born – one here, one there. Both are imminent. And I have a plan.

Hazel came to a few hours later, still raving about her bad luck with men. I tried explaining to her that it was worse than bad luck; it was choice. (Hundreds of hours of group therapy have left their mark.) You actively pick them, I was explaining. You're obviously addicted, psychologically speaking, to a mean-spirited personality type who fails to meet the most fundamental requirements of interpersonal relationships. It's clearly your father's fault (that's you, Brendan), and if you don't come to terms with it – perform your own personal *Gestalt* – you'll never be what I would term a complete human being. But she was in no mood for advice. In fact I'm not sure she heard a word I said, or recognised who I was. She was taking huge swigs of brandy. Her make-up was all smeared across her face and she reminded me of how she looked when I dressed her up once for a fancy-dress party as a child – a hobgoblin, I think – but the greasepaint melted and she came home frantic and screaming because all the other little girls were fairies and Snow White. I can see her now, shouting at me, stamping, stamping, stamping that wee foot, with its shiny wee party shoe with the wee buckle, saying, 'I hate you, Mummy, you made me look ugly and everyone laughed at me!' the tears skidding across the oil. Such a joke she looked, I couldn't help laughing myself. I didn't laugh at her now, though, lipstick all across her cheek, mascara smudged, because she'd done it herself this time. My conscience was clear.

Then she clutched her knees to her chest in just the same way as Monica Fletcher does when she's attention-seeking in Group, and rocked to and fro. She'd had this incredible dream, she said, all about being in Eden, an oasis of tropicana, where she was raped by an enormous snake.

'It went right up through me and emerged via my throat,' she groaned. 'And a wodge of white gob splatted out.'

Even her subconscious is a gutter. A pity Dr McAuley wasn't there; it would have been right up her street.

'Well, you got at least one aspect of it right,' I told her; 'you are in a sort of Eden.'

She glanced around her, but didn't seem to take it in. When I told her I had a master plan she just said I could do what the fuck I liked, whoever I was, she didn't care, as long as I just fucked off. I learned a long time ago not to expect gratitude from the likes of my daughter. Fancy not recognising her own Ma. I left her choking over the bottle, looking like the whore she is.

On the way to Group, I came face to face with our son-in-law Gregory carrying Billy on his shoulders. He told me he'd fetched Billy from the crèche and was taking him home for the weekend, with Hazel's agreement via Dr Stern. He looked happy: his eyes were glazed, and I could smell whisky on his breath. He read my thoughts, and told me he'd just been enjoying a 'quick aperitif' with Dr Stern. Chatting, colleague to colleague. Man to man. His eyes were darting about madly, and he seemed desperate to say something that wouldn't come out, but then it finally did.

'Discussing Hazel, actually.'

Surprise, surprise. If he jogs Billy up and down like that any more, I thought, the lad will vomit.

'Oh yes,' I said. 'You wouldn't recognise her. She's quite come apart at the seams.'

'So Dr Stern tells me. I'm sorry it's come to this.'

'Like hell you are,' I told him, and I gave him a look.

This was followed by what he would term 'an embarrassing pause', in which he joggled my poor grandson some more. Billy just sat there like Buddha and listened with his big eyes, serious, thinking: This is my dad, come to see me.

'Bye-bye, my poppet,' I told him.

I'm not much of a kisser, but I took his tiny hand in mine and gave it a squeeze. And I thought: Have a lovely weekend with the King and his new Queen, Ruby Gonzalez, MD., Ph.D., greedy eater of lemon soufflé, and usurper of my daughter's throne. And watch out for her, Billy boy. Her belly is a poisoned chalice.

'Cheerio, Moira,' said my gynaecologist son-in-law, and swung off with Billy in the direction of the car-park.

It's a Pay and Display.

Yours sincerely,
Moira Sugden

Manxheath Institute for the Morally Deranged,
Tuesday
Dear departed,

Spring is in the air and the greenhouse is a triumph: termites burrowing, bulbs shooting up, chrysalises cracking open, hormones whizzing about. My miscellaneous medications bed is inching into bloom; the Valium turns out to have pinky-green leaves and a fluffy puce flower that resembles cotton. I plan to send a photograph to that terrible gardening programme where the earth is never dirty; they have a competition. After a shaky start with germination, which I put down to the type of capsule, the Largactil is now in bud, and promises to be a flamboyant, cabaret sort of flower. I had high hopes of my Lithium, but it has let me down; it's hairy and covered in a black insect called bloat-fly. Hazel's so-called vitamins were equally disappointing. I put them out of their misery.

As if I didn't already have enough on my plate with the greenhouse and Hazel, things have been coming to a head *vis-à-vis* Isabella's birthing arrangements. Yesterday morning I was preparing a huge nest of ferns, exotic herbs and jungle moss for her labour when suddenly I heard a cry and saw her outside, capsizing. It was almost in slow motion. I hadn't realised how many petticoats were involved. I rushed out and heaved her up to a sitting position; luckily she'd fallen on a heap of peat. Peat is always useful. She sat and groaned for a while, then lay down again. It was then that I spotted what the problem was: her belly was churning in a frenzy. The wretched baby was writhing about like she'd swallowed a boa constrictor.

'Monster, monster,' she was crying. It was piteous.

'You're going to have a good old rest, Signora P,' I told her. 'That baby's more than your match.'

I took her inside and we had a cup of tea in the Day Room. Her abdomen was still in revolt, but the fit was over. I told her about the nest; it was going to be a secret but she was in such a state about the lack of facilities in Manxheath that I had to break the good news to her. Then I stormed into Dr Stern's pretentious office. He looked shocked. Like so many men, he shies away from confrontation.

'What the hell d'you think you're up to?' *j'accuse*.

'Did you *make* an appointment to see me, Moira?'

'Mrs Sugden, to you,' I tell him. 'I'm a so-called client, aren't I? I'm here on an urgent matter.'

I saw him press his buzzer to summon a nurse, so I did my best to spit it all out before I got dragged off.

'The way you're dealing with Isabella's pregnancy is a fiasco,' I told him. 'You and your staff are in a state of chronic denial. I know the line you're taking: the baby is a schizoid fantasy – official. Am I right or am I right? You seem to have been losing your grip on reality lately, if I may say so. Dating back to when my daughter Hazel started to pester you, I'd say. I used to revere you, Doctor, but you've let me down. Will the dirty nappies be a fantasy, too? Do we have to come and hang them up here in your office? Do you want ocular proof?'

'Mrs Sugden. I think you're forgetting your *contract* here. We supply you with care on condition that you, the *client*, as you so rightly say – ' He broke off, seeing the door open. 'Ah, art therapy calls. See you at our next *scheduled* session.'

I feel another effigy coming on. When I reported the gist of things to Isabella, she just smiled. She doesn't get worked up about these staff like I do. She's fifty-five, and she's had a hard life, starting with a thing her Uncle Paolo did to her in a laundry-room in Turin. She says 'experience has taught her'. Either that or she's finally lost her Marbellas, bless her. I put her to bed with the panda hot-water bottle she's so devoted to, and tucked her in like a wee girl. (Wee, my arse.)

Yours in all sincerity,
Moira.

Wednesday
Brendan:

Your daughter Hazel is indeed in a serious emotional mess: the alarm bells started ringing when I found a bill for £340-worth of '*soins intensifs*' in her coat pocket, which can only mean trouble. I phoned Linda at the Butter Mountain immediately and told her to avoid anything that smacked of sexual intercourse if she could.

'Keep your boyfriend's appetites at bay,' I recommended. 'It's the recipe for marriage.' The man in question seems decent enough, though as an under-manager at British Telecom's Swakely Gap office he hoes a tedious row in life.

'Don't worry,' she told me, 'I'm a born-again Christian now and I've imposed a sex embargo.'

Duncan apparently accepted it with alacrity, so obviously they're on a good wavelength.

'Why get yourself born again when you're so bitter about the first time around?' I queried, but she said a man called Mr Foley wanted her on the other line and he took precedence.

By coincidence, I bumped into Duncan shortly afterwards. He was in the Day Room, trying to fraternise with his brother, but Keith was ignoring him as usual, and doing *The Times* crossword. Duncan told me he's been mooning about in bookshops a lot lately, now that Linda's got religion, and BT has put him on compulsory flexi-time.

'More fool Linda, and more fool BT,' I told him supportively. Apropos the book world, of which I know a thing or two, I was about to share with him some of the fruits of my Strathclyde Municipal Library, Inverness Mobile Book Centre, and Gridiron City Library experience when Keith came and shoved the crossword under my nose, pointing to a clue underlined in red. *A toad-in-the-hole of the Vanities, sixteen letters.*

'Codswallop,' I told him.

And I meant it. Crosswords are a tragic waste of time for someone of his abilities. The thing about Keith is that he really needs to be stimulated on the highest philosophical level, or he fritters away his time on silly brain-teasers. Which is why his whole life has become a displacement activity. Others of us set ourselves complex questions in Manxheath. Call me a conspiracy theorist, but I reckon we ended up here for asking them out loud in the first place. Society has a history of punishing the bearers of bad news. The ones who apply the tin-opener to the can of worms. I tried to transmit this idea to Duncan but it was like talking to the wall. He'd become obsessed with the sandwich machine being on the blink 'for the umpteenth time'.

'OK, if you'd prefer a conversation on a more practical level,' I told him, 'you can give us a hand getting in a few baby supplies.'

He finally agreed to buy a second-hand pram for Signora Pimento 'as a present from the Sugden family'. It was the idea of being part of the family that persuaded him; he's obviously quite hung up on Linda, sex embargo or no. I even told him he could have the pram back when Isabella had finished with it, as he and Linda might find a use for it once they were married.

'She's pushing forty,' I reminded him, 'and her biological alarm clock has been ringing loud and clear for some time. I could do with some more grandchildren, since it transpires that Billy's not exactly normal.'

'I'll take that as a sign of approval, if I may, Mrs Sugden,' he said.

It was a rash assumption to make, but I didn't say so, as there were other things on the shopping list – namely nappies, baby clothes, Q-tips, etc.

'Hang on,' said Duncan as I checked off the list of essentials from Dr Rosemary Pithkin's Baby Bible. I could tell that all this was beginning to try his patience. 'I thought this was supposed to be a phantom pregnancy,' he said.

And do you know what I replied, quick as a flash?

'Well, there's just the Ghost of a chance it isn't!'

When he'd gone I wrote a letter to Linda outlining

my grand plan and asking for a decent book on aquatic horticulture.

I added a PS: 'Probably better the man from Swakely Gap than no man at all.' I underlined the 'probably'. But he must be doing her some good; she's stopped wearing clothes from Oxfam, and a weird light has begun to shine in her eyes.

Yours sincerely,
Moira

TEN

O Ishmael, Ishmael. Lend me your stethoscope that I may listen to your heart.

We were in his office. I was sitting in a chair because I couldn't stand upright. A nurse was there.

He said, 'May I *ask* you, Hazel – have you been drinking? I'm told they found you wandering the grounds in quite a *state*. It's really not *advisable* to mix alcohol with the sort of drugs you've been taking.'

'Vitamins, you told me.'

'*Enhanced* vitamins. And something to calm you down. You've been through a lot.'

I looked at the calendar on the wall behind Dr Stern's head. It was Modern Art. By this I mean it was an abstract – a mess of blobby greys and browns, reminiscent of a baby's dirty nappy. I've never taken to abstracts, and I realised that I cared for them even less now. Like a lot of people, I prefer to know where I am with a painting. I wondered what Ishmael saw in it – and at the same time, I suppose, I wondered whether I really knew him as intimately as I'd thought. After all, if he liked abstracts – understood them, perhaps, even – he spoke a sort of language I didn't. While I was looking at the painting on the calendar, the greys and the browns began to fuse together. I thought I could see a face in it – a face that I realised, without being shocked, must belong to my father. He was smiling in a watery way, and his lips were moving as though he were trying to tell me something. But I couldn't make out the words.

Strange things were happening in my head. I realised with a thud that I couldn't even remember how I'd got there. How old I was. My full name. Where I'd left Billy. To be honest, the whole thing felt like skyscrapers exploding on film, with all the shattered breezeblock and glass falling in slow motion, and all the horror happening in utter silence, and all the mess being my fault. And the world was laughing at my inability to clear up the debris with the doll's dustpan and brush I carried in my hand.

When Billy was born, I blacked out twice with the pain. People die that way, don't they, parting with babies. It was something I remembered then, when Ishmael sat across from me at his desk and stroked the paperweight and told me Billy wasn't coming back. He'd be staying at Oakshott Road with his father. It was for the best. I wasn't to worry. And above all, I wasn't to feel in any way *guilty* or a *failure*.

'Your husband will be taking care of Billy until you're feeling better,' Ishmael said. 'I believe he's *hired* someone from an *agency*. It's really the best course of action. The Institute isn't the best environment for a two year old in the *long* term.'

My father's watery face disappeared from the calendar and I forced myself to look at Ishmael. He was writing something with a bulbous fountain-pen, his face set. The nurse was taking my blood pressure, feeling my pulse, banging my knee with a little rubber hammer.

'Stay still now, Mrs Stevenson,' she said. Her accent was Welsh. 'I need to see what I'm doing, love.'

'Don't call me love.'

'Oh sorry, love.'

So. Billy was gone. Dr Stern was explaining the rest gently, his round eyes blank as tiddlywinks. I looked at the forms he put in front of me, but it didn't cross my mind to read them. I was still struggling with my middle name. Surely I had a middle name? There was a jar of coloured biros next to the anemone paperweight, and I picked out a green one to sign on the dotted line. I remembered reading somewhere that official documents must be in blue or black ink, or they are null and void.

'Do you mind green?' I asked him, giving him a chance to realise his mistake, my small betrayal. But he didn't even notice.

'Any colour you like, Hazel,' he said in that voice of bedside comfort which only last night, beneath my sheets, had Song-of-Solomoned my breasts, my thighs, my belly a field of wheat set about with lilies. A voice that had sighed and groaned in greed and gratitude as he stormed the ramparts and collapsed the sky. My husband, by contrast, was more controlled – more efficient, I suppose. He never made any noise, except for his funny tune, and sometimes afterwards, when he'd ask if I wanted a Handy Andy.

He'd rather I had volunteered for treatment myself, Dr Stern was saying, but in the end a Compulsory Section would make me feel more secure.

'For you *own good*, Hazel.'

He had avoided meeting my eyes, but now he looked straight into them with a look that made me gasp. It was just the look he had – intense, dark and powerful – when we were making love. It seemed to reach directly from his soul to mine. I would do anything he wanted; of course I would. I finally dragged my eyes from his down to the piece of paper in front of me.

'Does it mean we can't go to bed together any more?' I asked him as I signed.

I tried to ask in a matter-of-fact way, but it came out messily garotted with emotion. When I looked up again I caught him with raised eyebrows, exchanging glances with the nurse. She sniggered unprofessionally, loading a hypodermic from a small blue bottle. When it was full she sent a little squirt of liquid into the air which descended in a mist of droplets.

'I'm afraid so, Mrs Stevenson,' he said.

I was shocked to see a smile tweaking at his mouth. The nurse giggled again, as though there were some kind of joke. She was slim and dark, with cushiony-looking tits. Her name-tag, strategically placed on the nipple area of her right breast, revealed an appropriate Christian name: Hope. Hope Westcott. The elastic belt of her uniform accentuated her trim little nurse's waist. It would have been ridiculous to kid oneself that Ishmael hadn't noticed this.

He said, 'But we'll have you back to your normal self in no time. I'll send someone to fetch your things from your hotel.'

'Just a little prick, love,' said Hope, and stuck a needle in my vein. She was much younger than I was, perhaps twenty-four or twenty-five.

Later she showed me my bedroom, a small cubicle with two narrow beds, a washbasin and a mirror. The toilet (in white – a hygienic design with a button flush) was down the corridor. A woman was crying in the room next to mine.

'That's Monica Fletcher,' said the nurse. 'She's probably been watching the news. Here's your pillow-slip, love. You'll be sharing with another girl. Her name's Peggy but your mother calls her the Ossature. From the Latin *os*, meaning bone, apparently. She's ever so quiet, but she's a bit of a vomiter so give the basin a good wipe every time.'

In the distance, the sound of an ambulance.

The nurse asked me if I needed anything so I said no, just leave Dr Stern alone, OK? She got my drift. When she'd gone I sat on the bed. The window overlooked the garden, and I stared out. Perhaps I should have been surprised by what I saw, but I wasn't. Nothing could surprise me much, now. Not with my father's face appearing in a calendar, and Billy gone to live with Greg, and Dr Stern finished with me and shagging some Welshwoman. You see the world one way, don't you, all your life, and then when something comes along to turn the whole thing upside-down your vision goes wonky and you start to see things, and recognise them for what they are. Or at least I did.

The thing I saw was Ma's greenhouse.

Its sharp outline was unmistakable. A huge cathedral-like dome, its glass like brittle transparent hide over a carcass of iron, shooting thin spears of light into the morning mist. From nowhere, the thought came to me that this was surely the pride of Gridiron. Through the glass panes I could see bright colours. Flowers. Trees. Things moving. This apparition, this building, this construction, so starkly before me now yet so well camouflaged before, defied logic. Its presence told lies, made wild promises, beckoned and jeered and sang.

Suddenly I felt powerful and fearless and born again. And I also realised that if I wanted to I could probably fly.

I stood up, spread the enormous coarse-feathered wings that had sprouted from my shoulders, and fell hard into a profound blackness.

When I woke up, my sister was sitting on the bed waving a huge Venn diagram at me. I felt very sick.

'I've put two and two together,' Linda said, glowing

with pride at her own intelligence. She'd always been that way about her brain, like it was some prize pumpkin she'd grown.

'So you'd better tell me everything, and no pissing about.'

So I did. The invisibility, the GR218 experiment that went wrong, my hunch that Ruby was pregnant, the decision to expose Gregory. The affair with Dr Stern. (She raised her eyebrows when I told her about the sort of sex I reckoned I'd had.) His betrayal. The vision of the greenhouse. Every now and then she groaned or gasped or muttered 'Idiot'.

When I got to the bit about what I was doing as an inmate in Manxheath she stiffened.

'Did you sign anything?'

'Yes, but it was in green, so it was null and void,' I said, but I didn't feel too sure of myself.

'Jesus, Hazel, how did you get to be such a moron?' she hurled at me as she scrabbled in her bag for cigarettes.

Her eyes were doing that strange thing they do when she's in a rage; going a dark colour and sinking dangerously deep into her head.

'Why didn't you tell me straight away about all this?'

'Well, I thought you might over-react.'

'OVER-REACT?' she shrieked, dropping her carton of Rothmans and grabbing me by the shoulders and shaking me with vicious gusto.

When she let me go, she retrieved her fags from under the bed, lit one and inhaled deeply.

'No smoking allowed in the bedrooms,' I said, pointing to the sign.

'Get fucked,' she said.

I said, 'You see, I thought Dr Stern was on my side. It seemed like such a nifty plan.'

'Yes, well, one person's nifty plan is another's catastrophic suicide attempt,' she muttered.

She showed me her diagram, which didn't tell me anything I didn't know.

'I see you have the same suspicion that Ruby's pregnant,' I said.

'Suspicion? It's a fact. I saw her in Bulger's.'

I felt the blood drain from my face, and the watery taste that is a prelude to vomiting rise in my mouth.

'How can you be sure she was pregnant?' I noticed I was shaking. 'She's pretty fat. It would be impossible to tell.' This had been my one hope.

'She was in the nude,' said Linda.

'What, walking round Bulger's?'

I could picture the scene perfectly. Ruby waltzing brazenly through soft furnishings waving her cheque book, tits all over the place and the fruits of my husband's adultery bulging from her belly.

'No, in a changing room cubicle, idiot. Buying maternity undergarments and looking very pleased with herself.'

I went to the basin and threw up what looked like coffee and biscuits. Then *chili con carne*, then cup-a-soup, then pasta followed by dry retching. At least my room-mate wouldn't mind. Linda turned her head away and held her nose.

'Jesus, Hazel,' she groaned nasally.

'Where does Carmichael fit in?' I asked when I'd cleaned myself up with an Institute flannel.

'He doesn't – yet. But as soon as he hears about this he'll be playing a key role, just you wait. It's your only hope of nailing these bastards. Leave it to me. Ma's made an interesting suggestion which I may follow through.' She took another deep drag.

I was flabbergasted.

'Ma? What are you talking about? She's a loony! Keep her out of this! Keep her out of my marriage!'

'Hazel, get a life. You haven't got a marriage. Anyway, I'm not sure how you'd fare against Ma in a sanity contest. Just keep your mouth shut, and refuse all medication. I'll work on getting you out of here but for the time being I think you should just sit it out. You're a liability in the real world in the state you're in. Stay in your room. Read magazines. Do whatever you housewives do.'

'But I'm not a housewife any more!' I expostulated, and threw myself at the basin once more.

I'd forgotten yesterday's muesli.

'I'm nothing!' I choked through it.

'Well, for Christ's sake *become* something then!' Linda spat, buttoning up an absurd bottle-green raincoat with flaps everywhere.

And she was gone, slamming the door and leaving her fag burning in the tooth-mug.

She's always been jealous of me.

*   *   *

True facts are hard to find, but there is one that is acknowledged by all: thirty-five is a desperate age for a childless woman, whether she realises it or not. It is half of threescore and ten, and heralds a time of unique crisis; the onset of middle age. See Linda as a victim of this age of desperation. See her preparing to cross the pain barrier into the second half of her life, and leaving Base Camp way behind. See her in Bollingate View Terrace, applying an unprecedented amount of make-up with a shaking hand. And see her now, four hours later, arriving at a London platform and checking her *A to Z*. See her at Channel Praise headquarters, flashing her Ministry pass at the bored security men. And see her pluck up courage and stomp purposefully towards a door marked 'Holy Hour Production Offices'.

Inside, the hum of computers and the murmur of competent telephone transactions. It could be a bank, if it weren't for all the stopwatches. Nobody seems to be over twenty-five. The people are blandly attractive, in the way that is required in television, on-screen and off. They all wear name-badges and sweatshirts with the *Holy Hour* logo – a huge mackerel – emblazoned across the chest.

'Do you have an appointment with the Reverend, Miss Sugden?' enquires an office minion. He is young, with the friendly, stupid face of a koala.

'Just tell him "eggs",' instructs Linda. 'He'll know who I am. I have some important information to pass on to him about Dr Gregory Stevenson, of the Genetic Choice project.'

' "Eggs". Right, I'll tell him "eggs".'

A minute later, Linda is ushered through a door marked 'Dressing-room', and stands face to face with her saviour. At first Linda thinks he is sitting down on an invisible stool, but he isn't. She feels giddy. She has dreamed of this moment. Fantasised about it, even, if the truth be known. The door closes softly behind her.

'Eggs,' says Linda, hopefully, clutching her Leningrad hat.

'Eggs,' smiles the diminutive Reverend.

'I threw them at you in Gridiron City a couple of months ago.'

'I remember it well. Quite a catharsis.'

'I've come to, to – '

'My dear young woman,' he says, reaching out a strong, thick hand, whose fingers are so short they seem amputated at the second joint. 'Welcome.'

'Thank you, Reverend,' says Linda, struggling with

a suddenly pounding heart. So much to say, so few words to reach for. 'Thank you for bringing me to Christ.'

'My dear child. Welcome to a new world of love.'

Love. That great trigger-word that betrays us all. Holy love, earthly love, love-is-love-is-love. They can smile now, and their eyes can meet. Nothing is more natural, at that moment, than to join in a Christian embrace. And after that to kiss one another on the cheek. And on the other cheek.

And then on the lips. Linda is shocked by the size and thickness of the preacher's tongue, and the minty taste of his mouth.

'I came to tell you something,' she gasps, finally breaking the vacuum clasp of their lips.

'Ah,' smiles the Reverend, cupping her padded breast and squeezing it gently.

'Something important,' she croaks, as she feels her nether regions falter.

'My dear child,' he murmurs, slithering his other hand beneath her vest and bra and pressing a nipple.

What could be more natural then, than to acknowledge the urgent requirements of the bodies God gave them and rejoice in the fire that springeth in their loins? What more in keeping with His holy will than to cast off one's Marks & Spencer blouse and matching skirt? And to raise one's cassock – beneath which frock the Reverend reveals the most hirsutely righteous evidence of his spiritual ardour? And then to fornicate against the light-bulbed dressing table, for a total of thirty-seven seconds, until the Reverend's Christian seed is joyously dispensed?

Which act committed, there is a moment of heavenly peace, broken by the phone. The Reverend reaches out for the receiver and snorts awake.

'Hello? Oh, rightey-oh. I'll be out in two minutes. Bye.'

Linda, still crushed against the dressing table by the Reverend's short bulk, opens an eye and remembers her mission.

'Er, I need to talk to you, Reverend.'

'Talk? What about?' He seems genuinely surprised.

'My brother-in-law.'

'Ah, families. A blessing and a curse,' he murmurs, slithering out of her. From the corner of her eye Linda glimpses the Reverend's member again. She hadn't realised that hairy penises existed – but before there is time for her to register it fully, its satisfied owner is hoisting his Y-fronts up across his belly's wad of flesh, and peering into the mirror to smooth down his hair with a dollop of gel.

'Go in peace,' he says.

And leaves for the studio.

Linda watches the show on the small television in the dressing-room. It is strange to think that the man who kneels before her on the screen was ten minutes ago thrusting energetically, if briefly, inside her. He is on form today, and is demonstrating proudly the maquette of the House of God, a nightmarish hybrid of Gothic, Municipal, Romantic and Eco architecture. The donations pour in. Linda watches impatiently. Her life has changed, thanks to this man. Love has ripped through her like thunder and left her bare soul hanging out. She sees a bright future of marches, causes, and militant evangelism. Let the show end, that she may wrap her arms about him and they may hasten to legitimate their union. Linda decides on a simple gold band for a wedding-ring: nothing ostentatious. The ceremony itself will have to be televised, of course, unless they can hold it discreetly, in secret, and announce it later. She will be a strong helpmeet to Vernon, she vows. A worthy First Lady to his spiritual presidency.

On the screen, a tiny pageant of worship enacts itself: a prayer, a phone-in about teen violence, then a jangle of tambourines to usher in the Surbiton Triumphal Choir, dressed as Easter chicks. Finally the credits roll, and Linda waits.

And waits.

At five o'clock the koala-faced minion pops its head round the door.

'All right there? We're just closing up the office now. Poets' day, you know.'

'Poets' day?'

'Piss Off Early, Tomorrow's Saturday. Er, can I offer you a Holy Mackerel sweatshirt as a souvenir of your visit? You look like a size twelve. We've got loads in stock.'

'Thanks,' says Linda in a daze as she follows the minion to the production offices. The place is empty, and Linda's heart tightens with a familiar spasm. She watches him hunt in a cupboard and emerge with a *Holy Hour* Gift Pack.

'So the Reverend isn't coming back?'

'Nope. He took the helicopter up north on a healing mission.'

There is a long pause, which the minion does not seem keen to fill.

'Did he leave a message for me?' Linda manages finally, faking insouciance as she stuffs the Gift Pack in her handbag.

'The Reverend never leaves messages.' The koala face gives nothing away. 'He has a lot of fans, you know.'

ELEVEN

The greenhouse came and went after that, as did my wings, of which there were four – two at shoulder-level, and two that sprouted from my buttocks. They were merely decorative, and didn't work *qua* wings. I reckon I must have got pretty adaptable since the Gregory thing, because I quickly got used to these phenomena, and to the daily injections from Hope, the Welsh nurse, and to the vomitings of Peggy, aka the Ossature, who shared my room. Hope was right about her being quiet; she hardly uttered a word, except to ask how much I reckoned she weighed. One of the things I learned quite quickly at the Institute was to tell people what they wanted to hear.

'About four stone,' I always lied. She was more like five and a half.

The other thing I got used to was the strange disjunction between my skin and the person within. You get tangerines that are like that, their loose peel attached to the segmented ball of fruit only by the most tenuous strands of pith.

I wasn't unhappy at Manxheath. And despite Linda's dark mutterings, I agreed with the psychiatrists that a secure environment was the best place for me while I was adjusting to the new drugs. I saw several doctors, chiefly a thin, insinuating female called Dr McAuley who always wore her hair in a bun, coiled on top of her scalp like a transplanted intestine. Ma maintained it was a wig, made from filaments of nylon. I didn't see Dr Stern, except in the distance sometimes, or when I looked out of my bedroom window and saw him below on the forecourt, greeting a visitor. He was 'too busy' for any more one-to-one consultations. The drug combination I was on seemed to filter away most kinds of negative feelings, so I wasn't depressed about this: just mildly regretful.

I lived in a new world now; a world of metallic coffee machines, foam-filled sofas, acrylic ashtrays, tables covered in different varieties of formica – objects with outlines and textures and a sense of purpose about them. You know where you are with a toilet-roll holder or a radiator – and I'm ashamed to admit that, until I became a client at Manxheath, this fact had never struck me with adequate force. In the meantime the invisibles and intangibles of life – fact, ideas, arguments, so-called 'concepts' – slithered off beyond my grasp. Feelings, too. They just didn't seem to be my bag any more.

In art therapy, I discovered three-dimensional work. Macramé is a sort of cliché until you try it. But, with the help of a book called *Get Knotted,* I found that the intricate twining of waxed pig-string had a beauty to it and – dare I say it – a 'meaning' that I found lacking elsewhere. I made two hanging flower-pot containers, and a small hammock for Billy. The sessions were supervised by a theatrical woman called Diane. She was very permissive, and let us get on with whatever we wanted. This meant she turned a blind eye to Ma's clay things, while she got on with her own projects, which involved making avant-garde earrings out of found objects such as milk-bottle tops and balls of old chewing gum. She said she had been a student at the famous Morgana

Hathaway Art Foundation, which I'd never heard of, where she had specialised in non-biodegradables and something she called text. She was a big wheel, I later found out, on the Gridiron craft caucus. She came on Mondays, Tuesdays, and Thursdays. We were her charity cases.

I think I could have gone on this way indefinitely, if it weren't for the fact that the drugs weren't quite 'cutting the mustard'. Dr Hollingbroke's words, not mine. He was in charge of the fine-tuning of our delicate internal ecospheres. He was a tall, balding man with a woman's bottom; you might have mistaken him for another loony, if it weren't for his name-tag and electronic bleep. He would have discussions with nurses in which he'd say things like:

'Has the Thorazine been pulling its weight in that female mania case?'

'Did we overpower that Lithium dose yesterday?'

'*Vis-à-vis* our new manic, I'm going to tweak that Valium combo with some Stymozopane.'

My drugs weren't cutting the mustard because some things still broke through to me. Things which, psychiatrically and pharmacologically speaking, should have shut up and stayed put. (The doctor's words again.) Things like Billy. I missed him with the numb aching of an amputee. And I realised with a certain weariness that I'd give up everything – the greenhouse, my wings, the memory of Ishmael – to have him back. Dr Hollingbroke told me he had some more chemical tweaks in mind to deal with this seepage problem.

Some days I'd wander about in the greenhouse. Looking back, I reckon I must have been trying, in a vague way, to find some sort of clue as to what was happening to me. It was an over-heated, steamy place with any number of doors, and odd ante-chambers which were either brimful with the most undisciplined kinds of vegetation, chiefly cheese-plants, or virtually empty. I don't know much about architecture, but even I could tell that none of it could possibly have had planning permission. Some bits didn't even have air vents or drainage facilities. One of the largest rooms I came across contained only a broken bench and a plastic watering-can. It seemed like a shocking waste of space, but when I mentioned it to Ma she got quite irate.

'What d'you mean? I've personally seen to it that every square centimetre in that greenhouse is used to the fullest effect!'

I was struck, as I sometimes am, by the Scottishness of her accent when she said those words. 'Foolest effayct', it sounded like. I let it drop. We were obviously talking at complete cross-purposes. In any case, I never saw the remotest sign of her or her disciples in there, and I began to suspect that all the self-aggrandising talk of horticultural industry was mere bullshit.

One day, on impulse, I knocked on Dr Stern's door. Actually it wasn't quite impulse. I was bearing a gigantic bunch of greenhouse flora – a riot of pink thrills and spills which Ma would have called 'whore's drawers' if she'd seen them. There was no reply from Ishmael, so I walked in. It was then that I realised that time must have passed: the Modern Art calender had turned a page. The sludge greys and browns of April, the cruellest month, had been replaced by the bright orange, yellow and lime-green smudges of May, the merriest. It was quite a shock. I left the flowers in a urine flask on Ishmael's desk. Borrowing his bulbous fountain pen and an Assessment Form, I wrote a note for him: 'I will always love you. Hazel.'

It didn't look quite right. He'd betrayed me, after all. So I crossed out the word 'love', and replaced it with 'be available for you sexually'.

I stole the anemone paperweight. If anyone had a right to it, I did.

It was arranged on the client-provider allocation sheet that I should have daily sessions with Dr McAuley, she of the intestinal chignon. There was something in her personality that I disliked, so when Linda next came to visit and asked if I needed anything, I requested a pair of her 'acoustic minimisers'. With their help, Dr McAuley's invasive questions were reduced to a muffled drone. The days would begin with half an hour in her presence. I kept my eyes closed and used the time to empty my mind, much as I used to in the supermarket, when bunches of bananas and tins of gourmet sauce would float by, beckoning the trolley that glided me down the aisles. The trick was to retain that emptiness, that almost transcendental state, at the checkout, while I was filling the bags, and hopefully for the rest of the day. It was in one of these states of higher meditation that, despite my preoccupation with objects, I began to develop two rather abstract ideas.

When I first started seeing Dr Stern, I used to wonder whether I was mad, or whether the world around me was. But suddenly it came to me that it doesn't have to be a question of either/or. It can be both. Inner and outer insanity don't rule each other out. Hence:

Idea 1. This idea I called 'the personal versus global insanity issue'.

Meanwhile, things had been taken from me one by one – my husband, my home, my son, my lover, my hotel room. Some of these things I wanted back. So:

Idea 2. This idea I called 'my rights'.

Because of the slippery nature of 'concepts' in my life at this stage, I decided to associate these thoughts with an object, as a sort of mnemonic device. The object I chose was the metal-framed chair I was sitting on. It had a red plastic foam cushion.

That way it would all stay in my head.

At the end of one session, Dr McAuley seemed to have something urgent to convey to me.

'I'm not hearing what you say, Doctor; you'll have to write it down,' I told her.

She pulled an exasperated face and mouthed at me again, 'Come to Group this afternoon.'

But I made her write it down anyway. Give these psychiatrists a centimetre and they'll take a hectare. Something Ma told me, and she's right. She wrote it on her pad in black biro. She had that bulbous, low-slung type of handwriting that they teach in secretarial colleges. I should know. Mine is like that, too.

'OK,' I said. 'I'll come.'

The socially vulnerable knitting circle, Ma called it. I reckoned that if I took my chair with me, I'd cope.

Later, at lunch, a strange thing happened: Keith flung his cauliflower cheese across the room and then stood on the table, windmilling his arms. Then he ran out, sobbing, followed by Hope.

'Hope rushes in where angels fear to tread,' Ma usually said when she saw Hope rushing anywhere. Or sometimes she'd say, 'You can put hope in one hand and spit into the other.' I don't quite know why. But she wasn't there to say either of these things, or to translate what Keith had said, so no one knew what it was about. She turned up later, with earth under her fingernails. When I told her about the cauliflower cheese incident, she said it sounded like Keith had had a premonition.

'A bad one,' she said, her already pasty face growing pale. 'Every once in a while, someone here makes an important statement. Keith's problem,' she concluded, 'is epistemological.'

'Are you sure, Moira?' bleated Monica Fletcher from somewhere near our ankles. 'I've always thought the food here was rather good.'

The socially vulnerable knitting circle met in a windowless room which might once have been a padded cell. I was awarded a place at the very end, nearest the door. I'd brought my red-cushioned chair. It had become a sort of mascot. Keith was there, looking composed, like nothing had happened. If I'd said to him 'Cauliflower cheese' he'd probably have gestured: 'Cauliflower cheese to you, too!'

Dr McAuley caught me chatting to Isabella about epidurals and remarked that my hearing had improved. Indeed it had; I'd removed the earplugs.

'Now,' she began the session. 'Does anyone here have anything they feel they'd like to share?'

So my mother let rip about how I'd wrecked her Valium display in the greenhouse. She'd been planting pills, apparently, in a 'miscellaneous medications' bed. Loony tunes.

'What greenhouse?' asked Max.

'An interesting figment,' said Dr McAuley, 'of Moira's fertile imagination.'

'Mrs Sugden to you,' snapped my Ma. 'And it's no figment. Hazel's been there. She'll testify to it. She stole my whore's drawers.'

A McAuley eyebrow lifted in sudden interest. She paid attention to anything knicker-related, being a Freudian.

'*Valium domesticum* is a bugger to germinate, you know,' Ma added resentfully, her glasses flashing at me. 'It was in its hour of glory.'

'I gave them to Dr Stern,' I said.

'In the hope of a quick shag?' asked Max menacingly.

Clearly Ishmael and I hadn't managed to hide our affair all that well.

'But it's romantic,' Monica sobbed. 'Romantic, romantic, romantic.'

'Don't talk to me about romance,' muttered a greasy-haired man called David, whose wrists were in bandages.

'Sweetie been screwing you for money again?' asked my mother, spotting it too. 'Och, she's a shameless hyena.'

'It's worse this time, eh, Dave,' barked Max. 'Dr Stern's signed the incompetence-due-to-insanity papers. Now she can annul the marriage. She's marrying that bastard accountant next week.'

There was silence. David hung his head; the Ossature shivered and pulled her crocheted blanket around her flesh-free shoulders.

'Thank you for sharing that with us,' said Dr McAuley. 'Now, everyone, I'd just like to tell you that Moira's daughter Hazel will be joining us for group sessions from now on, which I'm sure she'll find empowering-and-enabling.' She said this as though it were all one word, like 'cheese-and-onion' in the case of crisps.

'Hazel's been very unforthcoming on a one-to-one basis,' she told the loonies. 'But I think she'll really blossom here. Welcome to Manxheath, Hazel.'

'Welcome to my world,' added Max, and gobbed on the floor. Max's world can't have been much different from yours and mine, because everyone pretended not to notice.

I smiled around the semi-circle, like a contestant at a beauty pageant, and Dr McAuley made a note on her clip-board.

And so I became a member of the Group. Other perks followed: I was allowed a subscription to *Woman's Realm* and *New Woman*, and it was agreed that Billy would come to visit once a week, and spend the day, until such time as I was deemed well.

I'd taken against the wallpaper in the Day Room: I found its Regency design of stylised green flowers in vertical lines had an ironic, mocking tone to it, so I spent most of my time in my room waiting for the Great Pretender Ishmael to come and whisk me off to dinner in Mutton Acre. I kept myself to myself. Being invisible helped.

*   *   *

'I'd like to propose a toast,' announces the man on the podium. He is small and tanned and bald. He smiles to reveal a fortune in artful bridgework. 'To the success of our new partnership.'

His oily herring's eyes skim the throng of people before him, a sea of smart suits and little cocktail outfits. The Executive Club Lounge of the Gridiron City Hopeworth is the venue for the gathering of this elite section of the scientific and business worlds. Some have limousined all the way from London for the occasion. Cummerbunds encircle management paunches, earrings jangle beneath big hair-dos. There is a smell of marinated olives, taramasalata, and money.

'Raise your glasses, please,' says Mr Root Hooper, trillionaire, 'to the new Hooper Fertility Foundation. Long may it thrive.'

'To the Hooper Fertility Foundation,' murmurs the throng before they sip.

'Fuck you,' mutters Linda under her breath, wincing on a lemon slice. Her blonde wig is itching her scalp, and her huge rose-tinted spectacles keep sliding down the bridge of her nose.

'Fuck Hooper, fuck Gregory, fuck the Reverend fucking Carmichael, fuck everyone,' she adds, expanding on her theme. Linda Sugden is on what Trish would call 'the psychological rampage'.

'Would you care for an *amuse-gueule*?' asks an astonishingly handsome waiter, thrusting a silver platter of pineapple and cheese chunks on sticks, biscuits spread with olive paste, and pistachio nuts under her nose.

'And fuck you too,' says Linda, looking him full in the face. 'I only eat Twiglets.'

Root Hooper tilts his flute of champagne towards that of Dr Greg Stevenson, standing next to him on the dais. Their glasses kiss with a tiny ping and they drink. As small streams of bubbles forge effervescent pathways to gullets lined with hors-d'oeuvres, there is a smile on the face of each man. It is an important moment. Hooper plc and Fertility Management Inc. are going to bed together, as the jargon has it. And the white froth of champagne that shoots from the jeroboam of Bollinger (a stream of liquid whose Freudian significance the dark-haired man in the beige Armani suit in the corner of the room notes with a quite professional smirk) is the climax of their courtship. The papers have been signed, the deal struck.

Linda edges herself round to the table next to where Dr Ruby Gonzalez is sitting and pretends to be reading the Hopeworth's glossy brochure. She notes, in passing, the shocking prices at the *Soins Intensifs* Beauty Clinic, e.g., £30 for a bikini wax. She snorts, and focuses her rose-coloured lenses on Ruby Gonzalez, who is looking moronically self-satisfied in the way that only pregnant women can, whilst downing orange juice and blue cheese profiteroles. Linda notes with distaste that she's sitting with her legs spread quite wide apart, Sumo wrestler-style, her belly spilling over the gulf.

As Gregory Stevenson and Root Hooper approach, Ruby's generous lips broaden into a big smile. Linda shifts in her chair and narrows her eyes to observe. Root Hooper is lunging forward to kiss Dr Gonzalez's hand, but suddenly her smile has twisted into pain and she's pulling backwards into her seat as though to shrivel away from him, still holding a profiterole aloft in one hand. Something is wrong with Ruby. She appears to be arc-welded to her chair, and there's something panicky squirming in her eyes.

'I can't get up,' she says tremulously, her face red. 'Greg!' she calls plaintively. 'Help! Oh, do excuse me, Mr Hooper, I really shouldn't have come. I just wanted to – '

She shifts in the chair in an attempt to cross her legs; it's then that Linda notices the dark patch spreading across Ruby Gonzalez's silk dress. A pungent smell begins to spread. The woman is awash with liquid.

'I wanted to celebrate with you,' Ruby soldiers on bravely. There is a small, uncomfortable silence, and Linda slaps a hand over her mouth to prevent laughter, screaming or vomiting. She watches Ruby's thighs and sees the plastic chair beneath her fill with liquid which overflows and splashes on the parquet floor. Ruby's eyes, too, are fixed on the broad puddle that is spreading towards Root Hooper's polished leather shoes. Gregory, Spam-faced, is looking annoyed.

'I thought you'd like to meet our new partner,' he tells Ruby sternly – in much the same tone that he would adopt with Hazel when, as usual, she had put too much salt in the cooking.

'Yes, darling, of course I'm delighted to meet Mr Hooper.'

Linda gags. Hazel has told her about the gruesome business of childbirth. The prying fingers of midwives, the horror of the mucus plug, the excruciating agony of pushing something the size of a Yorkshire terrier through an unyielding sleeve of flesh, the moment you clap eyes on the juddering, livid afterbirth – the whole shebang.

'This is very embarrassing,' says Ruby Gonzalez at last, 'but my waters have broken.'

'Your what?' asks Root Hooper, genuinely puzzled. 'Beg pardon, Dr Gonzalez?'

'Oh Ruby,' intervenes Greg with a sigh of irritation. 'I told you this was a bad idea, coming along at a time like this.'

'My shoes!' cries Hooper, suddenly spotting the puddle. 'Hey, get a cleaner here pronto, someone. There's some kind of mess on the floor.'

Ruby begins to give strange strangulated gulps.

'And an ambulance,' she gurgles.

By now she is surrounded by people who have all come to look at the spectacle she's made of her chair, the floor, the dress.

'Good God,' gasps a Hooper executive, whipping out a small packet of Kleenex from his breast pocket and waving a lone tissue in Ruby's direction. 'We seem to be flooded.'

'I'll get an ambulance,' Linda calls into the back of the throng as she grabs her handbag and prepares to hurtle off.

'Don't worry – I've already called one,' says a voice.

Linda looks up and her eyes meet the yellow silk shirt, peacock tie and beige Armani suit of her mother's psychiatrist. Linda quickly adjusts her wig and whisks her scarf across her mouth.

'It'll be here in two minutes,' says Dr Stern. And he smiles at Linda. Beneath the dark moustache, a row of white and perfect teeth.

TWELVE

I've always been fond of jigsaws – perhaps because, as a child, I was better at them than Linda, who was supposed to be the clever one. Linda never had the patience. She was more of a diagram person. She liked to make associations swiftly and in broad, radical terms. But my story was one that had to be pieced together, doggedly, afterwards. This was a jigsaw story. Linda helped me with it, of course, by offering her own pompous self-glamorising recollections. But there were plenty of other pieces: my own experience, Ruby's article in the *Lancet*, the Inquiry report, Ma's loony letters, the scientific evidence that emerged at the trial.

Though I'm the first to admit that, while the shit was actually hitting the fan, nothing made sense. I couldn't see for whirling excrement.

What happened next took place in the greenhouse. The event itself was real enough, but the location –

To this day I don't know.

It seemed real enough at the time. To me, to Ma, to Isabella, and to Keith, at least. In that respect we were at odds with the rest of the world, which, with hindsight, went along with the theory formulated by the Inquiry. Its report states:

*The so-called greenhouse was a potent hallucina-
tive figment, created by Mrs Moira Sugden for her
own escapist and symbolic purposes but later shared
by weaker personalities, including her daughter, the
other key witness. Its function as an emotional refuge made it especially attractive to those clients of
Manxheath whose Lithium dose had been gradually
increased over the preceding two months, under the
auspices of Dr Donald Hollingbroke. Parallels can
be drawn between this phenomenon and the mass
hysteria evidenced when religious miracles, such as
the alleged apparition of the Angel Gabriel over
Birmingham last June, are 'perceived' by a gullible
and vocal section of the population.*

The shared hallucination theory about the greenhouse
seemed quite plausible to Linda and the rest of the
world. But then Linda and the rest of the world never
saw it. Ever since, I have borne something of a grudge
against them for that.

Even those of us who experienced it couldn't agree
on what it was like. To me, for instance, it had been
an ill-organised sort of place that was heavily sexual.
Ma reckoned it was functional – municipal, even, and
based on something which Dad, with his double glazing
experience, had in mind for Jaycote's Park. Keith wouldn't
comment. We never got to hear Isabella Pimento's version,
though in her own way she had the last word. Now that
it's all over, and the thing's in smithereens, I doubt all
versions, my own included. After all, thanks to the soft-
bottomed Dr Hollingbroke, I was a cocktail of chemicals,
a pharmaceutical arsenal. Put a lighted match to me and
I might have emitted green smoke. Touch my skin and the
moisture from my pores might have stung or shrivelled
you. Say a kind word and I might have disintegrated.

It began on a Thursday night. The Ossature had finished her evening vomiting session in the toilet down the hall, which seemed to be the most user-friendly, and we'd read our horoscopes. Mine said, 'Take advantage of this peaceful time to get a few household chores out of the way. And romance could flower unexpectedly, so hang on to your hat!'

I saw the word 'flower', in the context of romance, as a reference to Ishmael. It meant he had probably reacted well to my bouquet. The Ossature's said, 'It's time to tighten your belt,' so she was pleased, too. Then we'd said goodnight and gone to bed. As evenings spent on psychotropic drugs go, it seemed quite normal.

But I couldn't sleep. In the end I tossed and turned so much I fell out of bed. So I got up and drew the curtains. The greenhouse was there, as it sometimes was of an evening, but there was a light on inside. This was disturbing. I tried closing my eyes and opening them again, but it was no use. The light was still there.

I fought my way into my yellow flannel Institute dressing gown and staggered downstairs and out into the garden. It was chilly, but as soon as I entered the greenhouse I was struck by a blast of hot steam. The light – and the strange noises I began to hear – seemed to be coming from the centre of the building, and I followed them into a big domed room that housed a miniature jungle.

The noises alarmed me, because I swiftly identified them as emanating from a couple having violent sexual intercourse. The woman was laying it on quite thick, groaning and sighing and at times almost screaming, but the man was ominously silent: there were no grunts of accompaniment, and none of the fumbling, thumping, panting, sucking (or in my husband's case, tunefulness) that you might expect from a normal copulation. The woman didn't appear to be enjoying it much. There was an edge to her voice.

It was a while before I located the action. I saw the red thermos first, on a plant-stand, gushing steam. The whole place was a sauna. Then I heard my mother's voice whisper, 'Come on, Isabella, come on, you can do it!'

So that was it! My mother and Mrs Pimento were two lesbians!

Then I saw Ma. She was dressed in a doctor's white coat and sitting on the floor, putting on green washing-up gloves. Next to her Mrs Pimento was lying prostrate, starkers, with her knees raised and her legs parted. Her pallid, naked rump shifted as she moaned, and the huge moon of her belly shuddered.

Good God. She wasn't having sex at all. She was giving birth.

'Come on, Isabella,' whispered Ma as she dipped her gloved hand in a bowl of what looked like methylated spirit and then slid it between Mrs Pimento's thighs. Her whole arm seemed to disappear inside her friend's cavity. I was shocked. Ma hates physical contact of any kind, as a general rule.

And this!

I have visited an abattoir. I have miscarried. I have seen a huge sewer rat being run over by a moped. And Ma once dragged Linda and me to see a Shakespeare play called *Titus Andronicus*. So I've been round the block a few times, so to speak, when it comes to nauseating spectacles. But this was in the far reaches of the monstrous.

Ma was shrieking, 'You must be a good twenty-five centimetres dilated and I think I can feel its wee head now!'

'Don't you worry, Moira,' croaked Mrs Pimento through the pillow she gripped in her teeth. And the muffled voice added, 'I done this many times before, I can do in my sleep. I nearly ready to push.'

Keith emerged from the shadow of a castor-oil tree and grabbed the thermos. Catching sight of me he gestured to me to help. Quickly we began soaking towels and flannels. I found it hard to watch the birth. I remembered having Billy: bright lights, bossy nurses, the smell of antiseptic. Greg standing next to the bed, watching me critically as I got the breathing wrong. Then the stupefying need to force the baby out. Did you know that it kills millions of brain cells in one fell swoop, and your vagina is never the same again?

'Bear down, Isabella, bear down!' my mother was urging. And she called to me in a hoarse whisper, 'In the nick of time, Hazel!'

Isabella's moans were now clearly moans of agony, and Ma mopped her friend's forehead and her own with a monster sanitary towel.

'Keep your voice down, hen,' she told her. 'The staff'll hear your bawling and then we'll be in a fine mess!'

I wondered what she thought we might be in now. But at least she seemed prepared for the event. Apart from the hot water, towels, gloves and flannels, I could see a small Moses basket and a pack of nappies in a corner beneath a fig tree. I could even glimpse, behind a curtain of hanging geraniums, what looked like a pram.

I didn't really want to watch, but I found my eyes sliding over in the direction of Isabella's parted knees. She seemed to be thriving on her pain – riding on a wave of it. I had shrieked at mine, a craven jelly, a woman of straw who, if Satan had come along, would have signed away anything – her soul, her photo of Dad, her fondue set – to have it stop. Why not? But Isabella didn't see it that way; bizarrely, she was behaving as though childbirth were some kind of natural bodily function.

Just then she gave a different kind of groan, and suddenly, out from between her thighs shot a baby. It was striped with blood, and attached to a bulbous and knotted-looking umbilical cord. Keith, moving snappily, caught the baby in a towel, rugby-style, and passed it straight back to Isabella who folded it into the mountain range of her body while Ma applied two clothes pegs to the cord, and then cut it with a pair of secateurs. For a moment everything was jellied in time, and then:

'A miracle, the Lord be praze!' Isabella shouted, with surprising energy after what she'd just gone through. Then she gave a sort of primal scream – muffled sharply by my mother covering her face with the pillow – and disintegrated into smothered tears. Ma and Keith set to work dabbing at the baby with wet flannels.

My mother stopped to wipe her glasses on her apron, the one I remembered her wearing to roll pastry when I was a child. Then she put them back on and inspected the little thing, which was now bawling croakenly like a distressed sheep. Isabella Pimento heaved her weight on to her elbows and peered at the child through her parted knees.

'The Lord be praze again,' she said. 'A lovely, lovely girl.'

And as if in recognition of her mother's voice, the small creature, wrinkled and shrieking, let forth a long stream of black mucus from her backside.

At that moment, quite honestly, I could have done with my chair.

We were still clearing up the mess an hour later when a phone started to ring. Isabella and the baby were asleep on a bed of moss, exhausted from their ordeal.

'Get that, will you, Hazel,' called Ma, heaving a bucket from the tap. She was a new woman: brisk, matter-of-fact, in control. 'It's that portable phone of yours, in the pram, hen.'

I did what she said.

'Hello,' said Linda's voice. 'Just calling to see if everything's OK. Is that you, Ma?'

'No, this is Hazel,' I said. 'We're in the greenhouse.'

'What greenhouse?' snapped Linda, annoyed. 'Don't tell me you've fallen for Ma's absurd fucking idea about – oh, never mind. Just tell me the news.'

'It's unbelievable,' I said, and told her about the birth. After her more-than-scepticism concerning the greenhouse, I wasn't expecting her to believe that Isabella had just produced a baby, but I was in for a shock: she took the news calmly. It was clearly no surprise to her.

'I thought she'd have had it by now,' she said briskly.

'How come?'

'Because,' she said self-importantly, 'I gave Ma the signal to induce it a few hours ago. Looks like the drugs worked. I looked them up in a medical encyclopedia. Now, the important question. Girl or boy?'

'A girl,' I said.

At this, Linda gave a coyote howl of triumph and then a sort of cackle, which is her laugh. Fancy making such a fuss over an extra female in the population, I thought. She'd always been a feminist, but this was ridiculous. My head was spinning with unanswered questions.

'But how did you know Mrs Pimento was going to – ?' I asked, frantic for an answer, feeling I must be stupid, or lied to, or both.

'Ma told me.'

'And you believed her?'

'Not at first. But then I had a look, and I realised she was probably right. Anyway, the reason I'm calling is to let you all know that Ruby's had a baby girl as well.'

I think I said before that Linda was blunt on the phone.

'They must have delivered more or less simultaneously,' she said. 'I've just rung the hospital.' She sounded inexplicably jubilant. 'Pass me to Ma, will you?'

I flung the phone in Ma's direction and from the corner of my eye saw her catch it adroitly and begin an intense, whispered conversation.

I headed off. I needed that chair.

Memories.

When Hazel was six and Linda ten, they played dares.

'I bet you don't dare stay in the cupboard under the stairs for five whole minutes,' Linda said to Hazel.

I did dare, though. The full five minutes – though I came out crying and told Ma Linda had locked me in. The next time they played dares, it was Hazel who set the challenge.

'I bet you don't dare pee in the road.' But Linda did. She hitched up her skirt on a traffic island, shut her eyes and pissed. I, Hazel, watching from behind a bush, peed too but by accident, in my knickers, out of panic on my sister's behalf. Linda would dare do anything. If I'd asked her to crap on the pavement like a dog she'd have done that, too. It was pride.

Ma knew all about that, and had banked on it when she thought of her plan. That, and Linda's crusading zeal. Ma knew just how to egg her on.

'Dysfunctional behaviour,' Dr McAuley would have called it.

195

'Active Logic,' would have been Linda's definition. Active Logic was one of the buzz phrases of her guru, Klaus G. Armstrong.

* * *

The Sacred Bleeding Heart NHS Trust is a modern building, featuring reconstituted stone, acrylic sculptures, and an internal courtyard with a Japanese garden, complete with geriatric Koi carp and raked gravel. The maternity wing is calm and restful, painted in the muted, milky colours of courgette and pecan. There is a smell of flowers with a hint of rot, and the commercial fragrance of baby lotion. Flowers – yes, there is an abundance of flowers, though mixtures of red and white are banned. This is an old nursing superstition. The combination of the two colours is shocking, they say, like blood on a sheet.

That night, in the maternity wing of the Bleeding Heart, a blonde-haired nurse peers round the door of Ruby Gonzalez's private room to check she's asleep. And there Dr Gonzalez lies, hair Pre-Raphaeliting all over the pillow, a sweet smile on her waxy face, and flowers all around. She could almost be laid out for a funeral. The baby lies in a bundle in the perspex cot next to Dr Gonzalez.

The nurse works quickly. It doesn't take long to switch the two babies. Out of the perspex cot she lifts Ruby's sleeping infant, and removes the nametag from its ankle: Angelica Sofia Gonzalez. Then, from a laundry bag on her medicine trolley, she lifts another small bundle, around whose ankle she fits the nametag. She puts her own bundle in the cot next to Ruby, and places the bundle that was formerly Angelica Sofia Gonzalez in the laundry bag. This she replaces on the trolley, gently. Neither baby stirs. The nurse is just turning to

196

leave with the trolley when there is a yawn from Ruby, who is suddenly sitting up.

'I didn't ring,' she says. 'Who are you?'

'Night Duty Nurse Rogers,' whispers the nurse, adjusting her huge glasses and yanking at bed-linen. 'Just checking on all the first-time mums. Here, drink this.'

She thrusts at Ruby a plastic cup with a pale-green liquid in it, and observes keenly as Ruby swallows.

Ruby says, 'Yuk.'

The nurse says, 'Lime juice. Full of vitamins. Now, is everything all right for you here, Miss Gonzalez? Stitches not too painful?'

'Of course they're too painful. And it's *Dr* Gonzalez. You look familiar. Haven't we met before?'

'Oh, I doubt it, Doctor,' says the nurse. 'We all look the same in uniform. I'm from an agency. Now try to get some rest.'

Suddenly Ruby is feeling strangely groggy, but not unpleasantly so. It's as though someone has chosen to pack the inside of her head with mashed potato. She sighs and peers at the bundle in the cot and smiles.

'She's got a different face every time I look at her,' she says lovingly. 'With or without my contact lenses.'

'That's babies for you,' says my sister Linda.

And she turns out the light, wheels out the trolley with her bag on it, and disappears into the night.

*   *   *

'A baby is a baby is a baby,' Mrs Pimento had remarked cheerily to Ma as her sleeping offspring was smuggled out of reception that night in Linda's arms, to a life of vivisection for all she knew. 'I will have another one in a few months.'

She'd let her daughter go without a second glance. She was used to it, Ma said afterwards, darkly.

But how wrong Isabella was about babies. How wrong we all were. A baby is not a baby is not a baby. I've had four; three little ghosts and Billy. My mother has had three — me, Linda and a boy called Herman Paul, our brother, also a ghost. Cot death, Ma reckoned. Isabella — an untold number. The ghosts of babies past and present linger in the air. Little, elemental lives, foetuses floating in suspension, not of this planet nor of another, some beneath ground, some in limbo, some pickled in a jar in my husband's laboratory, some not quite dead, others not quite alive. There are too many children in the world, proclaims Gregory. Too many small parasitic mouths that cannot be fed and are doomed to scavenge. Our beef mountains are their hunger valleys, our milk lakes their dust-bowls of thirst. Let only the responsible breed. Let they be the inheritors of our fragile earth.

Isabella was perky enough the next day, or so it seemed. There were no outward signs that she might be about to shatter. At breakfast she consumed six cups of tea with two spoonfuls of sugar per cup, and five slices of toast heaped with Bovril. I watched the Ossature count them all in, then heard her count them all out again in the user-friendly toilet. Proxy vomiting was her forte.

Later, in Group, Isabella patted her belly proudly. It was still huge. You wouldn't have guessed.

'I give birth in greenhouse,' she announced with triumph. 'No problem.'

Silence. Ma shot me a look.

'Congratulations,' said a tiny woman called Monica, who was crouching on the floor.

'Boy or girl?' asked the greasy-haired David politely. I wondered if he was sticking to the Institute's Personal Hygiene Contract. Max didn't say anything, which was unusual.

'Little girl,' said Isabella. 'But she gone now. We swap her for Moira daughter Hazel husband mistress baby. Linda look after that one.'

More silence, punctured by a genteel cough from Monica.

'Linda, Moira other daughter,' Isabella explains, ignoring Ma's throat-cutting gestures. 'Work on Butter Mountain.'

'Shall we leave it there, Isabella?' begs Dr McAuley. 'But may I say I'm pleased – I think we're all pleased, and Dr Hollingbroke in particular I know will be pleased – that you've decided to *let go* of your pregnancy. I think, don't you' – she smiles with horrible gentleness – 'that it was becoming a burden to you.'

'Yes,' intervenes Ma with surprising coolness and poise, hitching up a corner of her blouse and polishing her glasses. 'What a relief for all of us. Does that liberate us to turn our attention to other matters?'

'By all means,' replies Dr McAuley, fiddling with her excruciating bun. 'Any suggestions from the Group?'

A pause. Ten seconds, eleven maybe. Dr McAuley never let it go much past twelve.

'Well, perhaps I could suggest a discussion topic then,' she smiled. 'What we might talk around today, I feel, might be responsibility. Taking Responsibility for One's Actions.'

She said this as though it were some new concept she'd developed.

'Does anyone have anything they'd like to share around Responsibility?'

Max heaves a loud, weary sigh.

'OK, confession time,' he announces with a strange smirk.

We all look up in surprise at the notion of Max confessing anything. Max clears his throat, and waits for complete silence to fall before he utters the four words that are to change the course of hospital-management history.

'I am the father.'

Bedlam!

'NO!' screams Ma, and rises from her seat and strides over to Max. She reaches up, snatches at the collar of his safari suit and begins to shake him violently. I have seen this kind of behaviour before, and I watch with something that's not quite nostalgia, but more a prickling feeling of recognition. I know this territory: Ma as severe gale force nine, Ma as hurricane, Ma as typhoon, tornado and tidal wave, Ma as an element in her element.

'No, no, no!' she's screaming.

David and Dr McAuley have hurled themselves in, trying to unclamp the two rocking bodies. But just as suddenly, Ma has pulled back and slumped down into a chair. I've never seen her look lost and hopeless before, and it's quite a revelation.

Max is brushing down his safari suit, stamping his feet like a frisky colt, and laughing uncontrollably.

Isabella has fled.

Dr McAuley reaches for her clip-board and makes a long note in her flattened handwriting. Then looking up, she explains gently, 'More painful personal growth.' And addressing Max, 'And some interesting reaction to it.' Max smirks. 'I think we should all take our hats off to Isabella for relinquishing her fantasy. She may be in for some "post-partum blues", so let's all bear that in mind, shall we?'

It was then that we heard the first huge bang.

We knew what it was – or at least Ma and I did, because in an instant we were both thundering down the corridor towards the garden. No one else followed.

As we discovered later, they never heard a thing, or at least that's what they claimed. Just as we arrived in the Day Room a second huge crack of noise rent the air, and outside, through the french windows, we saw the greenhouse explode.

Looking back later, there was something magnificent about the way the whole thing seemed to shudder before lift-off. The scale of it, too. It was operatic. It called for Wagnerian chords. But at the time it was like a glimpse of hell. Not least when a third blast shuddered across the blue air and a glittering shock of glass fountained up. Ma dropped to the floor and covered her ears. I just stood there. And we watched as a small human shape, like a doll, zoomed skywards. Isabella seemed to stay suspended in the air for a long time before she burst. With a faint pop, she became a red firework that blossomed in all directions.

Ma screamed and screamed and screamed.

THIRTEEN

On the other side of Gridiron, post-partum elation. It's the morning after the perfect birth.

'Another toast,' says Greg to Ruby, reaching for two disposable beakers.

When Root Hooper finally realised that Ruby Gonzalez was in labour, he had persuaded the ambulance to take a case of champagne to accompany the parents-to-be to the Sacred Bleeding Heart NHS Trust. My husband did full justice to the gift. Into the small hours he had drunk the best part of two bottles unaided, before finally crashing out on a plastic bench in the waiting-room. By the time Linda, alias Night Duty Nurse Rogers, passed by the open door with her laden trolley, he was sleeping like a baby.

Now, brain churning and stomach a-fizz, Gregory inhabits the shaky neutral zone between drunkenness and its aftermath.

'To Angelica Sofia Gonzalez, and to the Genetic Choice Programme of The Hooper Fertility Foundation,' he announces, twisting wire and sending a fat cork rocketing to the ceiling with a pop. He pours, and holds aloft two plastic cups of yellowish foam.

'May we bring hope of perfection to an imperfect world.'

There is no pride like the pride of a new father.

Especially when he believes the infant he has sired to be the world's first Perfect Baby. Without realising it, Gregory has begun to hum his sex tune.

Ruby smiles valiantly, refuses champagne, and drinks deep from a huge flask of water by her bedside. She too is feeling groggy and nauseous. As well she might.

'Feeding time in a minute,' she murmurs, joining in Greg's happy gaze at the little creature in the cot. All babies look beautiful to their parents. Even ugly ones.

'She doesn't look quite herself this morning,' Gregory remarks, squinting into the lace-quilted cot.

It's true. She isn't herself at all. She must, they agree, have had a bad night. Ruby's had a bad night, too. She had a weird dream, she's been telling Greg, about red and white carnations growing through her pillow, turning vicious, and choking her.

'Don't worry, darling,' Gregory soothes. 'You're going to be the perfect mother.' Ruby sighs, reaches for a fancy chocolate, unwraps it, and rolls it in her mouth, feeling the bitter darkness of it dissolve on her taste buds. Soft classical music is playing from the sound system, and Angelica is sleeping at last. Her parents' eyes, shiny with love and weariness, are glued to the sight of her compact body which snuffles, grunts, farts, and winces with weird grimaces such as you see on neurology videos.

'It's amazing,' Ruby is saying. 'How can a baby gain a whole pound in weight overnight? And even her hair's grown since yesterday! And don't you think her face has changed?'

Greg takes another gulp, and pronounces, 'Don't forget this is a very special baby we have here, darling. If her growth rate is remarkable, it's a sign that things have gone according to plan. I think we can say we have a professional success on our hands here, as well as a personal one.'

Dreamily, Ruby closes her eyes and gives a big satisfied sigh. Love and work, work and love. Two birds killed with one stone. No wonder, throughout the pregnancy, she has had a tendency to resemble the Virgin Mary, and to smirk.

The nanny arrives, bearing Billy and a fly-swat. Ruby and Greg have employed Mrs Goody on the '100 per cent availability option' indicated by four red stars in the agency's price range. This means she is on tap twenty-four hours a day, seven days a week. The agency comes recommended to Greg by none other than the vice-president of Hooper plc, a family man himself, and it specialises in the type of nanny who will not have an affair with the children's father. This means mutton dressed as mutton. Mrs Goody is certainly that. She has a 'thing' about insects, but apart from that seems quite sensible. Mrs Goody settles Billy on the floor and then withdraws discreetly to await further orders and consult the Gridiron City bus timetable.

Billy now begins to make infuriating car noises. He is playing with the expensive new set of Formula One racers that his father has bought him to cushion the blow of his sister's arrival.

'Brrrrr! MMMRRRMMMM! MMMRRRMMMM!'

It's clear that Billy doesn't think much of Angelica Sofia Gonzalez, with her little wrinkled face and tangle of black hair. Or of the way his dad and Ruby are cooing over her.

'She's got your solid legs, hasn't she?' Ruby is saying to Gregory.

'But your colouring. Your eyes. Almost black.'

'BBBRRRRRMMMMMM!'

'Quiet, Billy darling. You'll wake your baby sister. And she's got your chin. That's your chin! That is absolutely your chin, Greggie.'

Angelica is in fact the spitting image of someone else altogether.

From beneath the bed, more car noises, louder and more insistent: 'MMMMMRRRMMMMMM! MMRM-MRRM-MRRRM!'

Ruby says, 'It's not that I don't want him here.'

'I know,' says Greg. 'I feel the same way. We need some time together, just the three of us.'

Mrs Goody is summoned back.

'Sibling rivalry,' she pronounces. 'Quite normal.'

'I want my mummy,' says Billy.

'Well, Daddy's here,' snaps Ruby. 'And Aunty Ruby and Baby Angelica.'

Gregory rolls his eyes despairingly.

'Idea, Billy! I've got an idea!' announces Mrs Goody with practised excitement. Cunningly, she takes Billy to one side and whispers in his ear.

'Let's go on an insect hunt in Jaycote's Park! Zizzy wasps! Mosqitches! Daddy-long-legses! Now we're talking, eh, Billy?' she coaxes.

Billy looks up from his cars, weighs up what's on offer, then, without a word or a backward glance, abandons his cars and stomps out after Mrs Goody, fly-swat aloft.

'Bye, Billy!' calls Gregory as the door closes.

'Goodbye, Dr Stevenson!' calls Mrs Goody.

Gregory and Ruby heave a joint sigh, turn to one another and kiss. This I do not know for a fact. It was not in Ruby's confession. Or Gregory's. It's just a guess. But the next thing isn't: there is a knock at the door and a huge bouquet, all freesias and red roses and ferns and cellophane arrives. It is so big it has to manoeuvre itself in sideways. There is a small envelope attached, which Gregory opens to reveal a card with a picture of a stork carrying a bundle in its beak. 'A New Arrival', it says on the stork's bundle. Inside, elegant handwriting in navy ink. The message: '*With congratulations to two cherished colleagues on a successful collaboration. Very best wishes, Ishmael Stern.*'

They exchange a look.

It hadn't taken Dr Stern long, after I'd given him a copy of the GR218 file, to contact Gregory with a modest proposal. A threat, really, but eloquently packaged. His sugared pill, once boiled down, conveyed the message: share the glory, or be exposed by your wife, whose evidence will be backed up by me.

If you'd asked me at the time whether I thought Ishmael was capable of this kind of double-dealing, I'd have said no. Hence, with hindsight, the whole tragedy. You think you're dealing with real coffee and it turns out to be instant.

The phone call had been enough to send Gregory into a dizzying orbit of paranoia.

'Jesus Christ,' he'd shrieked, slamming down the receiver. 'What a fool I've been. I'll kill Hazel. She found the file and showed it to him. They're out to destroy my entire career. I'll murder her with my bare hands.'

And he stretched them out in front of him and stared at his scrubbed nails with new, aghast eyes.

Ruby had reacted more practically.

'You won't need to go that far,' she'd jostled him sweetly, her brain racing. 'After all, if we decide to join forces with this psychiatrist, he could perhaps decide that she's unstable enough to – '

'To be sectioned!' Greg finished the sentence for her. 'Which would mean she'd be locked away in Manxheath!' A sweaty outbreak of guilt appeared on his brow, but he wiped it away.

And so they had held a meeting. Discreetly, over

cocktails in the Thank God It's Friday on Bradall Street, where they wouldn't be recognised. There was no question that Dr Stern's expertise would be useful – especially in analysing what had gone wrong with Baby B. Dr Stern was, after all, a very eminent psychiatrist, with an understanding of neural chemicals ('See the brain as the uncharted ocean on a globe') which they, as mere geneticists and reproductive engineers, could not match. It was a union of minds, that left none of them diminished, and would even add credibility, in the long run, to the venture. Thus the silk-shirted Dr Stern, persuasively, over absurd cocktails with ice and parasols. And, he had reminded them, if he had not been prepared to 'sway the short-term moral obligation to my patient, Mrs Stevenson, in favour of long-term life-enhancement for all', they would both have had to stay in South America.

'Make no mistake,' Gregory had concluded after the first of several meetings in the excruciating nitespot, 'we're being shat on from a great height. But we're talking damage limitation here, and it's better to have him on our side than on Hazel's. And that's the choice we're faced with. Plus he's promised to keep her mouth shut.'

Keeping my mouth shut was an important factor.

'Mutual gratitude,' says Greg, arranging the flowers in a plastic bucket on the floor. 'Which reminds me. Consider this Day One. Our series of tests on Angelica starts today.'

And from his briefcase he pulls a file marked 'Baby A'.

Before them on the silent television, the sweaty face of the Reverend Carmichael communicates with the Lord. His mouth is an O, and his stubby fingers grasp at air.

'Where's the thingie, Ruby?'

She passes Gregory the remote control, and in the press of a button the evangelist has disappeared into the no man's land of the blank screen.

* * *

Manxheath Institute of Challenged Stability,
Wednesday
Dear Isabella, best friend,
How I miss you. And the reactive behaviour you've caused! I've not seen anything like it in all my years in the mental health environment. Compulsive hand-washing, blame/shame syndromes, inappropriate hilarity, obsessive witch-hunting – you name it.

On a practical level, the pathologists had to scrape you off the exterior surfaces with wee pooper-scoopers. Then into plastic bags and off to the lab for DNA fingerprinting and whatnot. You were everywhere. I was lucky enough to find one of your teeth on the outer-windowsill of the Day Room: I managed to pocket it before they forensically vacuumed. I shall have to check this in a dental encyclopedia, but what's the betting it's a molar.

I'm writing this slowly, as I have all the time in the world. I'm on a new drug that offers you that. You'd have thought I'd have worked my way through the pharmaceutical gamut by now, but Dr Hollingbroke always has an extra trick up his conjuror's sleeve. So, life in 'slow-mo': every message from brain to hand going sea-mail, every journey to the lavatory a snail's triathlon.

We're all in deep mourning for you here in the Manxheath Institute for the Socially Retarded. The team from London keeps interrogating Hazel and me, because we were the only witnesses to your gory death. Talk about style, my dear! Everyone else in the building denies they even heard the bang, apparently. The inquiry team is a 'Mr Nice and Mrs Nasty' set-up: they're addicted to caffeine and bring their own thermos into sessions. They put it next to their tape recorder, which despite being what David calls 'state of the art' has developed an infuriating buzz.

Questions, questions:

Q: (MR NICE) Have you any idea, Moira, where all the glass came from?

A: The greenhouse.

Q: (MRS NASTY) What greenhouse, Mrs Sugden?

A: My greenhouse.

Q: (MR NICE) But there is no greenhouse at Manx-heath, Moira, is there?

A: Not now there isn't.

Q: (MRS NASTY) Why were shards of glass scattered as far as the Natterjack mini-roundabout on Jobey Road, Mrs Sugden?

A: Simple physics. An explosion of X force sends detritus zooming across an area of Y square metres.

Q: (MR NICE) What d'you think caused this, er, 'explosion', then, Moira?

A: More physics. An irresistible force met an immovable object, I presume.

Q: (MR NICE) And can you tell us, d'you think, Moira, where your impressive collection of pills came from? The pills that were found inside your mattress?

A: I grew them in the greenhouse.

Q: (MRS NASTY) What greenhouse, Mrs Sugden?

Etc., Etc. Vicious circles are debilitating stuff. At half-past eleven, we stop for coffee and exasperation. Then a time-check, a here-we-go look, a scribbling in notepads, and the infuriating buzz resumes.

Q: (MRS NASTY) Mrs Sugden, how would you describe your relationship with the staff at the Institute?

You've got to laugh.

Who cares about all this, I say, now that the thing's happened. It's all too late, too late, too late. Why speculate about what physiological Armageddon Isabella wreaked on herself now that she's mincemeat? I warned Dr Stern, didn't I? Did I not go to his office and demand maternity facilities? If you're looking for a culprit for all this, I tell them, look no further than the door of the man himself.

Q: What man? What door?

A: Dr Ishmael Stern. *That* door.

Silence, except for the buzz.

From what I can gather, they're developing a theory about hallucinogens and group hysteria, in which they themselves figure as part of the 'psychological fallout'. Their whole inquiry, according to this theory, is a symptom of the disease they have been hired to invesitage. It's the only way they can square the circle on paper. It's what Linda, in her university days, would have called a deconstructive meta-inquiry.

Meanwhile the aforementioned Linda, nudged on delicately by me, is putting her ideological 'Operation Sabotage' project into its second phase. This involves sliding off the Butter Mountain for a while in order to play zoo-keeper to the Perfect Baby, having appointed herself guardian of the planet's morals. Did I tell you she was a zealot from the age of three? She disapproves of anything genetic. Her nickname for Gregory, by the way, is the Wanker.

Operation Sabotage is a purely personal crusade now, she tells me. It was all mixed up with religion at one point, but she's become inexplicably cheesed off with

Born-Againness, and that tubby preacher on the telly who she threw the eggs at has suddenly become the Antichrist in her book.

'The more fraudulent people like Carmichael are,' she stormed on her last visit, banging her fist on the formica, 'the more principled we evangelical atheists have to be about ethical issues!'

There were tears in her eyes. I smell sex again.

'So I take it the Greens are getting you on the rebound?' I asked.

'I'll be single-handedly putting human genetic engineering back ten years,' she sniffed, ignoring me. 'And if I have to steal twenty of Gregory's guinea-pigs to keep that drug out of Joe Public's reach, I'll do it.'

'Let us hope it doesn't come to that,' I told her. 'You'll get done for factory-farming, and be crowned Queen of Hypocrisy.'

She's named the Perfect Baby Katie-Koo, after a doll my husband Brendan and I gave her when she was a child. Hazel bit off its head, which is why the two girls have always hated each other.

'Some way of healing the rift!' I told her. For an intelligent girl, my daughter Linda can be transcendentally stupid.

'Where's the baby now?' I asked. I'd seen no sign of a pram.

'Back at the flat,' she snapped. 'She's asleep.'

'That's illegal!' I informed her. I should know, having done the same thing myself and been hauled in for it.

'Katie-Koo's different,' she explained. 'She's not an ordinary baby. You can leave her and she just sleeps.'

All right for some, eh, Isabella?

The other daughter, Hazel, is being paranoically schizophrenic about the whole thing. On the one hand she is delighted we've landed Gregory and Ruby with your offspring, but on the other she is bitter and scathing about Linda's new role foster-mothering the fruits of adultery. To the point of derangement.

'Why should she have to look after the Perfect Baby?' she screamed at me over breakfast the next morning. 'Couldn't we just dump it somewhere, or kill it?'

She had a crazed look, and wouldn't let go of her wretched chair. She has developed a way of sitting on it with her feet gripping its legs. I offered her some Valium but she just put her hands over her ears and shouted, 'No more pills! No more pills!' over and over again.

Families. Strange, don't you think, Isabella, that family trees are not the other way up? I would put the babies at the top, like fresh shoots. The dead, their ancestral roots, below. I read that the remains of a prehistoric man were found, frozen. His testicles were miraculously intact after thousands of years. The contents of these testicles, carefully refrigerated, are still viable. My son-in-law would no doubt like to get his hands on them. Use them to impregnant a woman: muddle up past and future, in-breed across time-zones, turn the family tree into a tangled bush, roots and shoots all arse about face. As if he hasn't buggered things up enough already. Did I tell you, he brought a pocket calculator to his own wedding?

Ciao.

Yours affectionately,

Moira.

* * *

Belief in the creed of the Reverend Vernon Carmichael thrives, like woodlice, in the most unexpected places. But the heart of my sister Linda is no longer one of them. She has declared it a 'crap-free zone'. The Lord has let her down, and has been relegated, along with Jesus Christ and the Holy Ghost, to the rank of those who need their heads examined.

Since the day the Reverend betrayed her, not a single Love Heart has passed Linda's lips.

Nor can she look an egg in the face again.

But she still watches *Holy Hour*. It's part of the cathartic process. When John Two ran off with that bitch from Corporate Accounts, she forced herself to sit near him in the canteen every day. And when Terry called her a harridan, she checked its exact meaning in the dictionary, photocopied and blew up the definition, and pinned it above her bathroom mirror, near the Mensa certificate. 'Harridan: A haggard old woman; a vixen; a "decayed strumpet"; usu. a term of abuse.'

Face the fear. Feel the pain. It can make you born again.

The ashtray is full, and the bells of St Manfred's clang their monstrous din, all but drowning out the sound of the revving cars on television. Linda has been watching the desperate swerving of stock-car racing for an hour, and seen five muddy, bloody crashes, two of them spectacular. She squats at one end of the velveteen sofa, legs apart, knees up, cigarette hanging from her lower lip, holding Katie-Koo's bottle at arm's length. The baby, propped at the other end of the sofa, is feeding quietly. She is magnificently pretty, with black eyes and a mass of dark curls.

' "Your daddy's rich and your mama's good-looking," ' croaks Linda as the Perfect Baby finishes her milk, smiles radiantly, and immediately falls asleep. 'So get fucked.'

With no great affection, Linda wipes Katie-Koo's cherubic little mouth with a soiled tea-towel, heaves a disgruntled sigh, and jerks the cushion from under her. But the baby just shifts position, and smiles in her sleep. Linda has not yet managed to make her cry.

It is two weeks into her new life as a mother-figure, and the day stretches before her, long and vacant – as do the six weeks of leave that lie ahead. Time hangs heavy on Linda as it never did in her busy days at the Butter Mountain, so unexpectedly curtailed by her mission to sabotage the Perfect Baby Project. In fact she has begun to refer to the compassionate break she has taken (citing 'family problems' as though these were a temporary aberration rather than the backdrop to her life) as 'my eternity leave'.

There is nothing to do, except smoke five packets of cigarettes a day. It's costing her a fortune.

Two more cars collide on a muddy slope, and Linda cheers as one bursts into flames. Then she reaches for the phone and dials British Telecom in Swakely Gap.

'My name's Linda Sugden,' she announces through her dangling fag. 'I want to speak to Duncan Proutt.'

'He's in a meeting, I'm afraid,' says a voice with a pension plan.

'Well, when he gets out, ask him to come round with a dozen roses,' she orders him. 'And tell him I've decided to lift that sex embargo.'

Linda breathes out smoke into the receiver, and miraculously enough, a fit of coughing is induced on the other end.

'Did you get that?' she barks, annoyed.

'Right you are, Miss Sugden,' manages the strangulated voice. 'I'll pass the message on to Mr Proutt. I'll tell him you – '

But Linda has slammed down the receiver.

The stock-car racing has finished and *Holy Hour* is beginning. Linda steels herself and reaches for her cornflower-blue knitting. It's a cardigan for herself. Katie-Koo sighs and puckers her dimpled lips in a sweet smile. Linda looks at her with loathing, and then, with a sudden flash of inspiration, stretches out an arm and jabs at Katie-Koo's bare foot with the end of the needle. Hard.

'And bugger me,' she told me later, 'if she didn't fucking giggle, like I was tickling her or something! Jesus, when *you* were a baby and I did something like that to you, Hazel, you at least screamed the house down.'

Motherhood really wasn't her bag, she told me. She'd speed-read all the books, in particular Dr Rosamund Pithkin's Baby Bible (a gift from Ma), said to be the definitive work on baby care. And it must have been, because Katie-Koo did everything Dr Pithkin said she should and nothing she shouldn't. She'd done it, too, at the recommended times and in the recommended amounts, to the minute and to the gramme. Katie-Koo fed well, grew as the charts indicated she should, and slept twenty-two hours a day. Most astonishing of all, given Linda's stock of small cruelties, she had not yet shed a single tear.

Linda had heard about sleepless nights, and crying that shatters the nerves and will not be appeased – stories of skin rashes, diarrhoea, wind, colic and infantile *Weldschmertz*, but Katie-Koo was immune. The Baby Bible's extensive section on 'problems' remained unread. Katie-Koo was placid. She was no trouble. She was trouble-free and trouble-less. She was untroubled, untroubling and untroublesome. That was the trouble. There was nothing that prompted in Linda the maternal urge to soothe and protect, and to quell her own exasperation with a martyrish shrug of the shoulders and a nice warm feeling. The Perfect Baby stirred no tugs of conscience, no calls of duty. It was the way Gregory had designed her. 'To meet the needs of the busy professional couple,' as his Perfect Baby brochure would have put it.

The Perfect Baby was like a landscaped garden or an apartment rabbit — a living thing specially designed to require minimum maintenance, and create maximum decorative effect. Even Katie-Koo's bowel products were odourless. Linda could picture the questionnaire that led to this depressing combination of characteristics. It would have corresponded to the market research the toy manufacturers did when they came up with the original Katie-Koo, the crying, pissing doll. There is no doubt that this was a perfect baby.

Linda hated her.

If she had bothered to read the section of Rosemary Pithkin's Baby Bible entitled 'Problems Big and Small', she might have come across a section she could relate to. It was a Problem Big, under the heading 'Bonding, Lack of'.

> *Symptoms: various, incl.: Mother's lack of interest in, and affection for, the child. Child's lack of specific mother-related response.*
>
> *Causes: various, incl.: Disturbed pregnancy, difficult birth, perinatal shock, early trauma.*
>
> *Treatment: You really mustn't give up on this one. One theory in modern paediatric psychology is that some mothers and their babies are simply a 'bad fit'. I do not subscribe to this theory. Call me old-fashioned, but I have only one answer to your problem: you and your wretched baby must both try harder.*

Just as well, perhaps, that Linda hadn't read the problem section; she might have tracked Dr Pithkin down and personally deep-fried her in baby oil. But Dr Pithkin's diagnosis, had she been there to make it, would have been correct: Katie-Koo and Linda had not bonded. Katie-Koo smiled at Linda and nestled in her arms as any loving babe should, but she did just the same with complete strangers. There was a seed of mistrust in Linda's heart that came from she knew not where. Mistrust, and envy: *she* had cried endlessly as a baby. *She* had been too hot or cold, or feverish, or bored, or uncomfortable, or uncontrollably angry, ever since she could remember. That was life, wasn't it? Life's a bitch and then you die, as one of Linda's favourite sayings goes. (Or as my bachelor brother-in-law John always said, 'Life's a bitch and then you marry her.') So why should this child escape it? Why should Katie-Koo's life be so wonderful when Linda's had been, on reflection, a valley of toil?

When a woman gives birth, a bag of guilt is born with the baby, like an extra placenta. This bag is surely made heavier when the baby is not the woman's own but one she has stolen.

Linda takes a cold hard look at her little charge, stubs out her cigarette in the overspilling ashtray, and grinds it down with a twist.

On television, the Reverend Carmichael has fallen to his knees, writhing about in ecstasy and sobbing in a sweaty heap. Linda, eyes narrowed and cheeks puckered, shudders uncomfortably for thirty-seven seconds, tears welling glassily in her eyes.

The programme erupts into a jangle-twangle burst of music and spontaneous applause from the studio audience. Close-ups show that some of them are crying, too. As the *Holy Hour*'s theme hymn becomes a crescendo, a flashing number on the screen reminds viewers of the number to dial to pledge their minimum of £50 to the House of God.

'Well, Reverend Fucking Carmichael,' sniffs Linda as the credits roll over the prostrate form of the man of the cloth. The studio audience, arms aloft, stands behind him like a swishing field of green wheat. 'Tell me one thing, dickhead. Did the perfect infant Jesus drive his mother mad?'

Just then the doorbell rings.

Duncan to the rescue!

The *Holy Hour* credits are still rolling when, on the other side of the city, Ruby turns her gaze away from the television screen, her beautiful face a blank round cheese of misery. She flicks the remote control, rolls over, and lies still. The room is piled high with boxes of chocolates, fruit, flowers, and cards from well-wishers. Every inch of shelving space is adorned with roses and greetings and little baby-presents: a frilly jump-suit in pink, a musical rabbit that plays 'Rock-a-Bye Baby', a miniature water-wheel for the bath. The maternity wing of the Sacred Bleeding Heart is well placed for sunshine, and bright rays stream through the net curtains on to Ruby's crisp, scented linen and the lace-adorned cot where lies the babe.

The babe. Still there. Still ugly. Still grizzling. She has cried almost non-stop for fourteen days and fourteen nights, and Ruby is at the end of her tether. Even the nurses are shrugging their shoulders and murmuring about 'natural misery'.

'Perhaps you should be thinking of going home soon with Baby,' said the ward sister to her gently – but Ruby had begged to be allowed to stay another week.

'I'm not ready to go home yet,' she said. 'I'm not sure I can cope.'

And she raised such a pleading face in the sister's direction – quite a different face from the confident, arrogant Dr Gonzalez who had arrived on the ward a fortnight earlier and demanded cable TV and fresh guava juice – that the sister relented.

'It's your money,' she said. 'You can stay as long as you like.'

So see Ruby now, hunched in a foetal ball, the bedclothes bunched around her, her sloping shoulders shuddering as she sobs. On the floor lie reams of computer paper covered in complex graphs and analyses and tables which Gregory had thrown down before he stormed out, sobbing himself, destroyed with rage before the infallibility of the data, setting in stone the unmisinterpretable figures which formed proof of what Ruby had already suspected, but dared not admit to herself: that the worse-than-unimaginable, the barely-believable, the 99.9999-per cent-improbable has happened. Angelica is a normal baby. In all respects – motor functions, weight, eyesight, hearing, muscle tone, appetite, and intelligence, she is completely and tragically average. 'Pig-ordinary', to use a phrase of Gregory's when our son was a baby.

'Months of work down the bloody drain!' Greg had stormed, hurling the papers at her. 'And now we're stuck with this – mollusc!'

He was adamant: they must leave the hospital before Angelica was placed on a register of babies 'at risk'. The nurses had already been whispering about Ruby and Gregory's bizarre attitude problem towards their daughter. Nothing must draw further attention to them. They would take her home and keep quiet about her and eventually . . .

'Eventually what?' snapped a tearful Ruby.

'Well, you know,' said Greg.

'No, I don't,' wept Ruby. But she was lying.

'There's always the possibility of – '

The word 'adoption' was not spoken. A wall of ice had grown between Ruby and Greg since the first few days after the baby's birth. The three dozen white lilies he'd bought for Ruby began to emit a powerful odour just the wrong side of rottenness, but he came with no fresh bouquet to replace them. In fact he came to visit less and less, citing pressure of work and his paternal duties to Billy. When he did come, it was armed with tape measures and auriscopes and rubber appliances for weighing and measuring all parts of the body, and pages of instructions for testing Angelica's IQ, which he did between her bouts of screaming. Then he went off to analyse them. He was spending more and more time at the Hooper Fertility Foundation. Ruby hadn't even seen the spanking new laboratory that Root Hooper had bought for the Genetic Choice Programme. She had lain in bed most of the time, trying to appease the baby's ravenous hunger with her sore, cracked nipples, putting pillows over her head to shut out its crying, too awash with maternal guilt and too weak and harassed even to do her pelvic floor exercises to restore her vagina to its former glory.

And now Ruby, surrounded by pungent lilies, a touching icon of misery, raises her dark pleading eyes to the heavens, and weeps big tears of pure silver for the suffering she endures. Welcome, Ruby Gonzalez, to the State of Motherhood. There is no return.

FOURTEEN

We at Manxheath were faring no better. I began to understand why some people go mad. The world is an unpredictable, cavalier sort of place.

The staff whispered in corridors: the local press began to sniff about. How could it be, the Disciplinary Inquiry was to ask, that a woman in Mrs Pimento's condition of florid delusion could explode into shreds, standing on the lawn, witnessed only by two unsupervised mental patients? Where did all that splintered glass come from? And why was there not a doctor or nurse in sight? It didn't look good at all; Dr Stern's hair went grey overnight. His eyes, which used to be so dark and shining, turned the colour of an old anorak. Nurses said in low voices, glancing about as they spoke, that he was going to be hauled up before the Deciding Authority and risked disciplinary action, criminal proceedings, and having to make a public apology to Mrs Pimento's relatives, who were arriving from Turin in indignant droves for the funeral. One aged uncle seemed to be particularly affected. He came on a tour of Manxheath, growling '*Assassini, assassini*', but had to leave in a hurry when Ma chased him up a corridor screaming and waving a large piece of her clay work at him.

Finally, when the pathologists had sifted through

Mrs Pimento's splinter-filled giblets and the undertakers had filled a coffin with God knows what residual splatterings, there was a cremation ('They're turning her into haggis,' mourned Ma), and a private funeral ceremony to which patients were not invited. We were suffering from 'post-traumatic syndrome', and a new doctor was brought in to monitor our drugs. Dr Hollingbroke was shipped off on secondment to Coxcomb Hall for the Socially Disturbed, pending the Inquiry's report. Ma took to the Art Room with Keith, clutching a molar she'd found on the windowsill and muttering something about a 'memorial'.

'My world has fallen apart,' she told me melodramatically over breakfast one day. 'My greenhouse has been destroyed and my best friend with it. All in smithereens. Now is that a personal tragedy or what?'

She seldom emerged from the Art Room except for meals. She would eat nothing but Spotted Dick.

'Comfort food,' said Dr McAuley, who looked like she could do with some herself.

She had tried in vain to re-start the Group sessions. We were having none of it. Rumour had it that Dr McAuley was also facing disciplinary charges. Manxheath became a house of whispers. Nurses switched allegiance to a higher echelon of management and began to spy on the doctors rather than us. Even Hope did a U-turn, and refused to give me any more injections. Max took to patrolling the premises like a security guard, and would interrogate people about their movements. He had a stopwatch, and would ask things like:

'Why did it take you two minutes and thirty-five seconds to traverse the north wall corridor this morning when you did it in half that time on Tuesday?'

And: 'Is this going-to-the-toilet thing of yours some sort of elaborate double bluff?'

He avoided Ma, after she showed him the molar. She had taken to wearing it on a length of dental floss round her neck, to ward off evil spirits.

David sat in the Day Room, lizard-like, often motionless for hours, but sometimes he would scribble long letters to lawyers. Monica Fletcher wept snottily in the corners of rooms. She cried so much she had to be put on salt tablets. When my mother's huge stash of mind-altering medications was discovered in her mattress (far more, the staff swore, than they believed they had in stock; a whole arsenal of pills which she claimed were the harvest of the greenhouse), all patients were removed from drugs, pending 're-assessment'. We all went into terrible withdrawal. This took various forms; Max had to be strait-jacketed for a week, and my mother wouldn't leave the Art Room. The Ossature abandoned her sorrel-and-water diet for a full-scale hunger-strike. In my case, I just felt like I had a bad hangover. The tangerine feeling had gone and I seemed to fit into my body again, but it was as if someone had stolen my world in exchange. I had no place of refuge now the greenhouse had gone. I suppose my mother felt the same way.

'It was to be the pride of Gridiron,' she whispered to me one day as we passed each other in the corridor like ships in the night. And I knew what she meant. Her face was waxy and her clothes hung off her, giving her the look of a deflated hot-air balloon. The passages of Manxheath no longer echoed with noise, and apart from the hysterical music-'n'-chatter of TV game shows, there was silence. I spent most of the time in my room, thinking about revenge, missing Billy, or reading a book on personal management which Linda had lent me, written by her guru, Klaus G. Armstrong, but sometimes I'd come down and watch six hours of television at a stretch. I came to know game shows quite well.

Dr Stern walked in, and his eyes settled on mine like desperate search-lamps. I was still giggling from the anecdote on TV, and couldn't stop.

'Come to my office, please, Hazel,' he said. And he added, 'Please.'

He didn't sound like a doctor. He sounded like a man again. A man in trouble. His voice was hoarse.

'We have to talk.'

And so, almost like in the old days, but with sadness rather than sexual anticipation, I followed him into his office. It was still May, according to the bright Modern Art splodges on the calendar, but there was nothing to be merry about. The office was full of removal crates, and the shelves were bare. I was glad I'd stolen his paperweight. It could surely be of no use to him now. Ishmael reached in a drawer for a bottle of whisky and two glasses, and poured us each a large one.

He took a swig, ignoring me, and put his feet up on the desk. His suit was crumpled, and not in a fashionable way. His beard was streaked with grey. He was smaller and grubbier than I remembered him. There was a defeated look about him.

'Looks like it's all *over* for me, Hazel,' he said.

I didn't reply, and there was a long silence.

'I got your note, and your *flowers*,' he said. 'Thanks.'

'*Valium domesticum*,' I said. 'Ma grew them.'

Dr Stern made an exasperated noise, a sort of clucking sigh, like he was spitting out a locust.

'Yes,' he said, annoyed. 'I've *heard* that story, about how your mother got together her stash, and claims to have *propagated* it. We'll have to come up with a better explanation than that for the *Investigators,* though.'

'It's the truth,' I said.

The flowers didn't matter, but I found myself regretting the note. Since I'd come off my drugs I was more cynical about things. I looked at the man I had thought I loved with a more jaded vision. He looked frightened. His eyes were shifting about, restlessly, as though looking for a crack in the ground into which he could creep. All my respect for him had fallen away. Disillusion is a bitter, lonely thing, I have discovered. He wasn't even sexy any more.

'Look, Hazel,' he said, reaching in a drawer for a form. 'I'm going to burn something.'

And he tapped the sheet of paper.

He took a cigarette lighter from another drawer and lit the corner of the form. I saw the flame lick over a green signature and turn it, briefly, to violet. The handwriting looked familiar. Then he threw the flaming document in the metal waste-paper bin where we both watched it burn, mesmerised. There's nothing like a fire for intimacy and comfort – but Ishmael broke the spell.

'There,' he said. 'That was the *compulsory section* I put you under. See? It never happened.'

I shook myself out of my pyromaniac's trance, staggered at his gall.

'Yes it fucking well did,' I told him. I shocked myself, because I don't usually swear. I found myself shuddering with sudden, feverish rage.

He reached out to place his hand on my arm – an old trick – but it didn't work this time. I shook him off angrily. If I'd had a sharp pencil to hand I'd have stabbed it into his eye.

'All of it happened. You seduced me, you betrayed me, locked me up, you took away my son, and you filled me with drugs. And now you just burn a piece of paper and say it didn't happen.'

'Hazel,' he said simply. 'It *didn't* happen.'

'Yes it did!'

'No. You're quite *wrong*. Nothing happened. Certainly not *all* of it. But – '

'But what?'

I could see he was hedging now.

'But forgive me anyway.'

The nerve of it left me briefly winded. Then I stood up to hit him across the face. He sat there like he was going to take it. I was just aiming my swing when Dr Appleby walked in, without knocking, and I stopped. I couldn't do it with her there; like sex, it was too intimate.

'There's a smell of burning,' she said coldly.

'Yes, Dr Appleby. Just clearing things out, getting rid of some *junk*.'

'Well, it's a fire hazard,' she said. 'You should know that. Anyway, time to go, Dr Stern. You can clear out your things after the Inquiry has reported.'

Meekly, he stood up and brushed down his suit.

'Just discharging a *patient*. This is Mrs Stevenson,' he mumbled.

'It's for me to do that,' said Dr Appleby. And addressing me, she said, 'There will be an in-depth assessment of all patients within the next few days, and we'll decide then what the best treatment will be.'

She smiled at me unexpectedly, and I warmed to her.

'And don't worry, Mrs Stevenson,' she said, glancing icily at Stern. 'There will be no more drugs in this establishment for some time yet.'

I went back to the Day Room and my game show.

It didn't happen. Nothing happened. Hazel, you are quite wrong.

No, Dr Stern. Not this time.

There was a woman contestant on the show. It was called *Confession*. She was a quality control supervisor at a DIY concession called Grout-a-Matic, and her hobbies were knitting and scuba-diving.

'Not both at the same time, I hope!' chuckled the host.

That raised a laugh. The contestant was skinny, with bandy legs like a nutcracker in rather racy fishnet stockings. She had a page-boy haircut from the seventies, and a floral dress, and glasses far too big for her face. It was like she was wearing two televisions. The host, Tyrone Jiggers, wore a suit of pillar-box red and a spangled top hat. His tie had flashing light bulbs on it. Jiggers gave the Grout-a-Matic woman a giant banana that said 'The £300 Confession' on it.

'How do I hold it?' she giggled.

'Any way you like, my darling, but don't squeeze it too hard!' he replied, quick as a flash. That raised an 'Oooo!' and another laugh.

The idea was that she had to recount her most embarrassing moment ever. The one when she'd felt the most publicly humiliated. They have some interesting ideas, don't they, these television producers.

Mrs Grout-a-Matic was explaining how she's got two daughters, right, and one day they set up this blind date with Kim's brother's friend at a car-boot sale, right –

But that's always the trouble, isn't it. Whenever you get stuck into a good programme, something happens to interrupt you: a phone call, someone coming to check the gas meter, a mealtime gong, a scuffle. Quite a noisy scuffle, in fact.

It was Ishmael being pinned to the floor by two thickset males nurses and the slim Hope. Dr Appleby was remonstrating with him.

'Please, Dr Stern, you are abandoning all your professionalism here,' she was saying, trying to coax him to a sitting position. 'Try to retain some dignity, please, Dr Stern. This is very distressing.'

Ishmael was trying to grind his teeth and sob at the

same time. He was breathing in great theatrical gasps. I flicked the television off and observed him closely as he tried to stuff his whole fist in his mouth. Saliva ran down his arm, followed by a small stream of blood.

It looked fishy to me. Too many symptoms, I reckoned. He was over-egging it. Dr Stern knew a lot about breakdowns. They were his job. For someone like him, I realised, they would be quite easy to fake, if the alternative was a prison sentence for negligence. A World War Two prisoner in Colditz managed to escape that way, by posing as a harmful loony. The problem was, he stayed that way after the war; the mask fused to him. Dr Appleby clearly hadn't seen that episode of *Colditz*. No, she was insisting, there was no time for Dr Stern to fetch anything from his office or to change his clothes. He was going straight to London for the Inquiry Team to pronounce its sentence on his conduct as Medical Director of the Manxheath Institute of Challenged Stability. Did he really want to make a spectacle of himself in front of his staff and patients? Wisely, he didn't answer. Still, it's hard to see a grown man cry, even when it's pretend. Several of us were on our feet now, staring at him as he writhed beneath the weight of the two male nurses. Hope had given up.

'Well, well,' said Max. 'The fallen idol.'

And with an excellent aim, he spat a gob of greenish phlegm that landed in the middle of Ishmael's forehead. I wanted to cheer, but instead an older instinct took over, and I found myself coming forward with a Kleenex and wiping the brow of my former lover, feeling guilty as though I'd spat at him myself. Then I wiped the blood of his hand, too, and pressed the Kleenex to the small wound he'd made with his teeth.

'Thank you, Hazel,' whispered Ishmael. 'Can you forgive me?'

'No,' I said. And left.

Later, from my window, I saw them dragging him across the lawn to a waiting ambulance, and a sadness enveloped me. Maybe he really was having a breakdown. The dividing line between worlds is so thin: the normal world, and the world where the table is laid with its knives and forks the wrong way round, its cruet set askew, and its misshapen candelabra burning the noxious bright flame of things irredeemably amiss. And as I discovered – and remembered, thanks to my red-cushioned chair – you can straddle this dividing line, with a foot on either side.

*   *   *

Three weeks later, Ruby Gonzalez, head and feet propped on brightly coloured cushions on the sofa, watching television, eating chocolates. Beside her, the cot with its now frankly dreaded contents, the monster Angelica, whingeing of nature, spotty of complexion, disturbed of bowel, and average (tests clearly show) of brain. Crying again. And when, in all honesty, has she ever stopped? Only when her distraught mother, desperate for some sleep, has dosed her up with a teaspoonful of gin. The weary Ruby languishes in Hazel's home, which is now her own, and seeks comfort from God.

'I don't know why you watch that crap,' says Greg angrily, coming home to find her quite shamelessly absorbed in the Raving Rev on Channel Praise. 'He's the reason we had to turn to Hooper for funding, you know,' he adds bitterly.

Ruby knows. Ruby knows also that there is pressure on Greg from Hooper to produce results. Soon. But Ruby is less of a scientist now she has become a mother. She is less sure of things in general. She is less sure, for instance, that Hooper is all good and Carmichael is all bad. In fact, from what she has seen of the two men, her allegiances are beginning to shift. Carmichael reminds her of the dark, passionate world she came from – a world of mortal sin, of self-flagellation, of back-street chemical abortions, of Liberation Theology. A world she once longed to escape from into the cool rationalism of science. A world she is now being drawn back towards by a form of magnetism. The going is getting tough for Ruby Gonzalez. And when the going gets tough, all visitors are welcome. Even God, if he delivers the goods.

Root Hooper is impatient, Greg is explaining. He has his Perfect Babywear collection (pastels) all ready to go, and his team is working on a Junior Mind Gym (primary colours) for the Perfect Toddler. He doesn't understand why their productivity seems to have dropped.

'You promised this thing was in the bag, Stevenson,' he said to Greg, who now reports the conversation to Ruby. 'Don't forget our three-month get-out clause.'

Greg hadn't forgotten, and knew, indeed, that Hooper would use it in a flash if he had any idea that the Perfect Baby Project was now, far from being on the brink of success, back to Square Minus One. Root Hooper was not a scientist; he was a self-made man. And he wanted that Perfect Baby drug. Now. In fact, as he'd told Greg, he wanted it *yesterday*.

Greg had winced inwardly at the cliché, but he'd smiled with thin lips.

'I'm a scientist, Root, not a magician.'

'Well, I want some magic out of you anyway,' said Hooper. 'Before there's any more fuss in the tabloids from that Raving Rev git about Frankenstein's embryos. There's going to be a tidal wave of public opinion against this project pretty soon if he keeps this kind of pressure up. My researchers say the man in the street is getting pissed off with science. He thinks too many drugs have gone wrong, an excess number of galaxies has been discovered, there's more mass in the universe than there should be. It's confusing for him. He wants to get back to the days of pigs with eight teats. He's crying out for apocalypses, visions, crystal balls, a bit of tub-thumping, all that malarkey. And maybe he's right. The climate isn't looking good for our Perfect Babies. We need to get them out in the market-place quick, before the mood changes and they're as *passé* as growth hormones and titty implants.'

'Cold feet?' enquired Greg.

Hooper snorted in response, and the colour rose behind his tan. He was used to a bit of respect. Stevenson seemed to be forgetting that he, Hooper, had the 51 per cent share in this deal. And in business, Hooper was fond of saying, he who hath 51 per cent calleth the fucking shots. He shifted his sugar-free chewing-gum to a far corner of his mouth before he spoke. There was anger in his voice, but it was soft, and mint-scented.

'Cold feet? Root Hooper? It is well known that Root Hooper's feet do not get cold. Root Hooper thrives on controversy. I have balls, Dr Stevenson, of steel. I want this thing ready so we can time the launch right. That little Reverend fucker is a threat to this project, if we don't play it right. But don't worry. I'll deal with that part. Incriminating photos. We'll fake them, if need be. They're all at it, these evangelicals. Prostitutes, little boys, donkeys, you name it. So leave it to me.'

And he smiled briefly, the tongue flicking out over dry lips.

'Meanwhile, that "human trial" you were so hopeful about, what's become of that?'

'There's been a hitch,' said Greg. 'Something we can't explain. The first trial, as I told you, was promising, but

only a *partial* success, producing an average baby altogether, though one with what our psychiatrist colleague
has labelled a telepathy quotient of 160. That means the
child has some sort of extra-sensory perception, which
means that we're having some genetic impact, though
in this case not one that's useful for our purposes.
The second human trial has, er, miscarried. A late
miscarriage, I'm afraid. We're doing the pathology
now. Cutting it up, you know, sectioning off all the
pieces, removing the spleen and guts and heart and
other organs for dissection, analysing and measuring
parts of the foetal body . . .'

(Blind him with science and make him feel sick, was
Greg's strategy. Play for time.)

'All right,' Root Hooper said impatiently. 'I don't need
the gory details. How long's a baby take? Nine months?
I'll be wanting news of a new human trial by the end of
next month. You can go.'

Greg had smiled tightly, turned with an acquiescent
grunt, and left. How tempting it would be to snap and
bite at the hand that fed him. Softly, he had closed the
door on the office of Root Hooper, trillionaire and
ignoramus, with a feeling not of release but of being
trapped in an altogether smaller, more claustrophobic
place. He would be needing balls of steel himself.

'So that's the score,' he finished.

Has Ruby been listening to any of this? He notes
with dismay that she has started on another box of
chocolates, and is working her way through them with
a grazing rhythm that indicates she does not intend to
stop until she has ingested the lot. She is still staring
at the television, which is now showing midday adver-
tisements for housewives and the elderly: floor polish,
antacid pills, washing powder, slim-a-soup, denture
gel. Greg's heart sinks to a new low. This is not the

232

captivating, brilliant woman he fell in love with; this is an overweight, self-indulgent mamma with a bad case of post-natal depression. The feeling of claustrophobia tightens around Greg's gullet and throttles his larynx. He has to clear his throat.

'I'm off now. Got to fetch Billy and Mrs Goody from the station.'

They have been on a two-week holiday, to visit Mrs Goody's sister in Darlington, all expenses paid. Ruby is glad to be having the nanny back, but is less delighted about Billy. He has been missing his pathetically inadequate mother, apparently, and talking about her and 'Gwanny' an annoying amount. Apart from that he seems a happy, normal child – a sickening mockery of Ruby's own wizened little creature, who has this week lost weight and added late jaundice to her list of medical woes. Meanwhile her nappy rash, an angry constellation of spotty lesions, has spread to cover most of her body, and is inching towards her face. Ruby can hardly bear to look at her. She has been at home for a month, Angelica attached to her by suction for what seems like eternity.

'Oh, just one thing,' Greg says as he is leaving.

'Yes, what?' says Ruby through an Orange Velvet.

'When's your period likely to be due?'

'My what?'

'Your cycle, darling. Your menses. Your monthly flushing-out. Have you forgotten that women bleed? I was just wondering if, er, since the baby – ?'

It takes a while for the penny to drop.

With the help of chocolates, tranquillisers and *Holy Hour*, Ruby has managed to control some of her more explosive feelings about the baby. But now – no. No. Surely not. He can't mean it. Not another try. Surely, not after this – disaster. But looking at him, poised at the door, jangling his keys, she realises that he does indeed mean it. It probably all seems quite reasonable to him.

It is then that something snaps.

Suddenly Ruby has shot off the sofa and hurled herself at Gregory, knocking the baby to the ground where it lands with a sickening thud and begins to bawl. But Angelica's cries are nothing to the crazed shrieks of Ruby.

'No! No, no, NO! Get out! Get out of here! Get out!'

Greg holds her by the shoulders, grabs a handful of hair and twists. She is pinned against the wall, immobile with pain and shock. He stands looking at her for a moment.

'Ruby,' he whispers. 'If we don't get another baby on the way soon we'll lose the whole deal with Hooper. Come on, darling. Just a few modifications. We can do it this time. Angelica was just a freak accident.'

Ruby's eyes widen in horror.

'She's my baby!'

'And you can keep her, if you want,' Greg soothes. 'No one's taking her from you. And soon she can have a little brother or sister to keep her company.'

He lets go of Ruby's hair, muffles his face in it.

'Come on, darling. Think dates, now, love. Mrs Goody can baby-sit tonight and we'll go out, relax a bit. I'll book a table somewhere in Mutton Acre.'

Ruby's eyes are opening still further, round windows on a flabbergasted soul.

Finally she manages to croak, 'Get out. I never want to see you again.'

'Calm down, darling. Look, I have to go now, but you think it through, and we'll talk over dinner.'

And with a jingle of car keys, he has left.

For the last month, Ruby has been reduced to a womb and a pair of breasts. Since childbirth her wits have slowed, as wits do – but it doesn't take long to think this one through. With a sureness of step and a focus of vision that have been so lacking lately, Ruby picks up Angelica and forces her, whimpering, into the kangaroo sling around her chest. Into the child's mouth, towards which a slow larva-like stream of snot from its snub nose is making its way inexorably, she forces an enormous rubber dummy which fills its face like a door-knocker. Then she mounts the stairs, waddling two at a time, and drags out a large suitcase with wheels. From a drawer in the study she takes her Venezuelan passport, her credit cards, her address book, and her Bible. First things first. It doesn't take her long to pack the rest. And within half an hour she and Angelica have gone.

The bells of St Manfred's are crashing out one of their three tunes again, and Linda, cigarette in one hand, educational rattle in the other, is thinking murderous thoughts about the world. She has quickly discovered that there's no fun or mileage in being a martyr and a saviour of the sane society when nobody is aware of it to applaud her efforts. Katie-Koo doesn't seem to need a mother. She has got the hang of things on a physical level very quickly, and is already reaching out for her own bottle of milk, removing her own nappy when it is soiled, and applying talcum powder to her own dimpled botty. Linda and Duncan have begun to leave her for hours at a stretch, and she lies in her cot cooing gently, gurgling, or sleeping. She has not yet, in her six weeks of life, cried. Linda has been on the phone to the Ministry, saying the family crisis has ended and she's ready to return with all guns blazing. To be frank, she can't wait. She'd swap the fulfilment of motherhood for the fulfilment of a packet of fags any day. Katie-Koo doesn't need looking after. Katie-Koo is perfect. She can simply be left for the day, like a cat. A pile of books next to her bed, a change of nappies, an Activity Centre. She seems to be learning the alphabet. In fact, she seems to be starting to utter noises that sound uncannily like words. The trouble is, Linda doesn't particularly want to hear them. So Linda has taken to leaving Katie-Koo for the day, with Channel Praise on, which surely can't do more harm than those Junior Network cartoons in which robots with laser-guns on their index fingers rescue pneumatic women from cutlass-brandishing pirates. Katie-Koo has even started to hum the *Holy Hour* theme tune.

Yes: Linda has decided to become a working mum. Rosemary Pithkin says it's OK to go out to work, '*So long as you and your conscience can live with a decision which some would describe as selfish and irresponsible. I shall not pass judgement.*' Linda gets on the phone with Dr Pithkin's mixed blessing resounding in her head, to learn that not only will the Butter Mountain be delighted to have her back earlier than expected, but it will also be pleased to offer her a long-overdue Merit Award.

'Yes, it *is* none too soon,' responds Linda, trying nevertheless to hide the surprise in her voice. 'If that moron in Phase Two Marg. deserves one, then so do I.' And snorts.

The Merit Award has come about because while attending a 'Who Are We?' course, Mr Foley has experienced a management epiphany. He has learned that every organisation has to contain at least one person whom the others can hate: a focus of all hostility and loathing. In Linda Sugden's absence, Butter Mountain morale has been in decline, in-fighting and apathy on the increase. Mr Foley can now say to her, and mean it, that the place just hasn't been the same.

Linda is pleased, but does her best to hide it.

'See you later then,' she tells Foley, and crashes down

the receiver. 'Uh-huh,' she grunts to herself. Then mutters, 'They're probably giving everyone one. If Higgins gets one, I'm resigning on the spot.'

She swigs down the last gulp of her Nescafé, dons her bottle-green mac with the flaps, tethers Katie-Koo to the cot with a little silken harness (apricot) from Hooper Babywear, and strides off to the Ministry to claim her rightful due.

*　　*　　*

The next time I went to Dr Stern's office, his name had gone from the door, and there was no sign of the calendar, either. Dr Appleby let me in. She was in charge now. She had grey hair and a smile that seemed pinned to her face like a fashion accessory. Phoney, but welcome nonetheless. There hadn't been much smiling in Manxheath lately, and the laughter wasn't healthy. Whoever was doing it always looked like someone being strangled. But don't get me wrong: I didn't trust her. I wouldn't make the mistake of trusting a doctor three times, would I?

So when she started talking, I just listened. She was tense. The smile seemed to get out of hand, and started to crawl about her face. Her embarrassment grew until she was the colour of raw beef. She hesitated over each word, and faltered her way along the hazardous geology of what she was trying to say, as though at any moment she and her career might topple into a mammoth crevasse. My unlawful imprisonment at Manxheath was clearly a sensitive topic. She took half an hour to spit it out, so I'll summarise. Your assessment shows that you are a perfectly normal young woman and I have no idea why you are here. This is very serious. You claim that Dr Stern put you on a compulsory section, but we have no proof of this apart from some ashes in his bin. However, from what we understand, you were here originally to visit your mother. How you came to be an in-patient on medication, we cannot fathom. Can you help us, Mrs Stevenson? If there is further evidence of misconduct on the part of Dr Stern, we'll need to record it, I'm afraid. Never in my twenty-five years' experience of the mental health system . . .

By the end of it, she looked shagged out. I felt like offering her some chicken and mushroom cup-a-soup from the machine.

'Oh I couldn't testify against him,' I said eventually. 'We were lovers, you see. We used to do it here on the desk, sometimes.'

This seemed to be the last straw for the poor psychiatrist. In a strangulated voice, she asked me to excuse her. She had some urgent phone calls to make. Was I, er, considering pressing assault charges? And more words came creaking over the dangerous terrain: sensitive issue, jeopardise the reputation of, already severely embarrassed by, new management, press enquiries, detoxification of all patients. Regret. We deeply regret. We regret deeply.

She stood up to shake my hand, but I said, 'You don't understand.' I was enjoying myself for the first time in ages. 'Dr Stern was a wonderful lover. I had fabulous orgasms.'

The truth can be a killer.

She sat down in her chair with a plonk and went white. She told me, shakily that I was free to go, and that the Health Service apologised for the administrative error that had led to my being holed up here on heavy-duty medication for so long.

But I'm not stupid. I said I wanted that in writing.

She said, 'Of course,' quite coldly, looking at me sideways, and filling out a form.

And I want my file, Dr Apple Tree, I told her. The one marked 'Hazel Stevenson'.

'Appleby. But it's hospital property. And I haven't studied it all yet.'

'You have no right to,' I said. 'As you've admitted yourself, I should never have been here. I'm going to destroy that file personally. Or you'll be hearing more about my orgasms, and in public. My orgasms, Dr Apple Tree, will be on *News at Ten*. It will be the end of the Manxheath Institute of Challenged Stability.'

And I took the mustard-yellow file from the shelf right under her nose. I left. When I glanced back through the open door I saw she was slumped in the chair doing some sort of breathing exercise. So off I went.

This was nothing compared to what I was about to do.

I'd thought it all through, hadn't I.

FIFTEEN

Time at the Institute had been as long as a piece of string; the two months I'd spent there might as well have been two minutes, or two centuries.

When I walked out of reception there was a big sky with scutters of clouds, and a west wind bearing the burnt plastic smell of the Cheeseway Works. It evoked a strange nostalgia. Linda and I always used to know when they were mixing the beige. The smell of the plastic dye was different. They usually did beige on Thursdays, but today was Friday, Monica Fletcher had told me, because Friday used to be the day she had her hair done and it always gave her a pang of yearning for the days when the world was normal. I breathed in deeply, re-absorbing the pedal-bins of my past into my blood. But when I exhaled, it was with a new sense of myself – free, and cathartically changed.

Standing in the porch, I stared at the patch of lawn where I reckoned the greenhouse had stood. It was covered with clumps of daffodils with yellowing leaves and papery flowers past their prime. The grass was lush; it would soon need mowing. Birds pecked for worms, jostled by the wind. There was no trace of the greenhouse – not even a patch of destroyed turf where it had stood. I can't say I felt anything either way, in the emotion department.

I walked down the drive and out. At the front gates I swung round suddenly, on impulse, and looked back. The Manxheath Institute of Challenged Stability stood solid as a colossus, surrounded by noble swaying trees. Still nothing registered, except the reflection that, if you had the misfortune to have a friend or relative afflicted by insanity, you'd feel happy they were in there, surrounded by thick walls, sensible lino, and homely settees. And you'd recognise that this place, say what you will of its management practices, would do them proud.

I walked down the street, past the Pay and Display, and into Jaycote's Park. One of my few memories of Dad was rooted here, on this very path. He and Linda were throwing a frisbee – Linda with haphazard violence, he with precision and grace. When the man called Dad swung his arm to hurl the plastic disc high into the air I saw a huge hole in the armpit of his purple pullover, showing an orange floral shirt underneath. It was the sixties.

I reached the children's play area. There was no one else in sight, so I plonked myself on a tiny merry-go-round. It squeaked as I pushed myself round in a slow arc. I did five circuits, which on a clock, I calculated, is two days and a night, then stopped. The iron was cold.

Later, after Dad had gone to New Zealand with the woman from the petrol-station, Linda and I used to play here together, in the days when it was just a row of swings, a slide, and a see-saw, Ma over on a far bench with her shopping bags and her *Pocket Floral Encyclopedia*.

Me and Linda see-sawing: when Linda was up, I was down. When Linda was down, I was up.

Linda shrieking, 'Snot fair! You're up for longer because I'm heavier than you!'

Me shrieking back, 'Tiz fair! The one who's heavier can decide when to push. You could leave me stuck up here for ever if you wanted.'

Glamour versus control.

Ma calling, 'OK, wee brats, you can stop bickering, 'cos it's time to go!'

Now, another slow squeaking circuit on the merry-go-round.

Control was what I was after now. Look where patio furniture had got me. I would retrace my steps back to the Hopeworth. It could be my base for a week or so, while I firmed up my plans. I'd treat it as a sort of departure lounge – a decompression chamber *en route* to so-called solid ground. And it was right next to the park where I was sitting. From the merry-go-round I could see the window of the hotel room Billy and I had stayed in when we left Gregory. That's Gridiron for you. Everything's within spitting distance of something else.

The more I thought about the idea, the better I liked it. The Hopeworth's soothing muzak, laundered napkins, heavy ashtrays, and crisp sheets all stated, 'The world is a friendly place.' Adding, 'And you, Mrs Stevenson, are sane.'

Suddenly, I decided to change my name.

'Morning, madam,' chirruped two uniformed receptionists as I sailed in.

'I'm Hazel Sugden,' I blurted.

'Yes, Miss Sugden,' said the man with the big hair. 'We remember you from before.'

'I like the new look,' said the woman wearing a lot of gold. 'Been on holiday, then?'

'Sort of,' I replied. 'A rest cure.'

They smiled genially. Unlike the psychiatrists, they didn't care if I was lying.

'Any calls for me?' I asked gaily as I could. 'Under Sugden or Stevenson?'

Obviously I would never see the world in the same way again.

'No, Miss Sugden, I don't think there's anything in the message book as yet,' said the woman, riffling through. 'Nope. Jason will show you to your room.'

As I followed the narrow-hipped Jason to the lifts, I thought: So far, so normal. And no news from Greg. In fact, I wasn't too worried that he'd find me. With all the incriminating information I had on him, there wasn't much he could do. When we reached Room 308, double with cot, I tipped Jason, unpacked my suitcase (clothes, shoes, macramé work and forty women's magazines), showered with mauve shower gel, applied some Bloody Hell lipstick and fought my way into a strangely cut cotton dress I couldn't remember wearing before, let alone buying.

Before I went out again, I took a moment to look at my hospital case notes. I have to admit that I blushed with shame and anger when I read them. Among other things, Ishmael had written: 'A woman of average intelligence, capable of paranoia and neurosis. Mother-fixated, sexually frustrated, poss. de Cleranbault's syndrome. Depressed. Candidate for Section?'

That bit was dated the day after he'd taken me to dinner in Mutton Acre and I'd had that dream about us making love which was so real that it had had to be true.

Downstairs, in the Hopeworth Executive Centre, I photocopied the page. I didn't have any plans for it, except one day, when I had the courage, to do what Linda would do: frame it and hang it on a wall.

I still haven't got round to doing this.

I also photocopied a few other pages from the yellow

file I'd taken from Dr Appleby, and wrote a letter to go with it.

I'd spent quite a lot of time thinking in Manxheath. Thinking, mostly, about how to go about getting some dignity. Linda was keen on self-respect as a concept, and on revenge as a method of acquiring it, and I suppose it was her banging on about human rights that made me think perhaps I was owed some. Once I'd started to think that, it snowballed into a plan, with the help of the book Linda lent me. I'd read it in between TV game shows.

The book, *Ready, Steady, Go For It!*, by the American educator Klaus G. Armstrong, turned out to be quite heady stuff.

'Put yourself first,' he writes. 'Because your first duty is towards YOU. Prioritise your needs, e.g.,

1. Money
2. Power
3. Self-fulfilment
4. Security

etc. Now focus on that. Run through that list every night before you go to sleep, and tell yourself: I CAN HAVE ANYTHING I WANT.'

I did what he suggested, focusing particularly on the money because I reckoned most other things would be attainable once I was rich.

'Lay solid plans,' writes Klaus G. Armstrong, 'and your fantasies can become reality.'

His revolutionary ideas, coming when they did, turned out to be quite a godsend.

It didn't take long to get the letter ready. It was friendly, firm and businesslike ('Dear Root'), and it outlined the deal in what I thought was quite eloquent language. Nothing overtly threatening: just the facts of the matter ('Please find enclosed copies of some relevant pages of the GR218 document'), and a list of pros and cons, to save Root Hooper the trouble of working them out for himself. I don't know much about business, but I do know, thanks to Klaus G. Armstrong, that if you're a successful businessman you'll recognise when some discreet damage limitation is necessary.

A quarter of a million is nothing to people like Hooper, compared to shame, vilification and a possible jail sentence.

I explained in my letter that what I was sending him was just a small sample of what was in the file. As he would see, his name featured prominently as a projected sponsor for the experiments my husband had incubated. Experiments which not only by-passed the law, but operated in a different orbit altogether. I was quite prepared, I explained, to tell the whole story to the police. The only thing that would stop me was a great deal of money, in cash. (Sincerely yours, etc.)

I prepared an envelope for the personal attention of Mr Root Hooper, President, The Hooper Fertility Foundation, wrote 'Private and Confidential' on the back, and slipped it into my handbag with the letter.

'The phrase "Why not?" should be your catchword,' writes Klaus G. Armstrong in his conclusion. 'So ready, steady, GO FOR IT!'

Later, at the bank, it turned out to be surprisingly easy to withdraw all the money in the 'Dr and Mrs Stevenson' account and put it in another bank account in the name of Hazel Sugden. So that was another ten thousand pounds. Well, you need money to start a new life, don't you.

Kidnapping my son was no problem, either. I did it by taxi, mid-morning, when I was sure Gregory would be out. The street was quiet. The flowering cherries were in bloom and fallen petals covered the pavement, so that when I stepped out of the taxi my feet sank into a mish-mash of pink snowflakes. There is always something poignant about late spring: it's the time of year when you may accidentally step on a newly hatched baby bird, toppled from its nest by a cuckoo or kamikazed on its virgin flight. I told the Zippikab driver to wait there while I fetched my son. It had been raining, and the smell of the Cheeseways had been rinsed from the air and replaced by a smell I love: wet tarmac.

I opened the side gate and trod as quietly as I could down the narrow gravel passageway that leads round the side of the house to the garden. Halfway along, I heard Billy talking to himself in his little piping voice. I couldn't make out all the words. Then suddenly I clapped eyes on him: a curly-haired, stumpy little shape in muddy yellow wellington boots with frog faces on them. I caught my breath. He was bigger. The sight of his hooded anorak brought a painful lump to my throat. He was trying to stuff an earthworm into the cabin of a toy bulldozer. His face showed deep concentration. I heard him say, 'You be the driver.'

Then I caught sight of someone else: behind a line of flapping clothes, an auntyish-looking woman in her fifties was hanging out washing. Briefly distracted, I screwed up my eyes to inspect it, but saw no sign of the satin red knickers with fancy bows and huge whaleboned peek-a-boo bras I imagined Ruby Gonzalez wearing; just Greg's slightly worn Y-fronts. The nanny-woman stepped out to reach for another pillow-case and I dodged behind a forsythia. Neither Billy nor the nanny-woman, who later turned out to have the absurd name of Mrs Goody, had seen me.

I waited till she ran out of pegs and as soon as she went off to get more I plunged out through the dwarf conifers and grabbed my little lad by the scruff. He dropped his bulldozer but kept a tight hold of the worm. He started to scream but I slapped my hand over his mouth and kept it there until we were in the street and he recognised me and forced it off to fling his arms round me and cover me in a mixture of saliva and snot. Then we jumped in the Zippikab and whooshed off into town, hugging each other until we nearly choked.

Over a Big Mac, I got my breath back and sobbed with relief. How he'd grown. He was talking now, proper words.

'I love you, Mummy,' he said. 'Mummy, I'm a big boy now. Bigger than a lobster but smaller than a cupboard. Aren't I?'

'Have you swallowed a junior dictionary?' I asked through my tears. He was sitting on my lap eating a huge burger, posting french fries into my mouth, and smearing ketchup on his face, and needing his nose wiped, and wanting apple pie, all at once. I loved him so much my heart hurt.

'Ruby's in an aeroplane. Ruby's a silly bum-bum, and I'm making her mud soup. Baby too. Daddy went all funny. Chips, Mummy, I want chips as well. Mrs Goody's a smelly lady. She's a silly bum-bum as well, but I can kill flies now. I just want my mummy. And chips. One for you and hundreds for Billy.'

'You're staying with me from now on,' I told him. 'You're going to live with Mummy.'

'For ever and ever?'

'Until you're about eighteen, I should think.'

'I'm two.'

'Well then. We've got plenty of time.'

'Mum.'

'Yes, Billy?'

'D'you know something?'

'What?'

'I only wear nappies at night now. Not in daytime.'

So Mrs Goody can't have been all bad.

At the post office, we discovered that Billy's worm had died in his pocket. It smelt bad, and had dried somewhat. After a moment's hesitation I agreed to let him put it in the envelope before I sealed it. Billy posted the letter to Root Hooper. I lifted him up to the mouth of the letterbox and we watched the envelope slide down its throat.

Then we went back to the hotel room and pretended to be stegosauruses until Billy was so exhausted he fell asleep in my arms. I settled him in the cot, dialled Linda's number, and left a message on her answerphone telling her I was out of Manxheath and off the drugs. She could reach me at the Hopeworth in Room 308, double with cot.

'Give me a call when you've accomplished your mission,' I said. 'And we'll celebrate.'

Linda was cooking something, too.

*   *   *

Linda was boarding a train bound for the West. She was wearing a loudly patterned scarf fastened by a giant buckle brooch, and carrying a Moses basket containing a sleeping baby. She entered a second-class smoking carriage, and settled herself down as if she wasn't planning to move from her seat during the three-hour journey. From a large striped nylon bag she hauled the *Daily Mail*, some anchovy sandwiches, a thermos of Nescafé, and a bottle of formula milk for the baby. Departure had been delayed slightly, and the man who was seeing her off at the platform hung about near the window, looking gangly and foolish.

'Go away!' she mouthed, her lips so close to the glass

that her breath formed an oval patch of condensation. 'I'll see you when I get back.'

And she gave a small, annoyed wave. Duncan was wearing his dark-blue blazer bearing the British Telecom logo. His arms were too long for its sleeves. He reached on tiptoe to take another look at the baby, and blew it a sad kiss as though it was the last he'd see of her. Which, if all went according to plan, it would be.

Linda sank back in her seat, lit a cigarette, and heaved out her reading matter. Linda had never shared Ma's dangerously omnivorous taste in books; she was always strictly a spy thriller and management handbook reader. But today's reading matter was different. This was more like a work project. Projects have always been Linda's forte. We are talking about the woman who dreamed up a new kind of Arctic iceberg, clad in shark-proof plastic. We are talking about the woman who decided that a pulverised locust product be incorporated in margarine as a thickening and proteinising agent. We are talking about someone who takes her projects seriously.

Today's project is less of a challenge, perhaps, than Fatberg or Protomarg, but it's fascinating nonetheless. And it begins with some basic research, in the form of a thick brochure and a collection of articles and photo-features organised in a cardboard file, each with text highlighted and colour-coded in marker pen. She lays them neatly on the table in front of her and starts to read methodically. Duncan shrugs his shoulders and begins to shuffle his way up the platform to the exit. Just then the train starts to move, and he turns to wave, but as the carriage slides off, Linda has already entered the extravagant and bizarre new territory of her glossy brochure, and left Gridiron far behind.

She is in the House of God. The building she once saw in maquette form on the fateful day of her visit to the

Holy Hour production offices is now a gleaming reality, thanks to Ron's wizardry and the tireless voluntary work of born-again carpenters, electricians, engineers and painter-decorators. Certain weddings, those that celebrate a marriage doomed to fail, always feature an extravagantly optimistic multi-tiered wedding-cake, next to which the then-happy couple are photographed. Hazel had one, with ribbons and knobs on. The House of God, reflects Linda, resembles such a cake. It is built largely of a white cement and granite-chip composite called 'reconstituted stone'. Linda polishes off her sandwiches and unleashes a belch whose odour permeates the carriage. Then she lifts her head to glare accusingly at her fellow-passengers.

The House of God is, say the background articles, a triumph of market research, thanks to interactive computer technology. Witness the platforms and revolving doors, the laminated glass floors, the mirrored walls, the *trompe-l'oeil* ceilings, and the impressive central stage which boasts a host of ingeniously devised and cunningly crafted design features. Witness the state-of-the-art gymnasium, the two-, three-, and five-star restaurant facilities, the Terrestrial Communications Centre with its bank of telephones and faxes for the busy executive worshipper, and the Fantasy Garden for the kiddies. Witness a miracle.

Pilgrims have been flocking to the House of God in their thousands. It's cheaper than a theme park, and better for the waistline. To mention nothing of the soul.

Linda puts the brochure down, inhales smoke deep into her lungs, and gazes out of the window at the red-brick of Gridiron suburbia streaking past.

The soul. Following her brief and bruising encounter with religion, my sister is scathing about the idea of the soul. In the aftermath of her betrayal by Vernon Carmichael, her problem-solving mind has wrestled valiantly with the old chestnut of the existence of God – this she confides to me later – but has reached an epistemological cul-de-sac. Being a Mensa member is no help.

So fuck it all.

And fuck the Reverend Carmichael in particular.

She'd told me about her plan.

'See it as a form of slow-release capsule,' she'd said mysteriously. 'By the time it all dawns on him, it'll be too late.'

Now she re-opens her research file and smiles over her anchovy sandwich crusts with so much glee that the ticket-inspector has to take a second look to make sure she isn't suffering from colonic cramp, featured in the First Aid manual. There's certainly a pungent smell in the vicinity. The countryside skitters past, and as Linda speeds towards the House of God with her bundle of perfection, she sings a thumping religious ditty, with tambourines, a light, Eurovision drum-beat, and soprano parts for the ladies.

Today's the day
The time is now
Let Jesus in
It's bollocks hour!

This is her own variation.

*   *   *

Manxheath Institute of Total Dysfunction
Dear departed Brendan,
    Holding up there OK? Treat you well, do they? Good. Well, that's enough of your news. Here's mine.

Who'd have thought it: a new member. From the wrong side of the tracks, this time. An old face from days gone by. Remember Dr Ishmael Stern? Well, you wouldn't recognise him now; his wardrobe's taken quite a nosedive. Gone is Armani. The silk shirts, likewise, *disparus*. Goodbye, Fifth Avenue chic, hello, M & S leisure slax. Our cardiganed friend sits in a chair, most days, watching television. This seems to be the standard routine for newcomers. It's what Hazel did, before she buggered off without so much as a wee hanky-wave. I asked our son-in-law Gregory where she was, when he dropped by like a grim reaper, but he said how should he know, he'd come looking for her himself, seeing as she'd 'stolen' Billy from a certain Mrs Goody when her back was turned.

'Goody for her,' I said, but Gregory didn't get the joke.

A fog of guilt seemed to cling to him, like that visible body odour you see on the TV in the anti-perspirant ad. He turned on his heel to slope off, but Dr Stern, who'd been sitting all morning with his eyes glazed over, nursing a cup of cold Horlicks, suddenly tuned in at the sound of his voice.

'Colleague!' he called out from the deep wing-sided armchair, the best one in the whole joint, which we clientele had agreed to let him have for old times' sake.

Greg didn't recognise him at first, and when he did, the shock on his face (the cleanest shave in the North, I always thought, which all goes to show you should never trust a well-shaven man), the shock and the horror were a sight to see. His eyes had the look of sheep on the way to the abattoir. To Arabs, apparently, those thunderstruck eyes are a delicacy.

'Good God!'

That's our son-in-law Greg, expostulating in Ishmael's

direction. Ishmael is what we've taken to calling Dr Stern, now he's minus his dignity. It's friendlier, and it makes him seem like someone else – not the man we all knew as Dr S., who wore a white coat, and had us all stored on floppy disc, and broke my daughter's heart. This is Dr Stern normalised, pared down to the bone, the thing we laughingly call personality laid bare, a live, vulnerable specimen on the shiny lino of the Day Room.

'What on earth happened to you?' asked Greg stupidly. 'Why aren't you running the hospital?'

Ishmael's laugh was dry as a central-heating cough.

'Don't you read the newspapers? I've been *struck off*. Incompetence due to insanity. A patient of mine killed herself rather messily, and they found your *mother-in-law* here in possession of a whole arsenal of mind-altering medication. Enough to cook anyone's goose. So now I'm a voluntary patient in my own hospital. It's a sort of poetic reincarnation. I've been relaxing. Watching television. A bit of *clay* work. Observing the new management flushing out the old, and learning to Think in New Ways. *Dr Apple Tree*, we call her. Quite the *green fascist*, but effective. I expect you're worried about those incriminating *files*.'

He paused, for full effect, while Greg grabbed on to a handy Zimmer frame. He stood motionless, turning the colour that I call 'white with a hint of urine'. I swear, I could hear his aortic sphincters thundering away. Now watch this bit. He staggers along with the walking frame, towards Dr S., or should I say ex-Doctor. His knuckles are clenched on the aluminium, bloodless.

'Where are they?' he hisses, his voice all cracking up with strain.

But Ishmael just cough-laughs.

Then suddenly Greg's cast off the Zimmer frame and

grabbed him! And there they are rolling around on the floor wrestling, with the television blaring *Holy Hour* behind them.

Talk about entertainment.

Thump. Crunch. Praise the Lord. Weugh.

Did you ever see that dirty film, *Women in Love*, directed by Ken Russell? It was showing on the TV last week. A passionate story of sexual obsession, the *Radio Times* called it. Well, it was like when they wrestled there, the two men. One was Oliver Reed, naked. The other one, the good-looking one, he was naked too. You kept trying to catch a glimpse of their appendages, but Ken Russell is a clever director and doesn't show you too much of a good thing.

'You'll have to video it and do a freeze-frame if you want a proper look,' I told Monica Fletcher. So we'd sighed and just settled for the muscular buttocks, and Monica had snivelled at the violence.

Bam. Geuk. Clonk.

On and on it went, until you couldn't tell one from the other; they merged like a ganglion of Plasticine, the colours all squoilering together, and lots of grunting. But it all comes to a lurching halt when Dr Appleby enters and stops them with a single bark. They separate into individuals; one grey pinstripe, the other casual. Greg stands up and brushes himself down. He loosens his tie, which is half strangling him, with a tug. Ishmael has lost two buttons off his cable-knit cardie but he's sitting on the floor there and laughing painfully and showing his nice teeth.

'What's going on?' says Dr Appleby.

Her face is hard as a gingernut.

My turn to stir the excrement a bit, with my huge ladle. Old habits die hard, as they used to keep telling us in the socially vulnerable knitting circle, when it was a going concern.

'Fighting over my precious Hazel,' I tell her.

'Who is this man?' she asks, pointing at Greg, who's now gathering up the contents of his wallet.

I see a cheque book under the sofa, but I don't say anything.

'He is my son-in-law, Gregory Paul Stevenson.' This loudly, with the contempt it deserves.

'May I ask what you're doing here?' she asks him.

All the staff have a normal voice and a special one reserved for visitors. It's the speaking-to-visitors one she directs at him now, but there's something held in check about it, like it could quickly go the other way.

'I was looking for my wife,' says Greg shiftily. 'And then this patient of yours attacked me.'

But Ishmael said nothing. His eyes were on *Holy Hour*. He was looking for bargains in another department. Before she left, Hazel said she reckoned he was just pretending to be a person of challenged stability, to escape punishment, but my bones tell me he's a true convert. What's this if it isn't punishment?

'Have you signed in as a visitor?' Dr Appleby was asking Gregory snakily.

The smile had returned, but it wasn't the full works.

'I'm terribly sorry, Doctor,' Greg was saying. 'Please forgive me. As you've no doubt diagnosed, I'm in a bit of a distraught state.' He tried to force a chuckle, but he wasn't fooling anyone. 'My wife Hazel – I thought she might be here. She was a patient – '

'Hazel Stevenson? I've discharged her,' smiled Apple Tree. 'There's nothing wrong with her. She was misdiagnosed and then inappropriately medicated. And then suffering withdrawal. An appalling mistake, due to an administrative error on the part of Dr Stern here, who as you see is experiencing deep regret. There's been a full inquiry. We're currently making sweeping changes.

In the meantime we do apologise to you, Mr Stevenson. Your wife says she won't be pressing charges against the hospital. We've allowed her to take her file with her, which is standard policy in such cases.'

Which was all he wanted to know, of course. He was out before you could say hidden agenda, with a wobbly look about the jaw that spelt big trouble. Ishmael and I settled down in front of the television. It was either that or scream some more over Isabella. I've screamed myself hoarse lately; I deserve a break. Monica joined us. *Holy Hour* is about the only thing she can watch without getting hysterical. (Her Ken Russell days are over.) Actually she doesn't so much watch, as stand in front of the television with her eyes closed and her arm in the air, pushing upwards, palm out, in time with the music, like there's an invisible tent above her head. Sometimes she tries out her tongues, or goes into a caterwauling routine that she calls 'harmonics'. It's all quite experimental. What do you think of the Reverend Carmichael's House of God, then? Is it as good as the real thing, or wouldn't you know? Monica sent off for one of those T-shirts with a huge mackerel on.

Yours sincerely,
Moira Sugden

PS: Vegetarian lasagne and fruit cup with live yoghurt again tonight!

SIXTEEN

Billy and I were playing hunt-the-miniature-soap when the phone rang, and I had to crawl out from under the bed to get it. It was Linda calling from a phone box in the House of God's Terrestrial Communications Centre.

'Quick, switch on the TV and see what the Wanker's done now, to cover his tracks!' she shrieked down the line.

Not quite what I was expecting to hear.

'Who's the Wanker?' I asked, and she explained it was my husband.

Apparently she'd always called him that, behind my back and his. Despite everything, I felt slightly stung.

'Have you dumped the package?' I asked.

'Not yet. After the Service. She's asleep. Everything's fine. But I think you should see what he's up to. Turn on your television right this minute.'

I caught the sound of choirs singing in the background as she-who-must-be-obeyed hung up. I scrambled on to the giant bed and pressed the remote control; the screen flickered on above me.

And there it was, in flames, on live television: the Fertility Management Centre.

It was impressive; some of the fire seemed to be

burning blue, and the late afternoon sky was black-ened with rising tatters of detritus, while helicopters whirred above like hungry mosquitoes. It reminded me, curiously, of another, smaller fire, the one in which I'd burned Gregory's matchstick church. The Airfix models would have gone the same way if Jane hadn't intervened. But this was the real thing, and my adrenalin stirred. Belches of green and grey smoke formed noxious cumuli which sent the firemen scuttling for their walkie-talkies to say Alpha Roger; a wobbly camera panned from a cageful of barbecued laboratory rats to a general view of the disaster. It looked expensive. The chief fire officer on site was being interviewed by the local reporter, who was clearly having some sort of asthma attack. The fire officer, his eyes also streaming, agreed it was definitely the worst fire he'd seen in his long career in the fire-fighting services in this area.

'And will you be looking into the possibility of arson?' spluttered the reporter.

'Yes, as I say, we shall doubtless, hopefully, be investigating the possibility of arson.'

'Any clues so far, officer?'

'No clues so far,' coughed the fire officer.

'A possibility, then, that we can't rule out a link between the hostility of the Holy Task Force to the Perfect Baby Project that was partly housed here, and the present, er, fire?'

'Nothing ruled out for the moment, now if you'll excuse me.'

The reporter turned his sooty face to the camera and put on one of those expressions that they like to use at disaster scenes. He looked like he might die.

'So. Live from the scene, no clues as yet, but one thing is certain, nobody will be coming to any conclusions as to the nature and cause of this fire until they've managed to extinguish it.'

A fit of coughing overtook him, but he soldiered on. 'Now back to Patrick in the studio.'

One last glimpse of the wall of flame, and then on to junior royalty competing in an egg-and-spoon race at a charity event. So Gregory was trying to destroy the evidence by sending the whole mess up in smoke. I'd better move quickly. I called a Zippikab, cancelled the cheese and pineapple pizza with extra mushroom I'd ordered from room service, and stuffed Billy into his duffel coat.

Soon we were speeding through the wet streets of Gridiron towards the Fertility Management Centre, moths to the flame.

You are what you make. Is it then stating the all-too-obvious to point out that when you burn what you have made, you are doing something of an enormity close to suicide? I could have watched Greg's life's work blaze all night. It hissed and burped a pitiful song of folly.

Billy was in seventh heaven: police cars, ambulances, firemen, sirens going, blue lights flashing, heat, flames, soot, smoke, and men of action with calloused hands doing brave deeds with elbow grease and technology, killing the dragon and wiping their brows on oily rags. A scene of heroes. I approached the least heroic-looking, a callow police officer with a weak and incompetent lower lip, perhaps a trainee, who was taking notes and stammering into a walkie-talkie.

I said, 'Excuse me, officer. I think I know who started this fire.'

He said, 'Beg pardon, madam?' The lip hung loose as though a muscle had died.

I said, 'Get your notepad and write this name down: Dr Gregory Stevenson. Got that?'

He said, 'Beg pardon, madam?'

I had chosen well. Eventually, despite his exploded biro, he got the name down, and a muddled grasp of why he was making a record of it.

'So you're alleging, madam, that a certain Gregory Stevenson deliberately started this fire as an act of arson, to destroy some kind of, er, evidence about another, er, crime to do with babies. Now, madam, can I take your name?'

But by then I was slamming the door of my waiting Zippikab. Through the window, Billy waved goodbye to the trainee policeman and we sped off into the night.

*   *   *

Linda slid out of the shadows as the organ began to tune up and squeezed into the last remaining space in a pew near the front. She put the basket containing Katie-Koo, three nappies and a bottle of milk on the floor, out of sight. She had given the Perfect Baby a hefty tranquilliser, supplied from our mother's emergency stash of drugs. It never hurts to be sure. Katie-Koo would sleep for at least five more hours. Long enough. The whole House of God compound was a smoke-free zone, so Linda was keeping her nerves at bay by chain-sucking her way through a packet of ultra-strong medicinal lozenges. Katie-Koo and Carmichael were made for one another, she reflected, inhaling a rush of searingly cold mint. The bogus angel and the bogus saint.

The cathedral was filling up with track-suited worshippers, some of them in wheelchairs, bearing gifts for the altar: cans of tinned tuna, mostly, from what Linda could make out; bananas, a lardicake, some smoky bacon crisps, a bunch of tulips. Every day was harvest festival at the House of God.

Slowly, the lights were dimming to almost black and for a second there was silence before the TV show countdown started and the giant screen ran the opening sequence of *Holy Hour*, while portentous music groaned from a specially modified organ steered by twin dwarfs in red velvet suits.

An elderly gent with abnormally freckled ears was seated next to Linda; as she stared accusingly at his profile, he began to babble something very fast as the music groaned and wavered to a plateau of vibration. Others around her joined in, and soon everyone was putting in their ha'porth. Linda exhaled in frustration. There was a time, not so very long ago, when the Lord had whispered to her soul, too.

Abandoned again!

A good slogan for a Love Heart.

She'd applied for a new job. Euro Ag. Planning in Brussels, in charge of a whole department. If there was any justice in the world, once this business was finished, she'd be an international commuter with an apartment overlooking the Mannekin Piss and her own space in the executive car-park. Sometimes you just know when it's time to move on.

Linda manoeuvred the lozenge to the back of her mouth, crunched and reeled in shock at the peppermint blast, which irrigated her nasal passages and temporarily deafened her. She reached for a baby-wipe from the Moses basket, blew her nose in it noisily, and stuffed the soggy mess in the suggestion box in front of her. The freckle-eared gent next to her was in a trance.

Now, up on the stage, a cloud of dry ice had begun to crawl across the stage, and from its epicentre a huge metallic rocket-headed cylinder was forcing its

way upward like a thrusting bud. It reminded Linda
of something, but she couldn't quite work out what.
The cylinder grew to twice the height of a man, and then
suddenly its sheath retracted to reveal the barrel-shaped
figure of Carmichael in flowing robes of royal blue. A
cheer went up from the crowd as he leaped out of the
contraption, which closed itself again and shrunk away
into its socket in the stage.

A penis, Linda realised suddenly: that's what. She
recalled the Reverend's unusual member and shuddered.

Meanwhile the Reverend's eyes were skimming the
congregation.

'Friends,' he said in that voice of oil and honey
Linda knew so well. 'Welcome. Welcome to God's
home.'

A sigh spread around the huge hall as the Reverend,
following a chord from a battery of guitars behind him,
began to croon the *Holy Hour* theme:

Today's the day
The time is now
Let Jesus in
It's *Holy Hour*!

The crowd joined in, and none sang more loudly and
with more crazed abandon than my sister Linda.

Today's sermon was apt, for Carmichael was nothing
if not a man who knew exactly when and how to cash
in on a news story. These things are an instinct, like sex,
or the knowledge of right and wrong.

When the applause and murmuring had hushed, he
pulled out a monstrously shiny red apple from his
cassock and held it aloft. In the television lights, its
redness was shocking.

Then he spoke. Pirated cassettes exist of what he said, and what happened afterwards, though the official videos have all been confiscated and destroyed.

He said, 'The Apple of Knowledge looked as tempting and as succulent, ladies and gentlemen, as this.'

There was a murmur. Carmichael brought the apple close to his face and sniffed it elaborately, breathing in deep.

'Mmmm!' he hummed slowly. 'The perfume! Wonderful! Gorgeous! Now, folks – wouldn't you just like a bite?'

The audience shuddered and recoiled with mutterings of, 'No way!'

'Come on now, don't be shy!' urged the preacher. 'You, sir! Come and take a bite of the Apple of Knowledge! That's what the snake said to Eve and then to Adam. Come and bite into my tasty fruit! Let yourself be tempted!'

The man shook his head vehemently as Carmichael thrust the apple at his face.

'Bless you,' murmured Carmichael, withdrawing, and made the sign of the cross in the air.

'Bless you, bless you, O ye folk. If only Adam and Eve had been like you.'

Now he shoves the apple under the nose of an elderly woman in the front row.

'You, madam! Bite into the Apple of Knowledge and taste original sin!'

The woman bellows, 'No, sir! I will not! Not for all the tea in China!'

Her friend, sitting next to her, adds for emphasis, 'No way, José.'

'And rightly not, dear madams, rightly not!' responds the preacher with *gravitas,* staring mournfully at the apple in his hand. He looks up and lets his eyes scan the crowd before him slowly, as though inhaling them individually.

'And why, folks? Because the Bible has taught us our lesson about knowledge and it's right there in Genesis!'

And he starts pacing the stage with sudden, violent energy.

'Chapter three, verse thirteen: "Eve has partaken thereof, and the Lord God said unto the woman, *What is this thou hast done?*"'

'And what did Eve say to that, ladies and gentlemen?

'She said, "The serpent beguiled me, and I did eat."'

'And so the Lord had no choice, did He, but to banish both her and Adam because of their greed and their curiosity. He sent them forth, saying thorns also and thistles may it bring thee, this knowledge, and thou shalt eat nought but bread and the herb of the field. Which is a strictly vegan diet, folks.'

He holds the apple aloft again.

'Now, ladies and gentlemen – still no takers? Well, I know of one man who partook. A man who, in his folly and pride, took it upon himself to bite into this Apple of Knowledge!'

A murmur from the audience.

'Shall I tell you his name, ladies-and-gentlemen-and-children?'

A hushed pause.

'His name is Dr Gregory Stevenson!'

The Reverend gazes up at the apple in his hand, and the camera projects its tempting wholesomeness on to the video wall behind him. Then suddenly he has spun the fruit round to reveal the other side.

A huge and greedy bite has been removed.

The audience gasps.

'Yes, ladies and gentlemen, and so you should be shocked. *That's what a bitten apple looks like.* And now we know what it's done. On the news today, ladies and gentlemen, as you may have heard, the extent of one man's folly was on display for all to marvel at. Dr Gregory Stevenson is on the run from God and righteousness, ladies and gentlemen. Let his folly be an example to us. He bit into this apple you see before you, ladies and gentlemen, and now he is paying God's price.'

The audience boos. The freckle-eared man next to Linda shudders in a spasm of indignation and lets loose a weird groan.

Carmichael is storming out the Bible.

'And Adam and Eve did weep, and God said unto them, "Be thou banished, unworthy children, from mine kingdom, unworthy in my sight. For thou hast tasted of the forbidden fruit and ye shall be outcast from Eden, to eat thistles, as I have said, and bracken and other blasted vegetables of the field".'

He refers to the fire at the Fertility Management Centre as 'God's wrath'. To the police hunting for the missing Dr Stevenson as 'the people's witnesses'. To the whole of Gregory's enterprise as 'an object lesson in grandiosity and vaingloriousness'.

While he preaches eloquently of 'the Frankensteinian folly of false-idol worship', and commits her brother-in-law to the fiery gulags of hell, Linda listens, smiles, and bides her time.

She has calculated that the moment to act is two minutes before the end of the service, when there will be no time for anything else. She sits like a coiled spring as the show continues with jokes, a healing session, a mass blessing, and a final sports prayer.

' . . . and may the Great One see his way clear to removing heretoforth this thorn of misery at the heart of our great national game,' finishes the Reverend, 'and soccer will thrive and flourish as the orange groves on the shores of Galilee.'

'Amen!' calls the congregation. 'Hallelujah!'

The organ music is striking up again, and the Reverend is taking a breath for the final hymn, when a blonde-haired woman, ignoring the glares of the congregation and the frantic waving of the producer, waddles up to the stage brandishing a comatose baby.

Carmichael spots her, and exchanges a look with the producer, who signals to the dwarfs; the rousing hymn-tune dissolves discreetly into soft chords of muzak.

'Please, Reverend,' begs the woman, falling to her knees and holding Katie-Koo aloft like a triumphant goalkeeper with a football.

'Please, Reverend. Bless my afflicted child.'

The producer, relaxing, gives the signal for the camera angle to tighten. Live television takes risks, but nothing much can go wrong when it's a sleeping baby needing a splash of holy water on its gob. Linda grabs the microphone handed to her by a lackey, and starts noisily kissing the hem of Carmichael's robe.

'Reverend. Bless her. Bless her, please,' she mumbles.

A standard enough request in the House of God. Carmichael doesn't recognise Linda. Why should he? She's wearing the wig and specs, and as the koala-man said, he does have a lot of fans.

The Reverend carries around his neck a gold chain from which hangs a small vial of holy tap water for occasions such as these. He unstoppers it and bends down, trickling a few drops on the baby's forehead and making the sign of the cross.

'Bless you, God's creature. May the Big One be with you now and always.'

A sigh from the congregation. Another soul individually blessed; another small but vital redemption in the Lord's name; another mother's heart at peace.

But this is no ordinary mother.

'Take her,' says the woman.

Her voice is suddenly different, harsher. The Reverend stiffens in surprise.

'Beg pardon, madam?'

The woman before him has stumbled ungraciously to her feet, nearly tripping over a footlight.

'Take her,' she says again, commandingly, and shoves the baby at him.

Carmichael clasps the bundle in a reflex, stunned.

Linda, microphone in hand, turns to face the camera.

'This man,' she says, pointing at the Reverend, 'is the father of my child. He seduced me. And may I say now and publicly, to all of you foolish women out there who may be harbouring sexual fantasies about the Reverend here, the copulation that produced this infant lasted precisely thirty-seven seconds and was no great shakes. In fact,' she pauses for effect, 'in fact, he has a disgusting hairy penis and the whole thing was fucking crap.'

Linda's timing could not have been more perfect. The theme tune wipes out the rest of her speech, and the credits roll.

Hallelujah for live television!

*　　*　　*

Linda told me the story breathlessly when she arrived at the Hopeworth later that night with a bottle of champagne, and a plastic replica of the Reverend Carmichael for Billy. She told me about the look on Carmichael's face, and the howl of anguish he gave, and about how the crowd mobbed him, and how she escaped in the mêlée and took the train back to Gridiron minus her wig and specs.

You have to hand it to her.

We filled our glasses and drank a toast to our future. Then we watched the news. Carmichael's love-child and his allegedly hairy penis made the lead story. The search was on for the mystery mother. The congregation were still milling about the House of God like lost sheep: police declared it a 'crisis zone', and installed camp beds for those who refused to leave. Another televangelist was on his way from the States to counsel the nation. Carmichael was said to be in hiding, and at prayer.

Linda was hugging herself with glee. If she could have kissed herself she would have done.

'I did it! He believed me! He thinks he's the father! I've got rid of her! I'm brilliant, brilliant, brilliant!'

Linda's prize pumpkin brain had scored again.

And as it turned out, my smaller, less efficient organ hadn't performed so badly, either. The second story on the news concerned my husband. It was an update on the fire at his clinic. To my delight, things had moved on: an anonymous tip-off had suggested arson, and police were still searching for the man they believed perpetrated it: Dr Gregory Stevenson, 'the controversial doctor at the centre of the Perfect Baby drug row'.

There was only one way to celebrate.

'Come on!' I said to Linda. 'Let's jump on the bed!'

Stifling our giggles so as not to wake Billy, Linda and I wobbled on to the mattress and then began jumping tentatively, with small bounces. The springs were ferociously tight, and shot us upwards with such energising vigour that we grew more daring, and soon we were jumping higher and higher, and then as high as we could, and in perfect synchrony, as though we'd done nothing all these years but practise for this moment, this time of sisterly abandon, in which as I shot upwards, I caught sight of my excited face in the mirror, and my hair flowing up, with Linda just a streak of paint in my side vision, and when I landed, I saw the hole in the knee of Linda's navy tights, and heard her small grunt as she made lift-off, and then I was up again, suspended in air, jumping, jumping, jumping, and the air around us whirled with a strange, speckled light.

When I was up, she was down. And when she was down, I was up.

When the room was spinning, we collapsed and just lay there panting. Feeling the glory and the control.

Gregory's arrest and downfall came about very quickly after that. It turned out that he'd been caught in a sort of pincer movement. In tipping off the callow police trainee, I'd been one half of the pincer.

The other half of the pincer turned out to be quite a surprise. A surprise to me, anyway. Looking at her sad-eyed photo in the scrapbook, though, you can see that it had a certain logic. After all, she'd suffered a betrayal, of sorts, at the hands of Gregory. And a fair share of hell, thanks to Linda and Ma, who'd lumbered her with a normal baby when she felt a perfect one to be her due. So *why not* go out with a bang, Ruby Gonzalez?

Yes. Ruby Gonzalez.

The remains of the Fertility Management Centre were still smoking the next morning, when the famous copy of the *Lancet* appeared. That, too, is in the scrapbook. The lead article is entitled 'Optimum Gene Selection: some Empirical Research', by Dr R. J. Gonzalez. (The J is for Juanita, I have since learned.) I read the article as a straight confession, though it was presented in scientific jargon, offering the facts without any moral interpretation, except for the last line, which was a pure cry for help. Ruby was clearly determined to be remembered as a scientist first and a silly woman second. But facts are all you need to damn yourself, and she did that all right. I sort of took my hat off to her.

The article made enough discrediting claims about her work with my husband to get Ethics Committees, church leaders, and Scotland Yard's Moral Affairs Unit hyperventilating with activity. Within an hour, all the fax machines had clogged. From now on, criminal arson was the least of Gregory's worries.

As I have mentioned, the last line gave some sort of insight into her state of mind. It said, 'This researcher has been forced to conclude that such experiments can only lead to personal tragedy.'

I have to report that when I first read that line I experienced a minor twinge of a grotesque emotion I could not identify, and can't to this day. It was very brief, and for all I know it might have been something else: a pang of indigestion, or my body unconsciously registering a minor earthquake on the other side of the world. I have to report also that, later on, an opaque and clinging burden of pity settled on me when I realised just how much trouble Gregory was in. In the old days I would have stroked his forehead, perhaps, got together something stodgy for dinner to help him forget. Now I just felt weary. You can't jump on a bed for ever.

As usual, the media took over. The hunt was on for Baby A and her mother. Prizes were offered, and several women with babies came forward claiming to be Dr Gonzalez. The answer to her whereabouts was finally provided by the Venezuelan Press Agency. Dr Ruby Gonzalez had issued a statement through her lawyers. She and the child were living in a Trappist nunnery somewhere in Latin America. ('Keeping their traps shut,'

Ma said.) According to the press reports, Ruby had given up medicine. It was the devil's work, according to the new, holy Ruby. She was taking a vow of silence as of today, following this final photo opportunity and press conference, at which the imperfect baby would be on display.

'Nappy rash permitting,' added the statement, reiterating what Ruby's article had stated so unequivocally: that Angelica wasn't perfect at all. Far from it.

Nappy rash did permit, and I have the photos and the cuttings. They, too, are in the scrapbook. Ruby's depressed, resigned look. The scrunched-up face of Angelica yelling at all the fuss. The way Dr Gonzalez finally said, simply, 'That is all,' lowered her cowl, and spoke not another word.

They tracked Greg down shortly afterwards. He was holed up in his new lab, where he'd locked himself into a cupboard full of Petri dishes with an electronic key. They found him clutching a file marked 'Baby A'. He was slapped in Gridiron Correction Facility and charged with arson until they could come up with a strategy to settle the Perfect Gene question once and for all, *vis-à-vis* the law. The great and the good were called in to form an emergency committee.

There was silence from Hooper. A spokesman said he was hunting in Kenya and could not be located at this moment in time. In fact, as a probing television camera dangled at the window of his penthouse discovered, he was at home, kicking the walls, smashing vases, shouting at his mistress, drinking gallons of Mexican beer and throwing darts at a cardboard cutout of a man he kept on the bathroom wall: generally relaxing. Even in disgrace, Hooper gave good television. When he finally emerged, it was with a 'No fucking comment' to the waiting press, before his lawyers whisked him off for consultations.

The consultations must have involved a discussion about damage limitation, because later that day a despatch rider knocked on my door at the Hopeworth and handed me a bulging envelope.

I counted the money.

All two hundred and fifty thousand pounds were there, in fifty-pound notes.

A year on, I look back on it all now with a certain affectionate wonder. There was no mention of me at Gregory's trial. I kept interviews to a minimum and made sure not to say anything interesting. I mumbled on the radio. They had to ask me to speak up.

'I was in a nuthouse,' I said. 'I know nothing.'

Some things are worth it for the money.

Gregory is still doing middle-class time in his white-collar open prison. He's decided to switch from medicine to fossils, and is taking an archaeology degree. I take Billy to visit him regularly. It's the least I can do. Boys need fathers, even if they're as bad as Gregory. I wouldn't ever dream of telling Billy what his father tried to do. They spend a couple of hours together in a special family unit and a new bond seems to be growing between them, which involves Lego. I don't see him often myself, since the signing of the divorce papers. I may have hated Ruby, but at least she did the decent thing. I still have fantasies of going to visit her and pouring out all the bottled-up stuff that's still there, and calling her a cow and all that. But she wouldn't be able to reply on account of the Trappist thing. I think this might take the edge off our encounter.

Even after the trial and after things had finally quietened down at Manxheath – even then I wasn't sure what I wanted to do with my life. Other people seemed to be making progress: Monica had suddenly turned cynical, the Ossature was now a fatted calf, David was now divorced from Sweetie and in love with Apple Tree, and Max had been transferred to a hospital for the criminally insane for buggering the Institute's guard dog.

As for Ma, she was out of the woods and back to her clay effigies with mammoth genitalia. The memorial she made for Isabella caused quite a stir: it was a huge green-and-yellow papier-mâché mausoleum to house Isabella Pimento's molar. The Gridiron craft caucus was alerted to it by the art therapist, and all of a sudden Ma was a leading light in something called Art Brut, with private views and drinks parties and even a small but passionate following of collectors, galleries and other hangers-on. Two art students came to study her 'methods'.

Ma had finally arrived. I was pleased for her, I suppose, but it all made me feel rather inadequate.

On a visit one day, I caught sight of a forlorn figure in the Day Room, bowed over some embroidery. It was a while before I recognised him. His hair was long, and in a ponytail. It looked dirty. He was wearing glasses. It was Dr Stern. I was about to walk away, but curiosity got the better of me. He didn't raise his head as I approached. When I spoke, my words shot out bluntly, like from a popgun, before I had time to think.

'Well?' I asked him. 'Are you mad or not?'

I noticed, staring past his head, that the green Regency striped wallpaper had been replaced by impressionistic dots in yellow, red and blue. It looked as though if you stared at them for long enough, reason might suddenly burst in.

'Mad is a word we prefer not to use here in Manxheath,' Ishmael responded automatically. 'Anyway, how should *I* know?' he added flatly, his eyes still on the tiny stitching of his embroidery. It was a square design, all in one colour – a deep, dingy purple-brown.

'I used to have this theory about the mind being a sea of *chemicals,* but now I'm not so sure. I think a *can of worms* is the metaphor I'd use now.'

He looked up, and I saw that his eyes were red, and brimming with tears. With care, he finished off a strand of silk and began a new one in the same colour.

'It's a Rothko,' he explained, stroking its lizardy surface. 'D'you know what your mother said to me the other day in Group? She said, "Healer, heal thyself." But I can't. I don't even know what there is to *heal.* I don't know what's *normal* any more, Hazel.'

So that Colditz thing was coming true, after all.

'What's de Cleranbault's syndrome?' I asked him.

'It's one of the delusionary complexes,' he said wearily. 'Involving the belief that one's having a *relationship* with somebody when one *isn't.*' He unpicked a stitch, and re-did it, then added, 'It's astonishingly *widespread.*'

Suddenly, the sight of him made me sad, and muddled. We sat for a while in silence. Despite myself, I took his hand and squeezed it. I didn't know what to offer him.

'Do you know what my sister Linda always says?' I found myself saying eventually. 'She says life's a bitch and then you die. So you see, we're all in the same boat.'

It was the most optimistic thing I could think of to say. And it seemed to give him heart, because for a moment, something that might have been a smile spasmed near his mouth.

I got up and walked slowly across the lino in the direction of the door.

'I think I love you,' he called out hopefully as I closed it behind me. But there was something that wavered in his voice, a hint of de Cleranbault.

*　　*　　*

I'd always wanted something of my own, something to strive for and believe in. Home improvement wasn't enough, I realised, after I'd paid a fortune to have the house re-vamped to eradicate all trace of Ruby. Nor was motherhood. With Billy at playschool five mornings a week, I needed something else. I was striving for sanity now. It's normal, isn't it, to want to be normal. When you've got lunatics in the family you need to stay on guard at all times. That much I do know about genetics.

In the end, it was memories of the greenhouse that inspired me. The idea hatched one Wednesday while Jane-next-door was giving me my geranium-scented aromatherapy. Because even though the greenhouse never really existed – can't have done – it felt right. Is that so wrong?

So I bought one, a real one, with Hooper's money and a bank loan. It's not so much a greenhouse, I suppose, as a garden centre. The Gretchenfield Garden Centre. You'll find it on Donkey Cart Road, in a prime location, next to Handiman and opposite Aqua World, by the pelican crossing. It's quite big. I have a basic staff of ten. I'm planning a new orchard section for next year, and I'm already famed locally for my range of ornamental shrubs. We do special reductions for pensioners and every now and then I bring in a well-known gardening personality to give a talk on germination or compost or what-have-you. You could say it's been a sort of lifeline, the whole thing. That business studies course I did all those years ago is finally paying off. And of course I'm rich. Last summer I took Billy to Disneyworld in Florida for a week, and I've waved goodbye to Marks & Sparks.

I don't grow any 'medications' at the garden centre, or any of that other weird stuff Ma managed to raise.

I imagine it would be illegal. She's a bit scathing about that, when she comes to help as part of what Dr Appleby calls a 'community enrichment programme'. You can't say she doesn't have green fingers. She comes to enrich us on Tuesdays and Thursdays, if she's not attending a private view, which she calls a *vernissage*. Sometimes Ishmael tags along, or comes to the garden centre for a cup of tea in our Koffee Korner before wandering off. He and Keith are allowed to leave the hospital sometimes, accompanied by Dr McAuley, for chess tournaments. Ishmael is getting pretty good, and is now an International Master, whatever that means. He keeps asking me to 'be his wife' but I change the subject and occupy him in potting up cuttings. His behaviour seems quite mad for a normal person, though I no longer trust my judgement in these matters. I don't know. It's dodgy territory. We don't really talk.

Linda, having received her Ag. and Fish Merit Award, has gone from strength to strength. She ditched Duncan not long ago. She couldn't tolerate sub-standard sex a moment longer, she told me. Now she's *en route* to Brussels for a promotion into something called Euro Ag. Planning. More strangely, I think I'll actually miss her. She said I could fly out and stay for a weekend, if I could get a baby-sitter for Billy, and if I could try to avoid irritating her. I'm hoping she'll try motherhood again one day, but she says her fingers have been burned.

It's Christmas Eve, and Gregory has been allowed out of the Correction Facility for two days because he's been a model prisoner and because a lot of suicides are predicted for the millennium. The theory is that families prevent, rather than cause them. We decided to have a ceasefire over the holiday season, for Billy's sake. It looked like I was being more generous than I really was, of course. After all, he didn't know about the baby-swap, and the extent to which my family had ruined his life. I decided to let him use the spare room, which now has an *en suite* bathroom with an aubergine toilet and matching bidet. He is Billy's father, after all. Later I'm having guests round for drinks and festive things on sticks.

I've been busy preparing the turkey stuffing (apple and chestnut with ginger) for tomorrow, but in the midst of it all I stop and remember one of those tiny moments of huge significance that stay with you for ever.

It happened this morning, when I'd finished vacuuming in the living-room. Billy and Gregory had built an impressive crenellated castle from Lego, and when by chance I found myself on my hands and knees peering through its tiny portcullis, I had a moment of sublime epiphany: a clear vision of the future, in which all my life was bright and new. Gazing down the corridor that led into the central courtyard, my heart lifted as I saw a little red soldier proudly standing guard over the castle entrance. He was wearing a crash helmet that belonged to another Lego scene – the garage one, I think. In his hand was a musket. He would keep that castle safe, you could tell, and guard the valuable furniture inside it with his life. And I realised then: I'm more in charge of things than I ever was.

So here we all are now, the night before Christmas: Ma, Linda, Keith, Gregory, Ishmael, Billy, and me. We're sitting around in the living-room. Despite the new peach-coloured carpet, I reckon you can still see the dark patch where the mustard and cress grew.

Gregory is stiff and polite with my guests. He sits in a high-backed chair, and avoids eye contact. Earlier he showed us his moderately interesting ammonite collection, a ring-binder containing photocopied photographs and diagrams of fossils found in Lyme Regis by other people. He hasn't changed much. That luncheon meat look is still there.

We've had our mini-sausages on sticks and our sparkling wine. There were quails' eggs, too, but I'd overcooked them, of course, and Ma had spat one out half-chewed, theatrically, into Linda's ashtray.

'It's hard as a wee gel capsule,' she'd complained. 'The kind you stick up your arse.'

Of course no one except Billy would touch them after that. Ma has a way of polluting things.

Now Linda wants to watch *Holy Hour Special*. I do, too, but I'm worried about what I might see. The Katie-Koo thing: it still haunts my mind. There's been much speculation in the press about the Reverend Carmichael's 'love-child', but he's managed to keep her out of public view by cloistering her in his Northumberland ranch.

The show is to be a sort of Yuletide re-launch after the Easter disgrace. The pre-publicity for the show has indicated that the Reverend will be surprising us all again. Needless to say, he has paid his dues, asked the Lord to forgive him his sins, and is Born Again again.

'He's bound to say something about her if he's re-launching himself,' argues Linda. She's clearly got over him: she's crunching on a Love Heart. 'How can he avoid it? Anyway, it'll be part of the deal to pull in the ratings.'

Linda has admitted to me that the Katie-Koo period of her life is now a bit of a blur. The Carmichael bit, too. She has forgotten, but not forgiven.

The public, surveys show, has done the opposite. They'll forgive him anything. Women, especially, will forgive. Pity the struggling and repentant single father. Blame the mystery slag mother who so cruelly dumped a child on him. Who seduced him in a weak moment. Who failed to use either modern birth control or old-fashioned self-restraint. Blame Linda.

The only one of us who doesn't have mixed feelings about seeing the show is Gregory, of course. He loathes the Reverend more than he ever did.

'You can like it or lump it here, sonny Jim,' Ma tells Greg.

'Can I offer anyone a cheese cracker?' sighs my ex, trying to make out it's his house we're in, with *his* wife, *his* new loose covers, *his* friends, *his* new dado railing, *his* aubergine bidet, *his* sparkling wine. We ignore him.

'Fancy a game of chess, anyone?' asks Ishmael. 'It's supposed to be very Freudian – all about killing one's father.'

'We'll kill him later, hen,' says Ma. 'Can't you see we're engrossed?'

Ishmael sighs, reaches for his embroidery bag, and pulls out the Rothko and a bodkin.

'The devil finds work for idle hands,' bitches Ma.

'So what does that make your *mausoleum*, Mrs Sugden?' ripostes Ishmael, but Ma pretends not to hear.

The music is thumping away; the Reverend Carmichael is looking jovial and serene; he is dressed as Joseph. Then the camera pulls out to reveal that he is surrounded by a whole nativity scene with real sheep and goats, and kneeling men dressed in shepherds' costumes. There is even a medium-sized cow, chewing lasciviously on some straw.

There is no Mary; just a crib.

We hold our breath.

'No!' yells Linda suddenly. 'He won't have the fucking nerve!'

Gregory is looking puzzled; I signal to Linda to shut

up and she valiantly restrains herself. The truth has gone no further than our family and we're keeping it that way. As far as Greg's concerned, the Perfect Baby never happened: Baby B was a 'failure', and Baby A, also a 'failure', was now a Trappist to boot. Gregory will never have any idea what really happened to his daughter.

Meanwhile, it transpires that the Reverend Carmichael does have the nerve. He reaches inside the crib and props up a cherubic, curly-haired baby on a golden cushion.

It's weird. Katie-Koo looks scarcely any older than she did a year ago. A design fault, perhaps. She is angel-faced.

'Rejoice!' cries Carmichael, his voice shuddering with paternal pride. 'For unto us a child is born!'

Linda groans, her eyes glassily fixed on the screen. And we all gaze in wonder and fear as the Perfect Baby sits up in her little cot, smiles benignly on Carmichael, the menagerie and the audience, and cries out in the tiny, tinkling voice of a wind-up toy, 'Happy Christmas to you from God's own Child! And a prosperous New Year to *Holy Hour* viewers everywhere!'

The studio audience gasps. What an extraordinary baby! Even Ishmael's eyes change shape in astonishment as the dolly-child gets to her tiny feet. She is wearing a white lace nightie and a headband with a gold star that flashes through her dark curls.

Then, in a small, quavery, breathy voice, she begins to sing.

Today's the day
The time is now
Let Jesus in
It's *Holy Hour*!

I look at Gregory. His face is all twisted.

'She's perfect!' he mutters. The tears are zig-zagging recklessly down his face. 'A Perfect Baby!'

'Almost a miracle, eh, Gregory,' says Linda, who also seems to be choking on an emotion.

'Looks like God won the race for perfection, sonny,' comments Ma. 'Who's for guacamole?'

On television, they're voting with their knees: members of the studio audience are descending into prayer posture, like a herd of resigned camels, before the miracle. For a ghastly moment I think Gregory is about to join them, but he grips the edge of his chair with white knuckles to stop himself. I've never actually seen him cry before.

Cry me a river.

Linda, Ma and I exchange a shaky triangular glance.

'Well,' declares Ma, sinking her chops into a pistachio-flavoured Turkish Delight. 'That's kakistocracy for you.'

Linda is wiping her nose on her sleeve and blinking back tears of what might be rage, nostalgia, envy, or a curious Linda-ish mixture of all three.

Now Katie-koo is waving and blowing kisses. Perhaps she sees the same sort of future I do: the one I saw this morning in Lego.

'Expect a new world,' the Reverend is pronouncing, 'and the Lord shall provide it.'

It's then that Billy appears like a little security guard in the middle of the room, brandishing the remote control, and presses the Off button.

The TV corner is suddenly cast into darkness, and into the darkness floods that gorgeous and unfathomable feeling of joy that is surely to be mine from now on.

My castle is safe. There it stands, fast and miraculous and inviolate as an egg.

And yes: I'm more in charge of things than I ever was.

A NOTE ON THE AUTHOR

Liz Jensen was born in Oxfordshire in 1959.
She has worked in Britain and the Far East as
a journalist and in France as a sculptor. She
now lives in South London. *Egg Dancing* is
her first novel.